W9-CDY-576

BBC

DOCTOR WHO™

THE VISUAL DICTIONARY

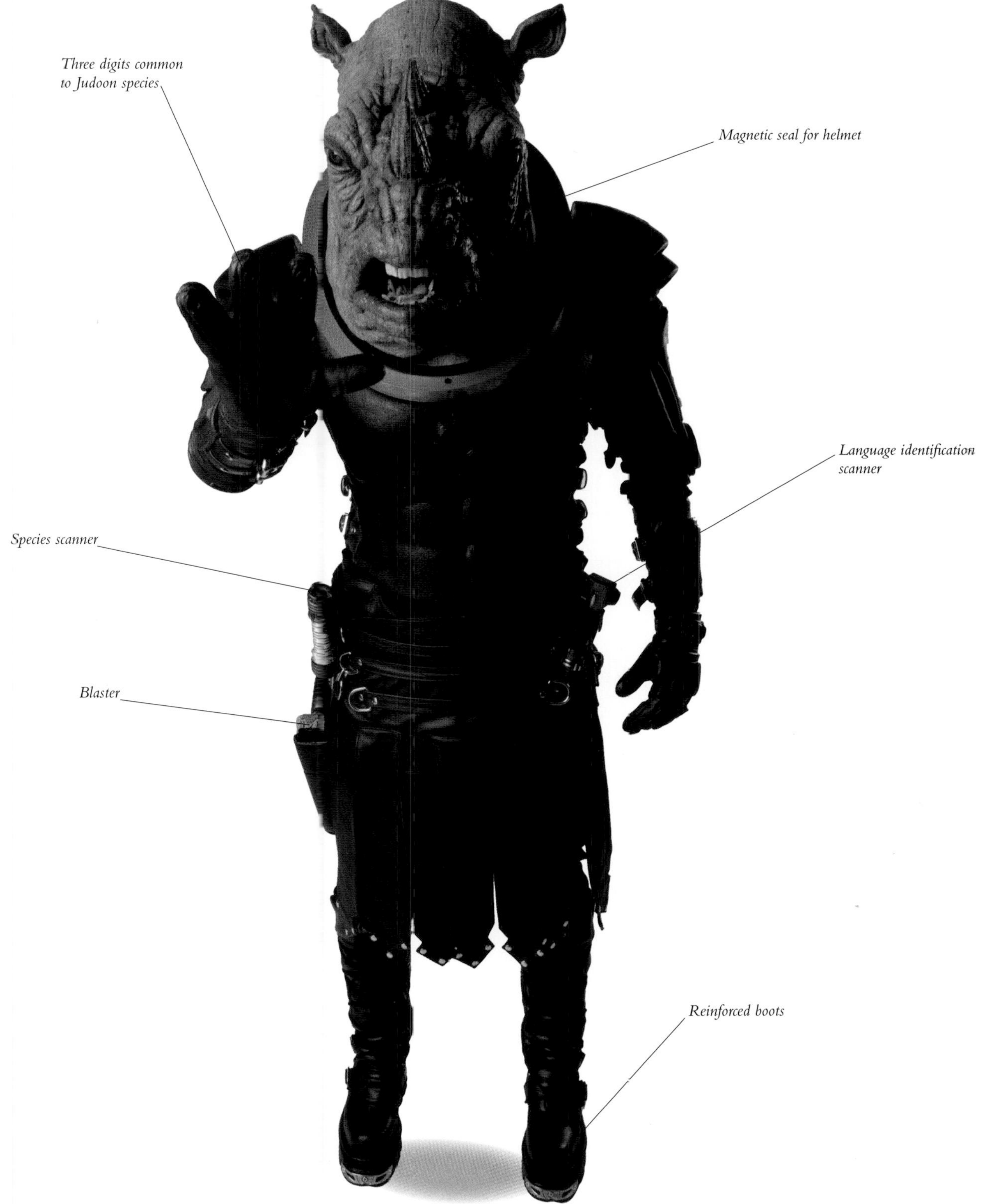

JUDOON OFFICER

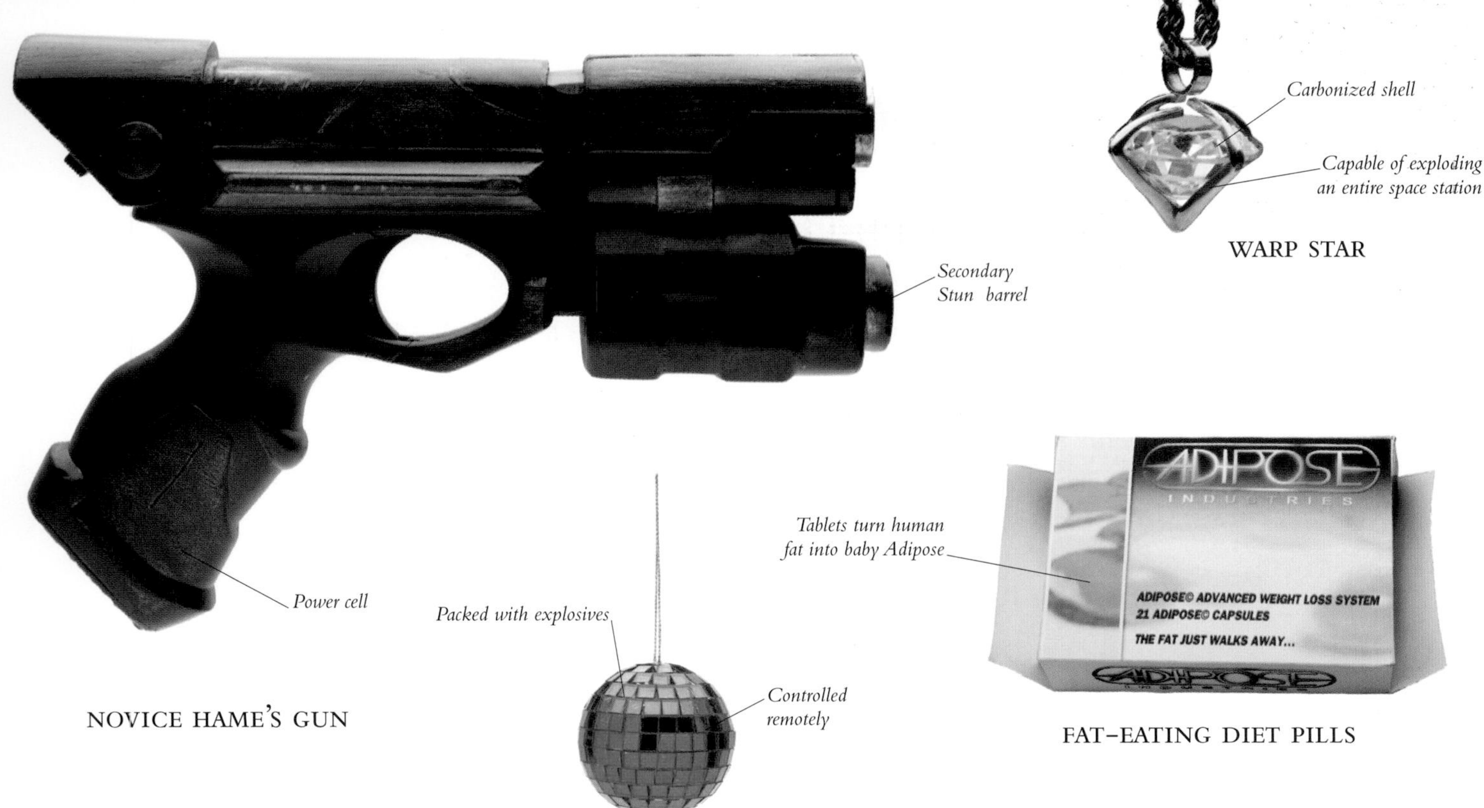

NOVICE HAME'S GUN

WARP STAR

CHRISTMAS BAUBLE

FAT-EATING DIET PILLS

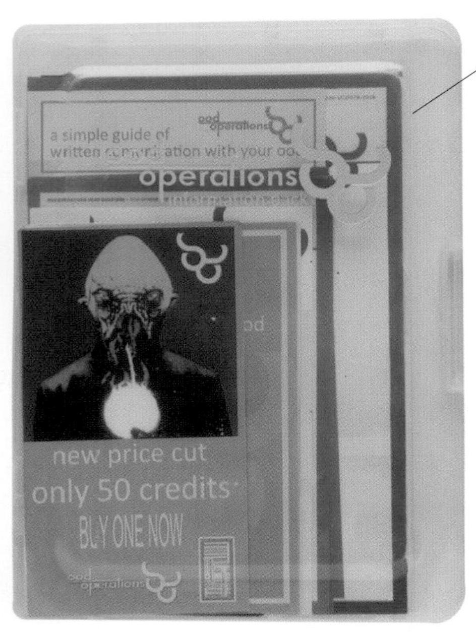

OOD OPERATIONS PRESS PACK

FREEDOM FIGHTER GUN

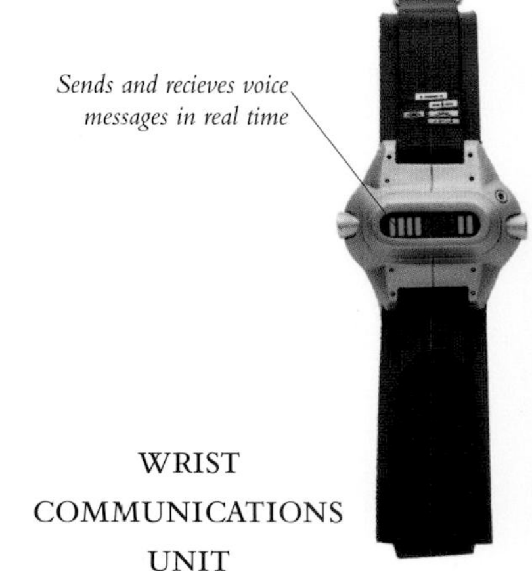

WRIST
COMMUNICATIONS
UNIT

RETROFITTED
BETAMAX VIDEO
RECORDER

CUFFLINKS OF VICTOR KLUM
(ABZORBALOFF)

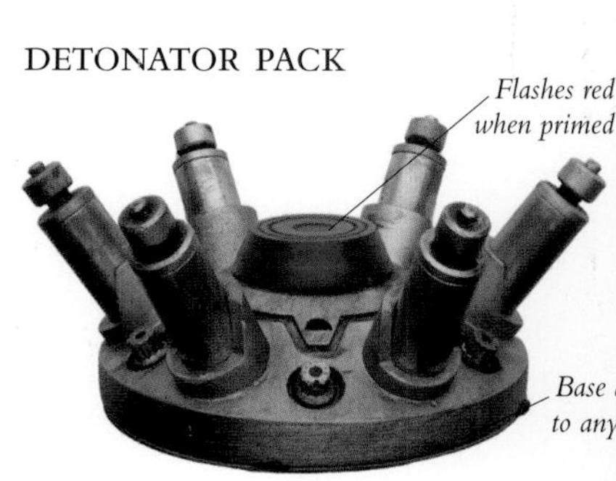

DETONATOR PACK

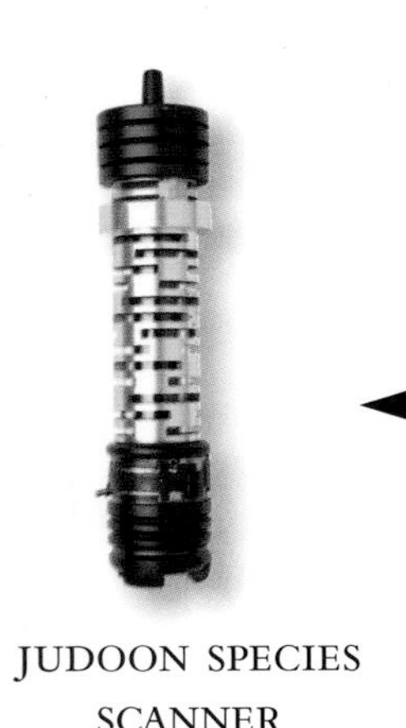

JUDOON SPECIES SCANNER

DOCTOR WHO™

THE VISUAL DICTIONARY

SONIC SCREWDRIVER

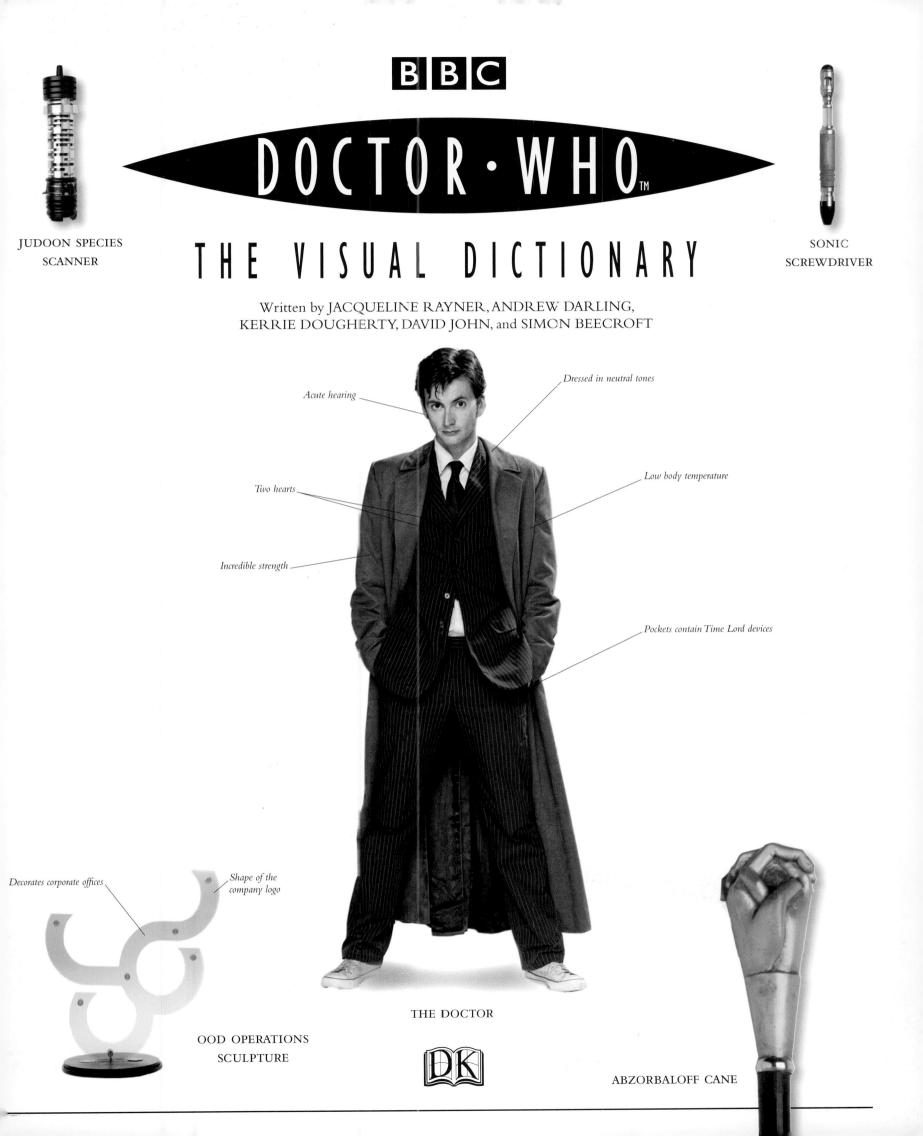

Written by JACQUELINE RAYNER, ANDREW DARLING, KERRIE DOUGHERTY, DAVID JOHN, and SIMON BEECROFT

Acute hearing

Dressed in neutral tones

Two hearts

Low body temperature

Incredible strength

Pockets contain Time Lord devices

THE DOCTOR

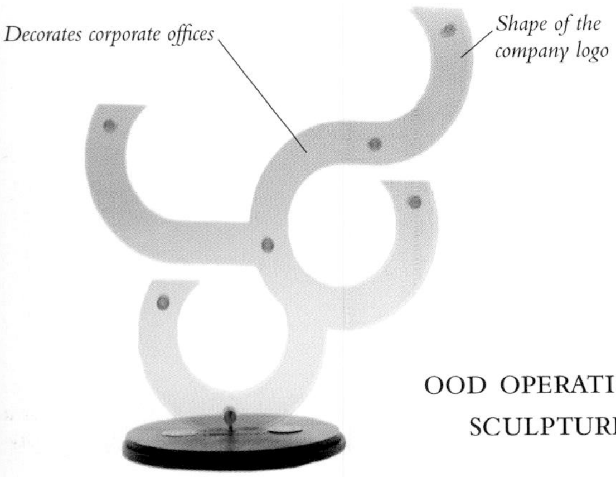

Decorates corporate offices

Shape of the company logo

OOD OPERATIONS SCULPTURE

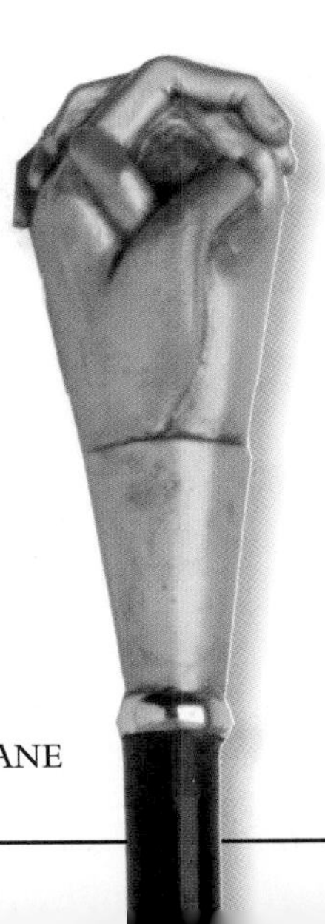

ABZORBALOFF CANE

DK

Contents

New Beginnings

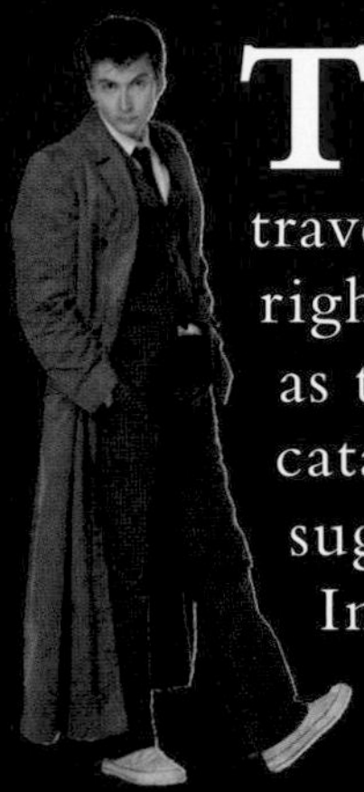

TIME AND TIME AGAIN, fate seems to thrust a mysterious time traveler known as the Doctor into the right place at the right time. However, as the Doctor always arrives at times of catastrophe, legends have evolved that suggest he is the cause of these events. In fact, he is usually instrumental in the resolution of crises, but like a storm, he can also leave damage in his wake. The Doctor was a crucial figure in the Great Time War, and witnessed the destruction of the Daleks, the Time Lords, and his home planet, Gallifrey. The Doctor continues to appear where he is needed to alleviate the chaos that is created in both time and space.

THE DOCTOR

Faces of Evil

Evil comes in many guises and sometimes it can be difficult to tell friend from foe. Since the Great Time War, the Doctor in his ninth and tenth incarnations has battled both new and old adversaries.

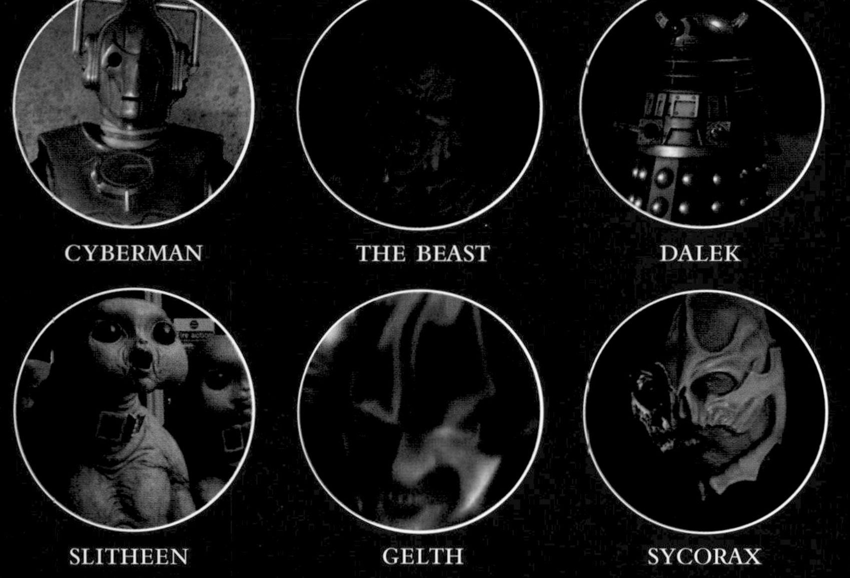

CYBERMAN THE BEAST DALEK

SLITHEEN GELTH SYCORAX

The Great Time War

After the Daleks discovered that the Doctor's people, the Time Lords, had tried to tamper with history to prevent their creation, they declared war and a massive conflict, the last Great Time War, began. The Doctor was the one who ended it. He destroyed the Daleks, but at a terrible price: Gallifrey, and all the Time Lords, burned, too.

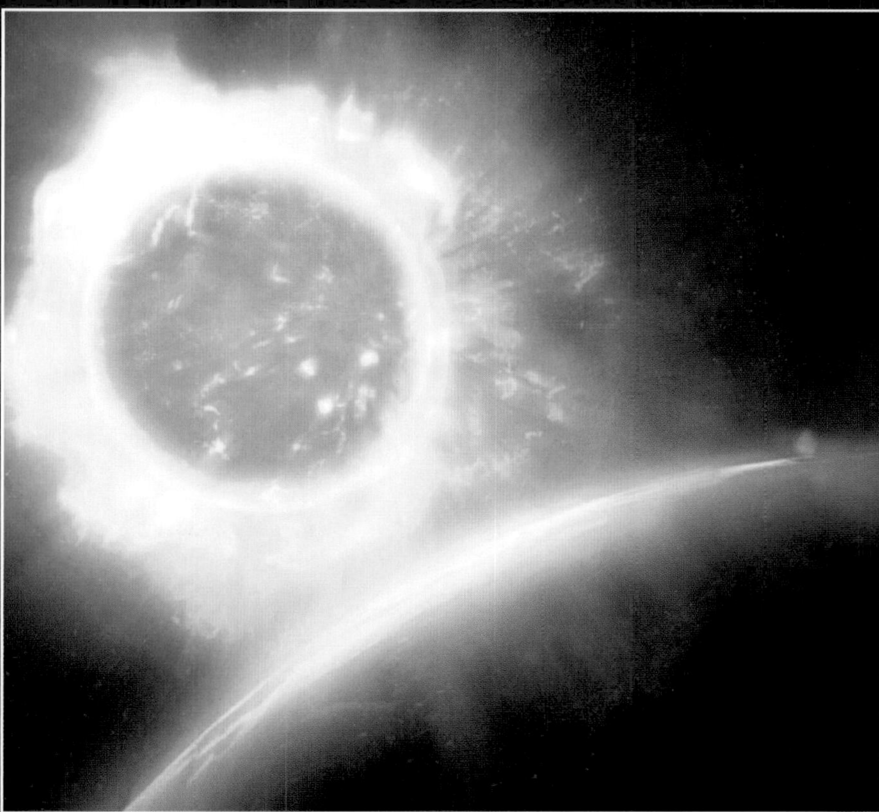

The Earth eventually ends in the year 5.5/Apple/26. It is destroyed naturally by the expanding Sun, not by an enemy.

The Dalek Fleet

Escaping from the destruction of the Daleks in the Great Time War, the Emperor Dalek fled to the far future. By the year 200,100 he had rebuilt his destroyed race using human genetic material. But the Doctor foiled his plan to invade the Earth with a massive fleet of warships and turn it into the new Dalek homeworld.

Target Earth

Many alien races have sought to invade the Earth, to enslave humanity, rob it of its mineral wealth, or simply to destroy the planet. Following the Great Time War, displaced beings such as the Nestene Consciousness and Gelth sought refuge on Earth, while in the far future the Daleks, reestablished using human genetic material, plan to invade Earth and make it their new homeworld. Fortunately for humanity, the Doctor has often defeated these plans and saved the world: in his absence, Earthly agencies like UNIT and the Torchwood Institute have also defeated alien aggression.

England, and London in particular, have seen more than a few attempts at alien invasion. However, few citizens of the 20th or 21st centuries would be aware of them, thanks to the efforts of UNIT and the Torchwood Institute to defeat and cover up the threats.

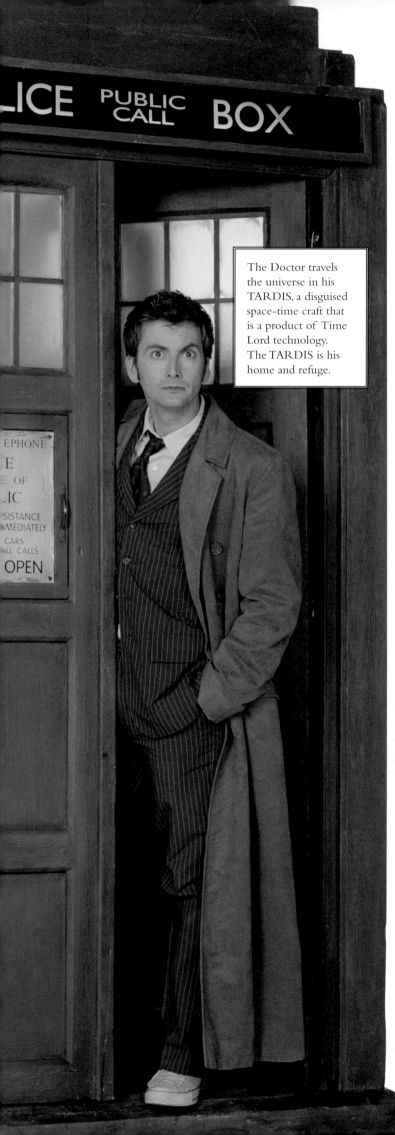

The Doctor travels the universe in his TARDIS, a disguised space-time craft that is a product of Time Lord technology. The TARDIS is his home and refuge.

The Time Lord

THE DOCTOR BELIEVES himself to be the last surviving Time Lord, a long-lived and incredibly technologically advanced society, which possessed the secret of time travel. The Time Lords preferred to observe the universe and rarely interfered in the affairs of other worlds. Unable to agree with this policy of nonintervention, the Doctor became a "renegade," stealing a TARDIS and using it to explore time and space.

There is Only One Doctor

Although each regeneration brings out different facets of a Time Lord's personality, the Doctor's essential character has remained unchanged for centuries. His affable and childlike traits conceal an extensive knowledge of the universe and deep wisdom born of experience. He has a strong sense of right and wrong and a firm conviction that he should intervene to prevent injustice. A pacifist who goes to great ends to preserve life and prevent war and violence, the Doctor has a great affection for humanity.

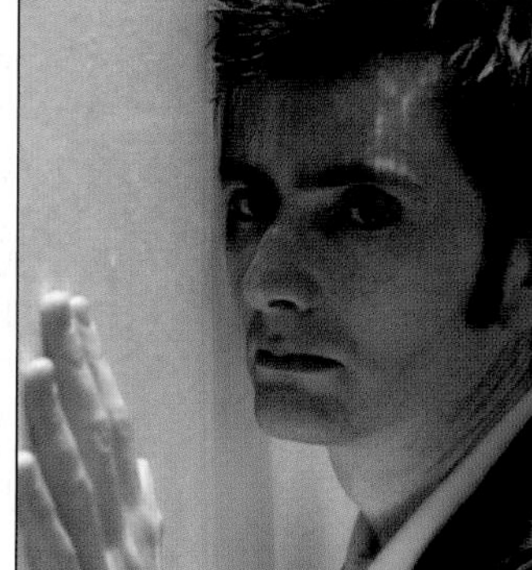

Despite his vibrant personality, the Doctor is sometimes overwhelmed by his belief that he is the last surviving Time Lord, following the destruction of his people and their planet in the Great Time War.

Moments in Time

The Doctor has a remarkable gift for appearing at critical moments in time, when catastophe is about to strike. He has, for example, been documented as a witness to the eruption of Krakatoa, in Indonesia, the maiden voyage of the RMS *Titanic,* and the assassination of President John F. Kennedy.

The Doctor at the launch of the *Titanic* (above) and at the eruption of Krakatoa (below).

Gallifrey—Planet of the Time Lords

The Time Lords came from the planet Gallifrey, located in the constellation of Kasterborous, some 29,000 light-years from Earth. Before its destruction in the Great Time War, Gallifrey was a divided world. The Time Lords dwelt in vast citadels enclosed in mighty glass domes, while the Outsiders, the outcasts of Gallifreyan society, lived tribal lives in the wilderness beyond the cities. Gallifrey's Capitol, the seat of Time Lord power, housed the Academies of Learning, the time monitoring facilities, the controls for the impenetrable forcefield that protected the planet and the Eye of Harmony—the artifical black hole that provided the energy needed for time travel. The technological emphasis of Time Lord society is seen in its complex script, which is mathematically based.

Time Lord engineering is so advanced it can transcend the normal laws of spatial physics, enabling the creation of "dimensionally transcendental" artifacts that are larger on the inside than the exterior would seem to indicate.

TARDIS

GENESIS ARK

GALLIFREYAN INSCRIPTION

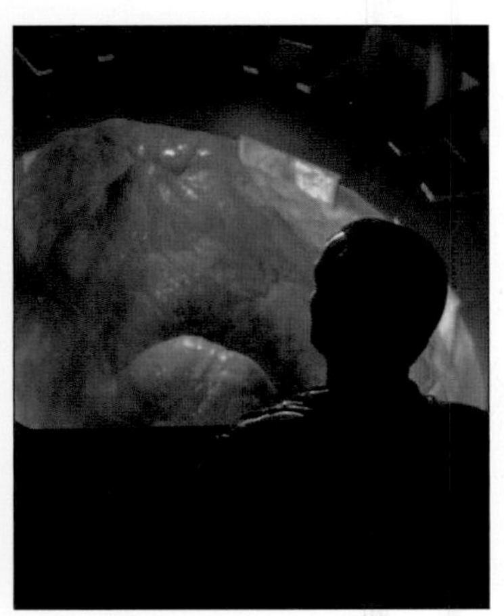

The Doctor's travels and the crucial role he has played in so many historical events across time, have given him an extensive knowledge of intergalactic law and protocol. For example, he was able to invoke the necessary regulations of the Shadow Proclamation in order to approach the Nestene Consciousness, who were invading the Earth.

More Lives than a Cat

In cases of advanced age, mortal illness, or fatal injury, Time Lords have the ability to regenerate their bodies, creating a new physical form that also expresses a different part of their personality. The regeneration process is hugely traumatic and can cause mental and psychological instability until it is completed, which takes many hours. In all, Time Lords can have 13 "lives" before their bodies are unable to regenerate any more, but it has been suggested that an entirely new regeneration cycle can be bestowed on a Time Lord, presumably by artifical means.

The Doctor's regeneration expels the energy from the Time Vortex that he absorbed from Rose

Rose witnesses a Time Lord regeneration for the first time

Anatomy of the Doctor

ALTHOUGH HE LOOKS LIKE a human being (and once claimed Earth ancestry on his mother's side), the Doctor is an alien being and his Time Lord physiology has many differences to our own. Physically, the Doctor is stronger, has sharper senses, and greater powers of endurance than a human being and can cope with heat, cold, radiation, and strange energies better than humans can. There are also some differences to his internal anatomy that have confused many Earthly doctors.

Highly developed Time Lord brain, with great memory capacity and telepathic ability

Highly evolved senses—he can identify blood group by taste and pinpoint historical eras by smell

Respiratory by-pass system allows short-term survival in airless environments

Two hearts, supported by a binary vascular system

Superhuman strength and stamina

Eye color—like all physical features—can change with regeneration

Lower body temperature than a human

Two Hearts

Time Lords have two hearts and a binary vascular system, which enables them to survive major accidents and many physical and temporal shocks that would kill a human being. They also have a respiratory by-pass system that enables them to survive without breathing for some time.

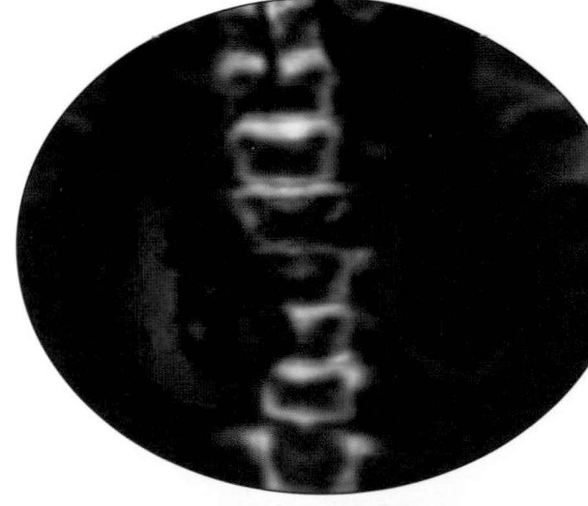

Time Lord life-energy is tremendously vibrant and powerful. When the TARDIS's power supply is almost totally destroyed, save for one cell, the Doctor recharges it by breathing his own life energy into the remaining power cell, giving up 10 years of his life in the process.

Nutrient fluid preserves severed hand

The Doctor's Hand

When the Doctor's right hand is severed by a Sycorax warrior, residual regeneration energy allows him to grow another. His friend Captain Jack acquires the original, which causes its surrounding liquid to bubble whenever the Doctor or a product of his DNA is near.

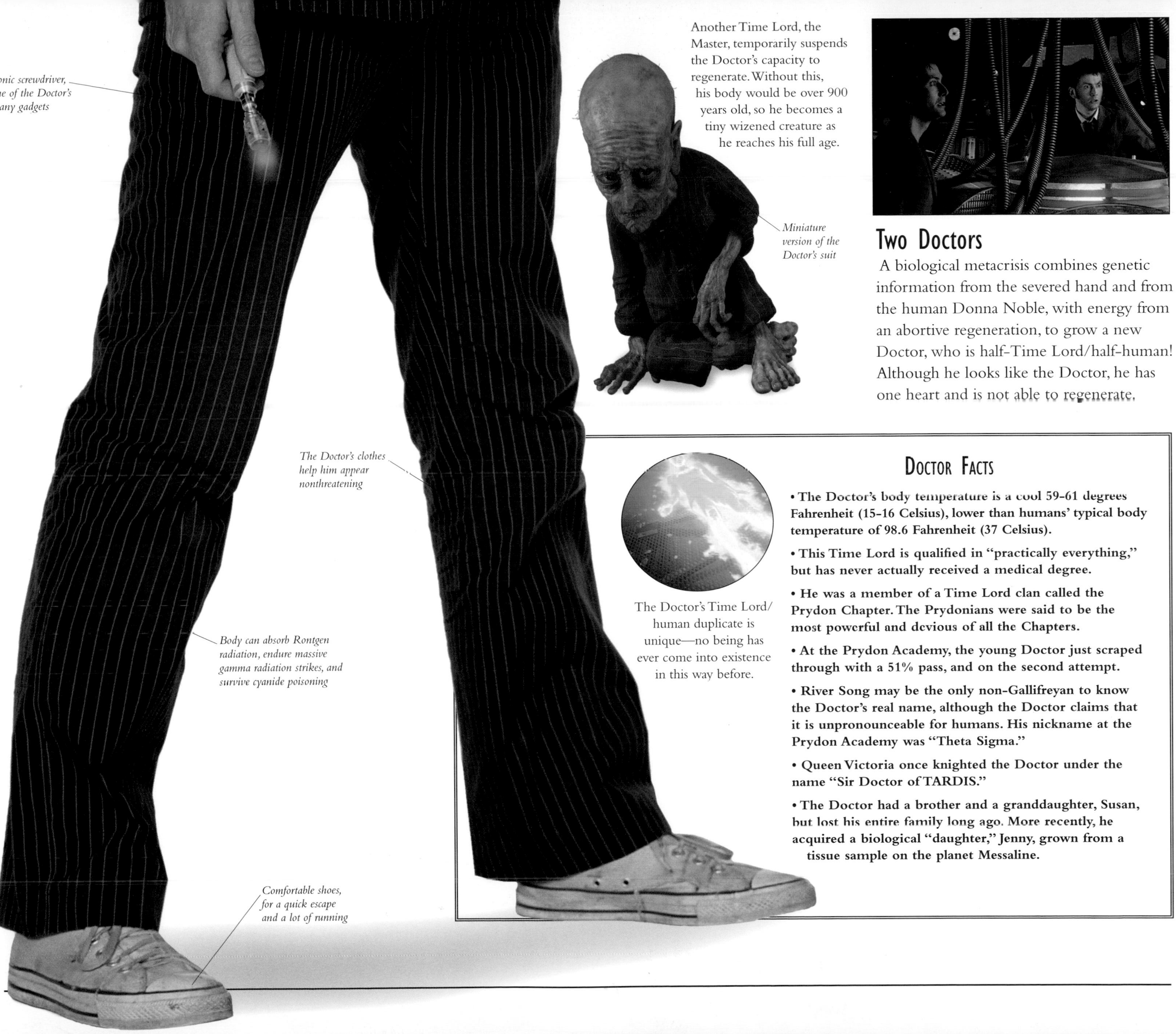

Sonic screwdriver, one of the Doctor's many gadgets

The Doctor's clothes help him appear nonthreatening

Body can absorb Rontgen radiation, endure massive gamma radiation strikes, and survive cyanide poisoning

Comfortable shoes, for a quick escape and a lot of running

Another Time Lord, the Master, temporarily suspends the Doctor's capacity to regenerate. Without this, his body would be over 900 years old, so he becomes a tiny wizened creature as he reaches his full age.

Miniature version of the Doctor's suit

Two Doctors

A biological metacrisis combines genetic information from the severed hand and from the human Donna Noble, with energy from an abortive regeneration, to grow a new Doctor, who is half-Time Lord/half-human! Although he looks like the Doctor, he has one heart and is not able to regenerate.

The Doctor's Time Lord/human duplicate is unique—no being has ever come into existence in this way before.

Doctor Facts

- **The Doctor's body temperature is a cool 59–61 degrees Fahrenheit (15–16 Celsius), lower than humans' typical body temperature of 98.6 Fahrenheit (37 Celsius).**
- **This Time Lord is qualified in "practically everything," but has never actually received a medical degree.**
- **He was a member of a Time Lord clan called the Prydon Chapter. The Prydonians were said to be the most powerful and devious of all the Chapters.**
- **At the Prydon Academy, the young Doctor just scraped through with a 51% pass, and on the second attempt.**
- **River Song may be the only non-Gallifreyan to know the Doctor's real name, although the Doctor claims that it is unpronounceable for humans. His nickname at the Prydon Academy was "Theta Sigma."**
- **Queen Victoria once knighted the Doctor under the name "Sir Doctor of TARDIS."**
- **The Doctor had a brother and a granddaughter, Susan, but lost his entire family long ago. More recently, he acquired a biological "daughter," Jenny, grown from a tissue sample on the planet Messaline.**

More Powerful than a Black Hole

The Time Lords artificially created a black hole called the Eye of Harmony. The captured energy of this black hole is the source of the TARDIS's power and is so strong that the TARDIS can escape from the gravitational pull of another black hole. The Doctor used this tremendous power to tow the Earth back to its rightful position, after it was moved to the Medusa Cascade by the Daleks.

The TARDIS

THE DOCTOR IS able to travel through time and space using a machine called the TARDIS. A triumph of Time Lord temporal engineering, TARDISes are "dimensionally transcendental," which means that the interior and exterior exist in different dimensions and they can change both their external appearance and internal layout. When the Doctor decided to flee Gallifrey and roam the universe, he stole a TARDIS that was about to be serviced for a variety of malfunctions and faults. He has never been able to repair it fully, which often makes his travels erratic and uncontrolled.

Materialization beacon indicates when TARDIS is arriving or departing

The Doctor's TARDIS is stuck in the shape of a 1950s London Police Box because its Chameleon Circuit is damaged

TARDIS exterior is virtually indestructible

TARDIS Facts

- The name TARDIS is an acronym of "Time and Relative Dimension in Space."
- The Doctor's TARDIS is a Type 40TT Capsule, considered obsolete by the Time Lords. There were originally 305 registered Type 40 TARDISes.
- The TARDIS has a "chameleon circuit," which is supposed to change its external appearance to blend in with its surroundings, wherever it lands.
- The TARDIS is able to use its telepathic circuits to translate almost any language for the benefit of its occupants.
- The exterior shell of the TARDIS seems to weigh no more than an ordinary police box: it can be picked up and moved with suitable machinery.

Sonic Screwdrivers

THE STANDARD TOOLKIT in a TARDIS contains equipment needed to tune and repair the ship. One of the most useful tools, the sonic screwdriver, uses variously focused soundwaves to make repairs where human hands cannot reach. In addition to turning screws, it can open locks, operate and repair ship systems remotely, and take many kinds of readings and scans.

The Doctor often uses his sonic screwdriver to interface with the TARDIS's central console. He can also do this remotely from outside the ship.

Time Technology

Sonic screwdrivers are a common Time Lord device—in fact, the Doctor has a number of them on board the TARDIS, though he usually favors one particular unit. To a Time Lord, their technology is simple: if need be, the Doctor could build himself a new one from scratch in almost no time.

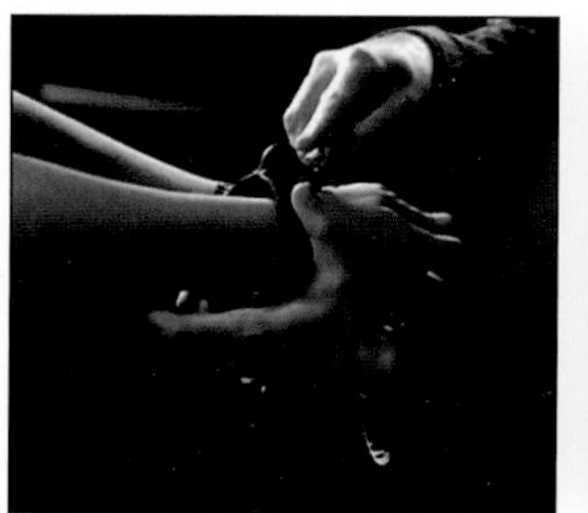

High-kinetic sonic waves can open almost all kinds of mechanical or electronic locks.

A reversed mode can also seal locks—useful when trying to keep an alien werewolf at bay.

Sonic screwdrivers are designed to be portable and functional

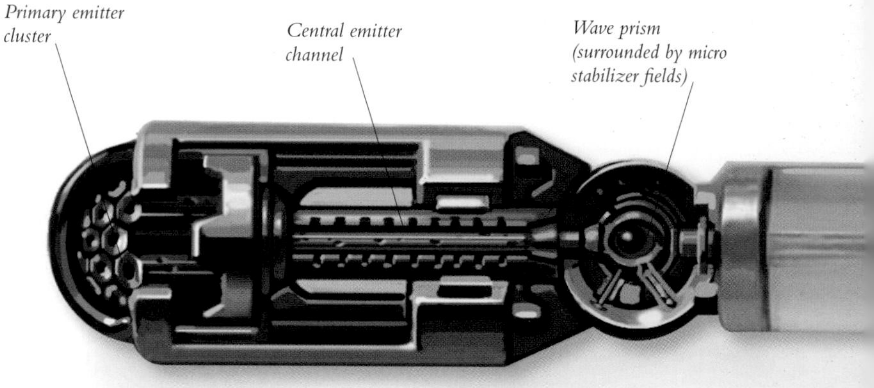

Primary emitter cluster

Central emitter channel

Wave prism (surrounded by micro stabilizer fields)

Curious to know how and why Donna Noble suddenly materialized before him, the Doctor sets the sonic screwdriver to scanning mode—though its range is limited.

The beam from a sonic screwdriver can interact at a molecular level with another object, for example, to "cut" a rope by unraveling the individual fibers at a particular point. It can also produce a high-energy beam capable of generating heat in order to burn or slice through many kinds of material.

Sonic screwdrivers can remotely detonate explosives, such as bombs, and activate missiles. At a certain power setting, it can even blast a door clean off its hinges.

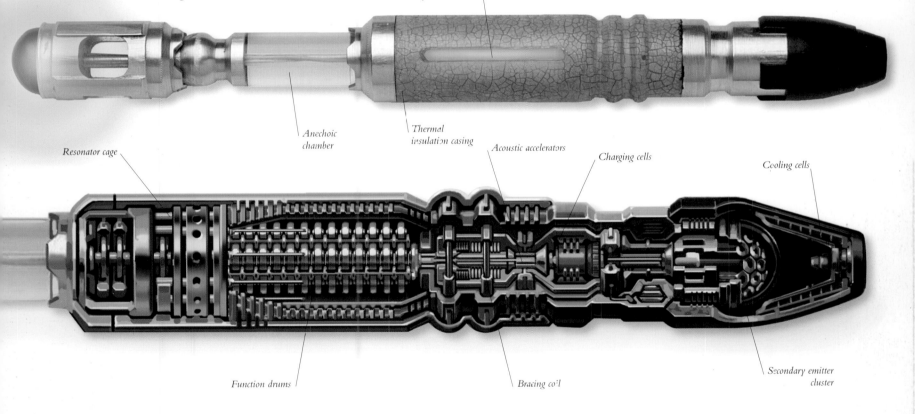

Screwdriver Operation

Sonic screwdrivers contain Gallifreyan circuitry, allowing their operator to switch between different functions using slight adjustments to the exterior casing. However, the device must be directed toward its object for maximum effectiveness. The Doctor keeps the tool on him for as long as its power cells allow between recharges.

Adjustment sensor

Anechoic chamber

Thermal insulation casing

Resonator cage

Acoustic accelerators

Charging cells

Cooling cells

Function drums

Bracing coil

Secondary emitter cluster

In the mysterious Library, the Doctor meets River Song. Although she knows him well, for him this is their first meeting. The fact that she has an advanced sonic screwdriver, given to her in the future by the Doctor, is a sign of their strong friendship.

Sonic Screwdriver Facts

Fragile housing cracked through use

- **The range of functions is almost limitless, and includes: interception of signals ranging from transmat beams to conscious thought; medical diagnostics and repair of organic parts; cutting, but also reattaching together materials such as barbed wire; operating Earth machinery such as computers and even cash machines; creating a spark to light a candle.**
- **The only locks that sonic screwdrivers cannot open are "deadlock seals."**

Tools of the Trade

IN ADDITION TO HIS TRUSTY Sonic Screwdriver, the Doctor has many devices to make life easier for him and his friends. His capacious pockets often produce a piece of technology that is just the thing for defeating a monster, but the Doctor also uses his high-tech knowledge to improvise weapons or handy gadgets. These are just a few of the things he has made use of in his travels.

Psychic Paper

Psychic paper appears blank but projects a low-level telepathic field, causing the viewer to see whatever they expect to see—such as an invitation or security pass—although it may also reflect what the holder is thinking. The Face of Boe and River Song contact the Doctor for help via his paper, and he has used it to gain entry to many places, such as Adipose Industries and Ood Operations. However, its use is limited: geniuses and individuals with psychic training are not fooled by the paper's trickery.

Page is blank until psychically activated to present an image

Clothes Make the Doctor

Every time the Doctor regenerates, he selects an outfit to suit his new personality. Each Doctor has a unique sense of style. Fortunately, the TARDIS has an enormous wardrobe from which the Doctor can pick and choose until he finds just what he wants to express his new identity. The Tenth Doctor prefers to dress in a manner that easily blends into many times and cultures.

Deadlock Seal

The TARDIS is secured with a deadlock seal, which is impregnable from even sonic forces. In addition to door locks, other objects can be deadlocked, such as the ATMOS device created by the Sontarans and the circuitry of the robotic Host onboard the spaceship *Titanic.*

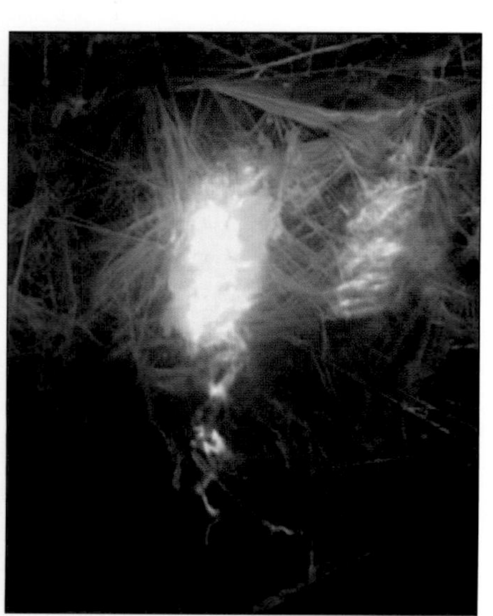

Huon Particles

An ancient form of energy, Huons were commonly used in the Dark Times by species such as the Racnoss for powering their webstar spaceships and teleporting. However, the Time Lords intervened and obliterated this deadly substance by unraveling its atomic structure. The only trace of it that remained was a remnant in the heart of every TARDIS. Billions of years after their destruction, the Empress of the Racnoss attempted to restore the Racnoss's power source by artificially constructing Huon particles using Donna Noble.

Handle can be used to lift two tons

Activation switch makes clamp stick to surface

Discovered on Earth by Torchwood Two operatives

Magna-Clamp

Alien magna-clamps cancel the mass of any object to which they are attached, rendering it virtually weightless. They form an unbreakable bond with any surface, which the Doctor and Rose find useful when they want to keep from being pulled into the Void, while every Dalek and Cyberman is sucked in.

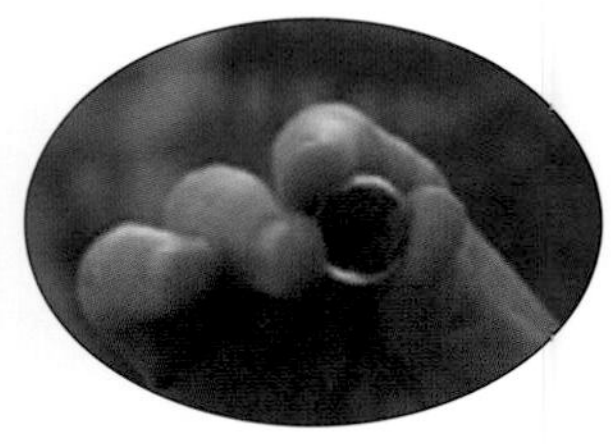

Biodamper Ring

A biodamper conceals the genetic signature of its wearer, hiding them from detection. It can only conceal known organisms.

Antiplastic

Antiplastic is a chemical liquid that breaks down plastic into its component molecules on contact. This makes it a useful weapon against creatures made of living plastic such as the Nestene Consciousness. When the Doctor tries to reason with the Nestenes, the fact that he is even in possession of antiplastic is regarded as a declaration of war.

Organic growth

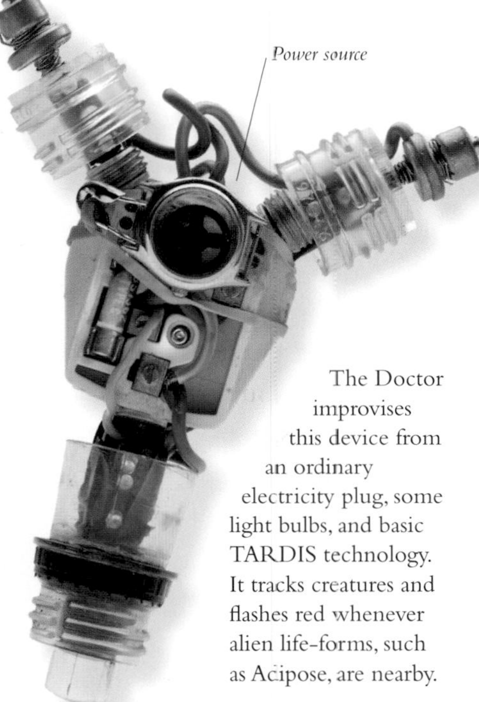

The Doctor improvises this device from an ordinary electricity plug, some light bulbs, and basic TARDIS technology. It tracks creatures and flashes red whenever alien life-forms, such as Acipose, are nearby.

ALIEN TRACKER

3-D Glasses

When objects pass through the Void—the space between dimensions—they attract tiny particles of matter, which stick to their forms. These remnants of the Void are invisible to the naked eye, but appear as red and green sparkling halos around objects when viewed through 3-D glasses.

Tribophysical Waveform Macro-kinetic Extrapolator

This extrapolator acts as a pan-dimensional surfboard, shielding its user in a force field and then riding energy waves to a preset destination. It can be programmed to lock onto an alien energy source and take its power. Integrated into the TARDIS, it emits a force field that helps the ship resist external forces exerted upon it.

Casing contains a shield generator

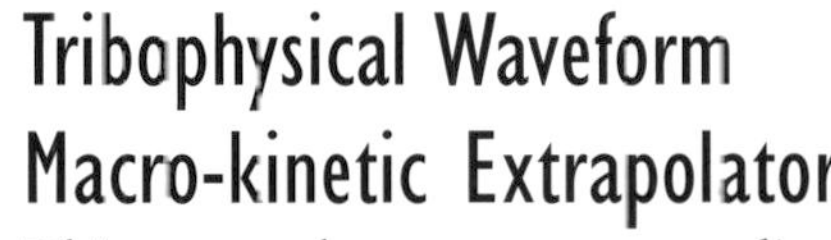

EMP TRANSMITTER

A core component of cyborgs (part-robotic and part-biological creatures), the EMP transmitter can be used to create a strong electromagnetic pulse that will scramble the circuits of any robot within a 50-yard radius.

Ice Gun

Named "ice guns" by Mickey Smith, these weapons emit a freezing vapor that extinguishes fires. They are a standard safety feature on 51st-century spaceships, such as the SS *Madame de Pompadour*, where they were also useful for temporarily disabling the Clockwork Robots, who went rogue while crewing the vessel.

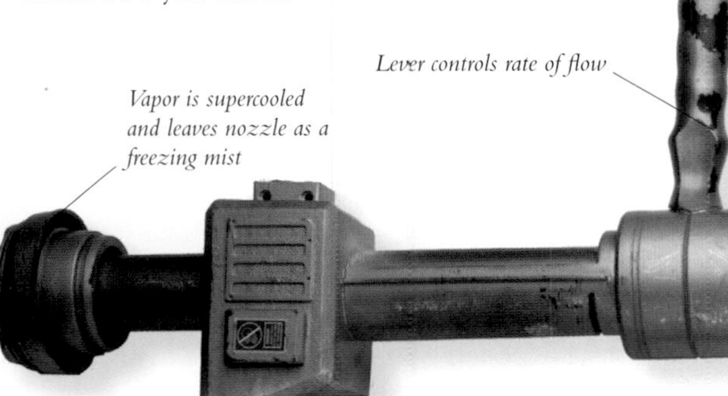

Pressing trigger turns liquid to vapor and propels it out of the extinguisher

Rose Tyler

THE WORLD OF London teenager Rose Tyler is transformed the night she is attacked by possessed plastic mannequins in Henrik's department store. A mysterious stranger called the Doctor saves her life and offers her a way out of her dull life as a sales assistant—a chance to travel with him across the universe. But this amazing adventure comes at a cost. Rose must leave behind her mom, who is also her best friend, her boyfriend, Mickey, and the life she knows on Earth.

Working Girl

At the end of her shift in Henrik's, Rose heads to the basement to deposit the store's lottery money. She is suddenly surrounded by deadly mannequins and freezes as they are about to kill her. The Doctor appears, grabs her hand, and makes her run for her life.

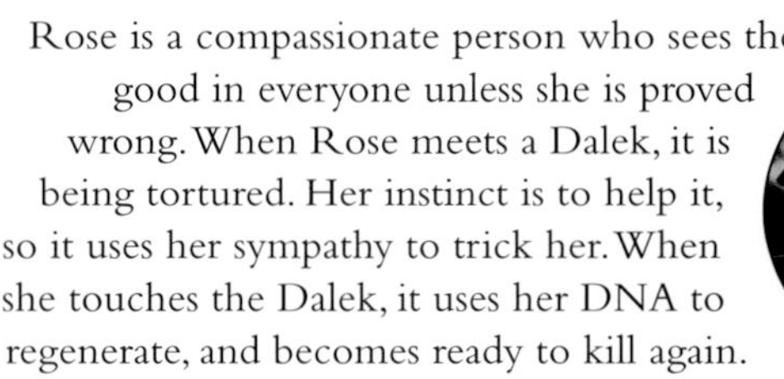

Rose is a compassionate person who sees the good in everyone unless she is proved wrong. When Rose meets a Dalek, it is being tortured. Her instinct is to help it, so it uses her sympathy to trick her. When she touches the Dalek, it uses her DNA to regenerate, and becomes ready to kill again.

Rose's mom, Jackie, is grateful when she remembers to call home

Rose's "superphone" is the only contact she has with her mom when she is traveling through time and space. The Doctor upgraded her cell to provide her with universal roaming so she could call home from five billion years in the future.

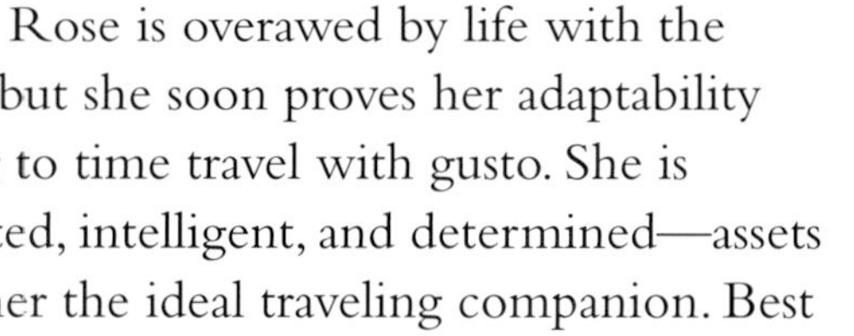

A New Life

At first, Rose is overawed by life with the Doctor, but she soon proves her adaptability by taking to time travel with gusto. She is quick-witted, intelligent, and determined—assets that make her the ideal traveling companion. Best of all, Rose has a wicked sense of humor that makes their adventures together fun.

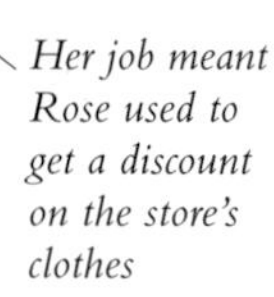

Her job meant Rose used to get a discount on the store's clothes

Rose Facts

- **Rose was born in April 1987. She was six months old when her father died, leaving her mother, Jackie, to raise her alone.**
- **She lives with her mom in an apartment on the Powell Council Estate.**
- **She was suspended from her school, Jericho Street Comprehensive, for persuading the choir to go on strike.**
- **She won a bronze medal in under-sevens gymnastics in elementary school.**

When she looks into the Heart of the TARDIS, Rose absorbs the energy of the Time Vortex, the medium through which the TARDIS travels. It gives her power over time and space, but starts to destroy her. The Doctor sacrifices his ninth incarnation to save her.

Rose is thrilled by her exciting life with the Doctor, whom she begins to realize she loves. But her time with him comes to a sudden end when she is sucked into a parallel world. But when all of reality is in danger, Rose returns to give the Doctor the "Bad Wolf" message—a warning that the end of the universe is imminent.

A Companion for Rose

Rose's foray into this reality helps foil Davros's Reality Bomb, but she still has to return to her parallel life. Despite their love, the Doctor is not able to join her. However, the Doctor's human version–created from his hand and a human–can. He is just like the Doctor, except that he is Rose's own kind.

Mickey's earring was a gift from Rose

Mickey Smith

Rose and Mickey Smith have been dating for a long time, so he is jealous when she leaves to travel with the Doctor. Mickey is loyal, sensitive, and a little sentimental, but when forced to rely on himself, and after facing many deadly aliens, Mickey becomes a brave freedom fighter.

Mickey Meets Ricky

On a parallel Earth, Mickey meets his alternative self, Ricky, who is tough and in control. He leads a gang that fights for humanity against an army of Cybermen.

At first Mickey is scared and overwhelmed by the Doctor's world. But a brief stint as his second companion, alongside Rose, transforms him into a heroic figure. He helps to defeat the Slitheen, the Krillitanes, Cybermen, and Davros's Reality Bomb.

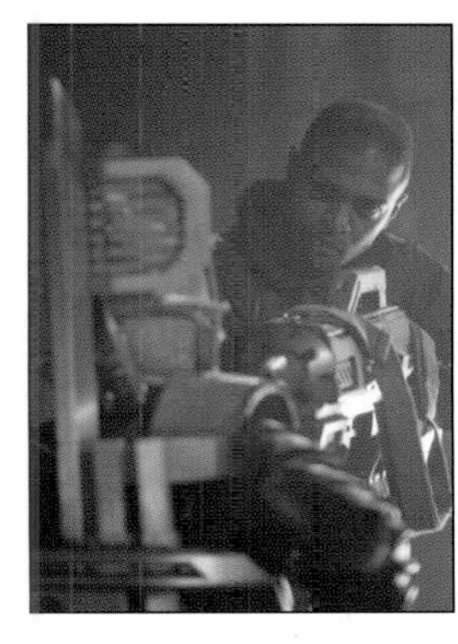

Jackie's feelings for the Doctor are complicated. She resents him for taking away her daughter, but she also feels affection for him and takes him in when he is sick.

Jackie Tyler

As a single mother, life has been tough for Jackie Tyler. At 19, she was left to raise Rose on her own. Jackie is funny, flirtatious, and very popular. Although she is sometimes brash, she is fiercely loyal and loves Rose more than anything.

Rose's father, Peter Alan Tyler, died when she was just six months old. When this world's Jackie and Rose are transported to the parallel universe, they are reunited with Pete.

Jackie is a licensed hairdresser

Dr. Martha Jones

CAPABLE AND INDEPENDENT, 23-year-old medical student Martha Jones impresses the Doctor right from the beginning. When the Royal Hope Hospital is transported to the Moon by the rhino-headed Judoon, Martha remains calm while all around her panic. Within hours of meeting the Doctor, she not only saves his life, but manages to save Earth, too.

Wears white medical coat with pride

UNIT call sign is Greyhound Six

Chic, fashionable appearance befits a professional woman

Medical student

From the start, Martha is less in awe of the Doctor than his previous companion Rose was. As a medical student, she is comfortable in the world of science and has a quick understanding of the complex concepts his world revolves around. She spends much of her time feeling second best to Rose, but her actions show that she is just what the Doctor ordered.

The Doctor and Martha quickly become friends, but when he kisses her—to complete a genetic transfer—Martha feels the first stirrings of love that complicate their time together.

Maid to Measure

Martha refuses to be "just a passenger" in the TARDIS, and the Doctor soon shows she is much more than that. When he hides as a human on prewar Earth, he gives Martha the responsibility of keeping him and everyone around him safe.

Martha Facts

- **When the Doctor first offers Martha a trip in the TARDIS she refuses—because of her exams! She soon changes her mind when the Doctor proves he can travel in time.**
- **Shakespeare is fascinated by Martha—could the medical student be the inspiration for his famous "Dark Lady" sonnets?**
- **Martha temporarily becomes a medical officer for the Cardiff-based alien-research organization Torchwood, under the command of Captain Jack Harkness.**
- **Initially, Martha does not know how to use a gun, but she soon learns and during the Dalek invasion UNIT gives her responsibility for twenty-five nuclear warheads.**

Martha keeps her trademark red leather jacket on, even when she visits Elizabethan England!

The Jones Family

Although Martha's parents are separated, she has a good relationship with everyone in her lively family.

Francine dresses up for Dr. Lazarus's reception

Francine Jones

It is clear where Martha gets her fiesty side from! Proud and unyielding, her mom distrusts the Doctor and will do whatever it takes to protect her daughter, even if that means betraying her to the authorities.

Clive Jones

Martha's dad seems irresponsible, leaving his family for a 21-year-old woman. But, he shows he can put his family first when he risks his own life to warn Martha that she is in danger.

Letitia Jones

Older sister Tish shows echoes of her sister's courage when she encounters danger. She is close to Martha and senses her unrequited feelings for the Doctor.

Leo Jones

With a girlfriend and baby, Leo is the most settled of the Jones family, despite being the youngest. But fatherhood does not stop him from getting into trouble from time to time.

Family Ties

Martha learns that families and the Doctor do not mix when her family is used as pawns by the Master. She feels responsible for their suffering and gives up time-traveling to keep them safe.

Spreading the Word

When the Master ravages life on Earth, Martha becomes a legend by spreading hope and telling stories of the Doctor around the world. But her success wipes out her celebrity: the hero is forgotten when the Master is defeated and time is reversed.

Not Second Best

The Doctor doesn't love Martha—and she realizes she cannot waste her life waiting for it to happen. Strong-minded Martha can succeed on her own, and her family needs her back on Earth.

A United Front

With Martha's record of saving the world, it is not surprising that the Unified Intelligence Agency (UNIT)—the organization charged with defending Earth—wants Martha on its medical staff. It might look like she has become a soldier, but principled Martha is working from the inside to stop the fighting. The Doctor taught her well.

Martha is compassionate and positive. When the war-mongering Sontarans create a clone of her for their army, it looks into her mind, with all her hope and dreams, and changes allegiance as it dies.

A New Life

Back on Earth, Martha moves on from the Doctor and falls for pediatrician Tom Milligan. Determined and hard-working, she builds a new life for herself as a doctor with a job at UNIT, and she and Tom get engaged. She learned a lot on her travels with the Doctor, but she suffered, too. For now, she is back on Earth, but Martha's life will never be the same again.

Donna Noble

SHE WAS A LOUDMOUTH who hated Christmas, could not point to Germany on a map, and deep down thought she was worthless. But being with the Doctor allowed Donna to see herself in a new way. She shows she has compassion and sense, and when she saves the cosmos from Davros's Reality Bomb, Donna is the most important woman in the whole universe!

Donna and the Doctor do not exactly hit it off when they first meet—Donna thinks the Doctor is kidnapping her and the Doctor is still missing Rose—but later they form a strong friendship.

There Goes the Bride

Donna's dream wedding ends in disaster when she disappears from the church and materializes in the TARDIS. Worse still, she discovers her scheming fiancé has been transforming her into a human key to help the Empress of the Racnoss regain her powers. The Doctor defeats the Racnoss but Donna is shocked by his cruelty. When the Doctor offers to take her with him in the TARDIS, she declines.

Donna missed the Sycorax invasion (hungover) and the Cybermen incident (scuba-diving in Spain), but she has front row seats for the Racnoss!

Fiery red hair matches her fiery temper

Confident face in public hides self-doubt

Well-groomed appearance inspires confidence when undercover

Chic suit for office work

Cannot believe how much running is involved in being with the Doctor!

Donna's Family

Donna is the only child of Geoff and Sylvia Noble. As a child, she used to go to West Ham soccer games with her Dad. Donna adores her maternal grandfather Wilfred Mott. Wilf's first encounter with the Doctor, when the *Titanic* nearly crashed into Earth, fueled his avid interest in aliens.

Sylvia cannot forgive the Doctor for helping to ruin Donna's wedding and does not want her daughter to be his companion. Deep down she is proud of Donna, but she is not very good at showing it.

SYLVIA NOBLE

WILFRED MOTT

An avid amateur astronomer, Wilf adores his only grandchild. Unlike Sylvia, he thinks that Donna should go with the Doctor as it is a once-in-a- lifetime opportunity to explore the stars.

The Little General

Donna comes to regret not going with the Doctor when she had the chance, so she sets off to find him. With her suitcases packed and ready in the car trunk, Donna investigates every strange occurrence and conspiracy theory that she can find.

Donna Facts

- **Donna has always been strong willed. On her first day of school she was sent home for biting, and aged six, she set off on a bus for Strathclyde by herself.**
- **Donna is the best temp in Chiswick. Her skills include shorthand, filing, and she can type 100 words per minute.**
- **Donna is the first—and perhaps only—human to witness the creation of the Earth.**
- **She has a flair for numbers—Donna mastered the library codes that make up the Dewey Decimal System in two days.**
- **Unlike Rose and Martha, Donna is not in love with the Doctor. She enjoys their time together, but just considers him a friend.**

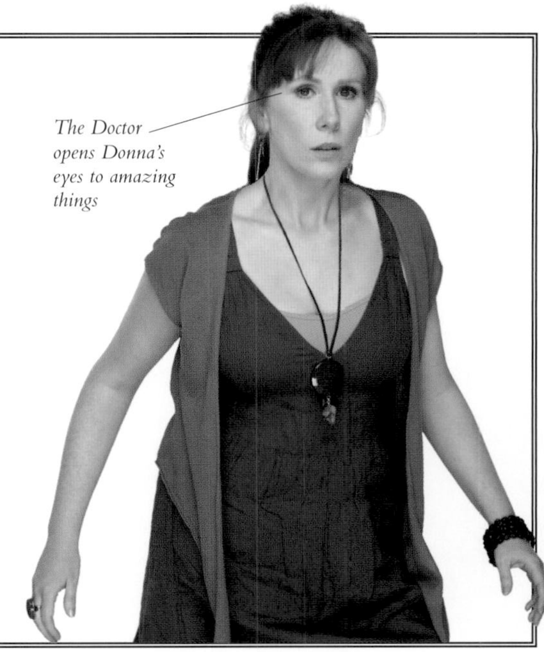

The Doctor opens Donna's eyes to amazing things

Life Without Donna

Being with Donna changes the Doctor and it turns out that without her there would be no Doctor at all. A beetle belonging to a being known as the Trickster reveals an alternate timeline in which Donna never met the Doctor and he was killed by the Racnoss.

TRICKSTER'S BEETLE

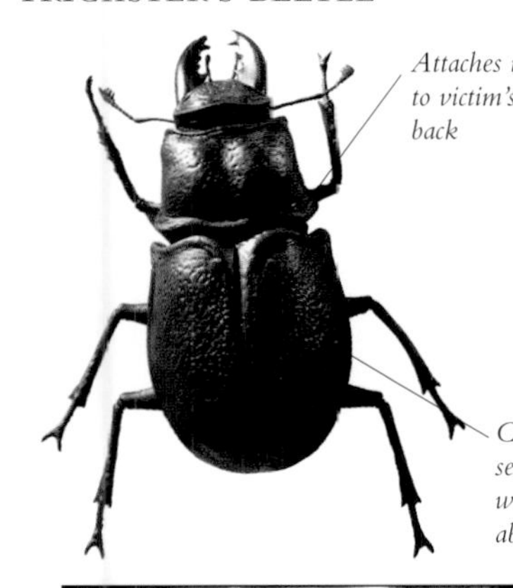

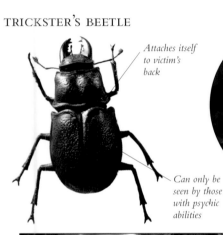

Attaches itself to victim's back

Can only be seen by those with psychic abilities

Donna's compassion influences the Doctor. When they visit Pompeii she convinces him to save Caecilius's family. She also shares the responsibility for destroying Pompeii so that the Doctor doesn't have to bear the weight alone.

Turn Left!

Donna truly believes she is nothing special. However, when she is caught up in the Trickster beetle's alternate timeline, Rose takes her back in time to sacrifice her own life, ensuring that the correct timeline plays out and the Doctor lives.

The Doctor-Donna

When the Daleks capture the TARDIS and take it back to their flagship, the *Crucible*, only Donna and the Doctor's severed hand are left on board. Somehow, the two entities fuse, creating a human Doctor and giving Donna the knowledge of a Time Lord. The all-new Doctor-Donna is the only thing that can save the universe from Davros.

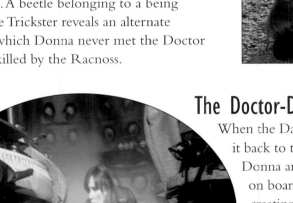

A Time Lord brain is so powerful, that its human host cannot survive. The Doctor reluctantly leaves Donna to save her life. If she ever remembers him, she will die.

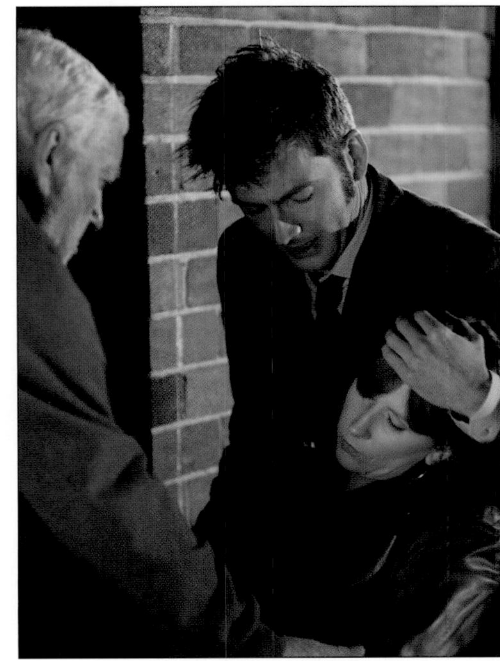

Captain Jack Harkness

Jack has never revealed his true name

Stripes for his fake rank of Captain

Jack favors 1940s' styles, even in the present day

BORN IN THE BOESHANE PENINSULA in the 51st century, "Jack" was recruited to the Time Agency, a mysterious espionage organization, but left after it stole two years of his memory. He put his enormous charm to work as a conman, taking the identity of a Captain Jack Harkness. After meeting the Doctor he discovers unexpected levels of courage and selflessness and leaves his criminal ways. He sacrifices his life defending the Game Station on Satellite 5 from the Daleks—but it is not the end of his story...

Stranded on Earth in 1869 after leaving Satellite 5, Jack moves to the site of Cardiff's Rift to wait for the Doctor. He is recruited by Torchwood Three. In 2000, he becomes leader and builds a team including Ianto Jones and Gwen Cooper.

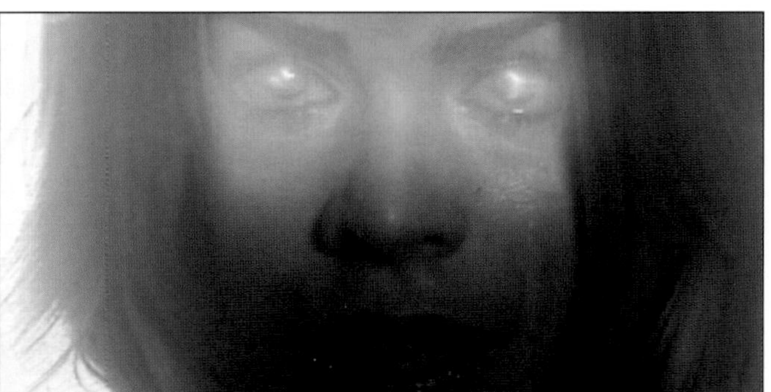

Immortality

When Rose opens the heart of the TARDIS and absorbs the Time Vortex, she gains its tremendous powers. With her abilities, she raises Jack from the dead after he is exterminated by the Daleks on Satellite 5. But she cannot control these all-consuming powers, and Jack is returned, not for one lifetime, but forever.

"The Man Who Couldn't Die"

Jack puts his immortality to good use, performing extraordinary feats to help others, such as entering the deadly radiation chamber on Malcassairo to repair the Utopia rocket and braving a Toclafane attack to destroy the Master's Paradox Machine.

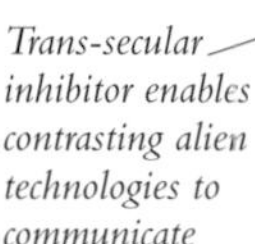

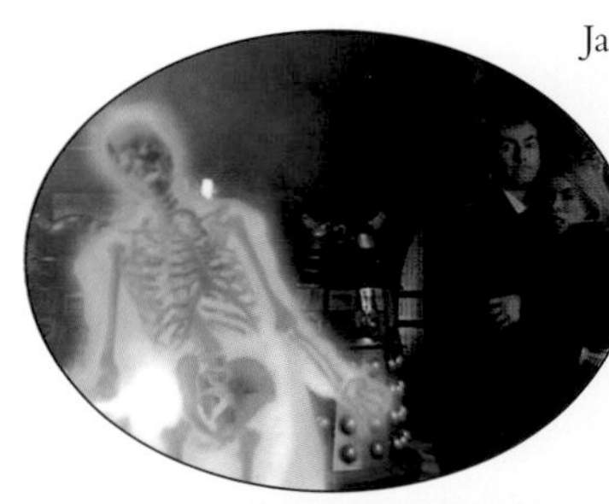

Jack engineers his death when he meets the Daleks again in their Crucible. Horrified, Rose does not know she made him immortal, but Davros is also fooled and resurrected Jack escapes.

Trans-secular inhibitor enables contrasting alien technologies to communicate

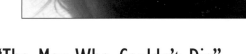

Central tracking transponder essential during surveillance

Main bulkhead

Ship A.I. personality matrix

Emergency cargo dump—essential for occasional extra-legal smuggling jobs

Life support

Yoke—only to be used when manual flight is absolutely necessary

Conning his away across the galaxy after leaving the Time Agency, Jack stole a Chula ship by telling its female owner he would be back in five minutes! In common with all Chula vessels, the ship contained subatomic healing robots called nanogenes, and had invisibility and teleport capabilities. The ship exploded after he beamed aboard a bomb to stop it from destroying Earth, but Jack was rescued in the nick of time by the Doctor in the TARDIS.

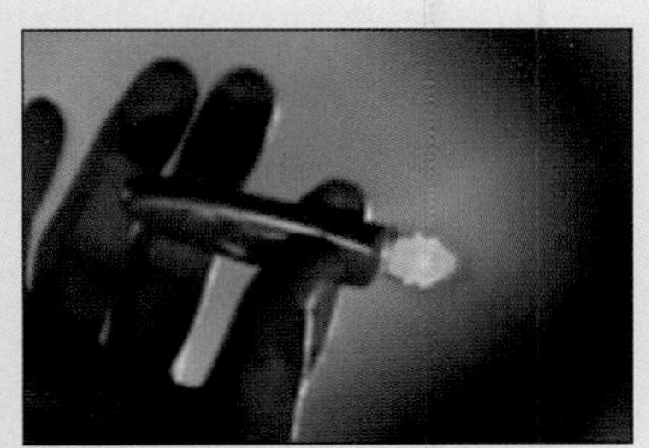

Zapper

- 51st-century technology
- Used to operate ship systems, including cloaking devices and music systems
- Bulb illuminates when the Zapper is activated

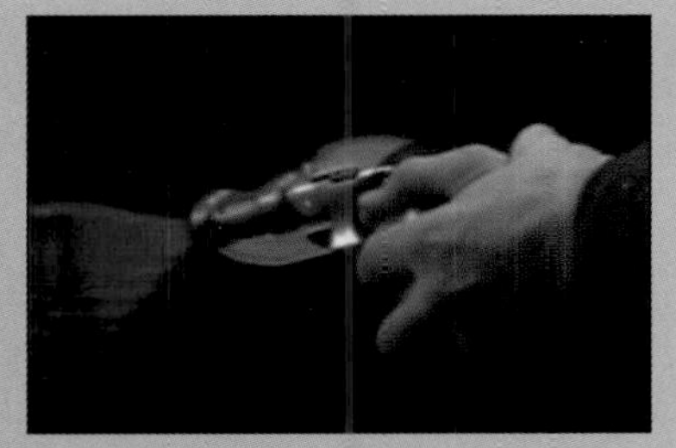

Digital Gun

- Manufactured in the weapons factories of Villengard
- Functions as a sonic blaster, sonic cannon, and a triple-enfolded sonic disruptor
- Battery life is short

Vortex Manipulator

- Scans for alien technology and overrides electronic devices
- Performs basic medical examinations
- Projects simple holographic images

Electro Binoculars

- Rented from a Martian store specializing in retro accessories
- Used by Jack to mimic Royal Air Force-issue binoculars.
- Feature incredible night vision and magnification

Traveling through the Vortex

There is no escape from Captain Jack! The Doctor tries to avoid him in Cardiff by dematerializing the TARDIS—but Jack grabs the outside! The immortal captain will not let go, even though the TARDIS travels all the way to the end of the universe trying to shake him off.

Captivating Captain

Used to the free and easy ways of the 51st century, and blessed with natural good looks and winning ways, Jack flirts his way through life. Martha and Rose are just some of those who have been captivated by his charm.

A Boy and His Toys

Jack has always been fascinated by gadgets, how they work, what they do and, most importantly, what they can do for him. At the Time Agency, Jack discovered all kinds of impressive toys, but when he sees something new, he will get it by any means—whether he has to steal, borrow, or haggle in a thrift store.

VORTEX MANIPULATOR

Deserted

To a Time Lord, who sees all the infinite possibilities of time, a fixed, "impossible" point—such as immortal Jack—is unbearable. The Doctor follows his instincts and flees, abandoning Jack on Satellite 5.

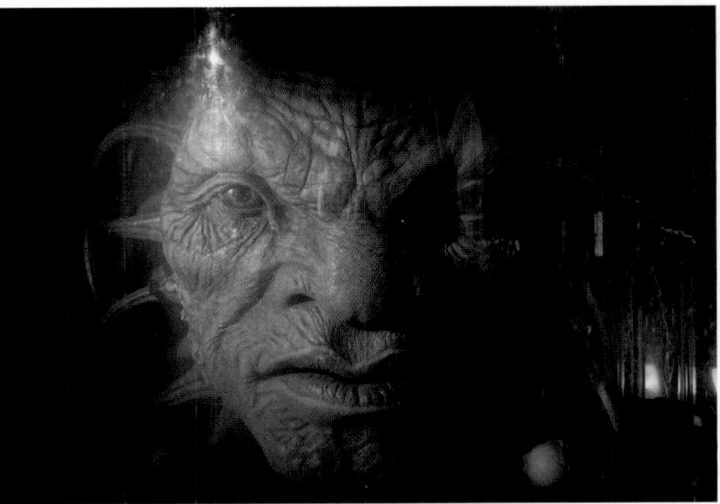

The Face of Boe

What happens to an immortal who keeps aging? Jack had been a poster boy in the Boeshane Peninsula, earning the nickname "the Face of Boe." The Doctor has met another Face of Boe—an ancient giant alien head. Is this who Captain Jack will become after billions of years?

The Face of Boe sacrifices himself to free the people of New Earth, and imparts his dying secret to the Doctor: "You Are Not Alone." This hint that the Master is living as Professor Yana at the end of the universe gives a clue to the fact that the Face of Boe has been to the far future as Captain Jack.

John Smith

JOHN SMITH—the most ordinary of names—has often been the Doctor's alias of choice when wanting to blend in. But, when he needs somewhere to hide from the deadly Family of Blood, he not only adopts the name, but actually becomes John Smith. The Family is able to track a Time Lord anywhere in time or space, so the TARDIS rewrites the Doctor's DNA so he truly is human.

The Doctor's real life seeps through into John Smith's dreams, which he records as fiction in what he calls his "journal of impossible things." The TARDIS, Rose, and many monsters all feature, as well as memories of the Earth's future, such as World War I (1914–1918).

From Doctor to Teacher

The Doctor has visited history but John Smith merely gets to teach it. The TARDIS places him in Herefordshire in 1913 as a history teacher at Farringham School for Boys. The disguise is so complete, that Smith believes he has always been human and is the Nottingham-born son of watchmaker Sydney and nurse Verity. He is an ordinary man of narrow experiences who knows nothing of the Doctor.

POCKET WATCH

Time Lord can communicate from within

Perception filter makes it seem like an ordinary watch

Decorated with Gallifreyan symbols

Mortar board is symbol of authority

A product of his time, Smith approves of corporal punishment

Human senses are dull in comparison to a Time Lord's

Teacher disguise built on Doctor's love of knowledge

Smith relies on books for historical information

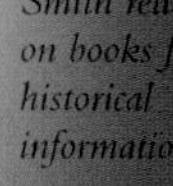

The Chameleon Arch

The TARDIS's chameleon arch can alter a Time Lord's physiology to any compatible species without affecting his outer appearance. Once transformation is complete, a Gallifreyan pocket watch—a symbol of the Time Lords' mastery over time—stores the original memories, personality, and biological data, which are restored the moment the watch is opened.

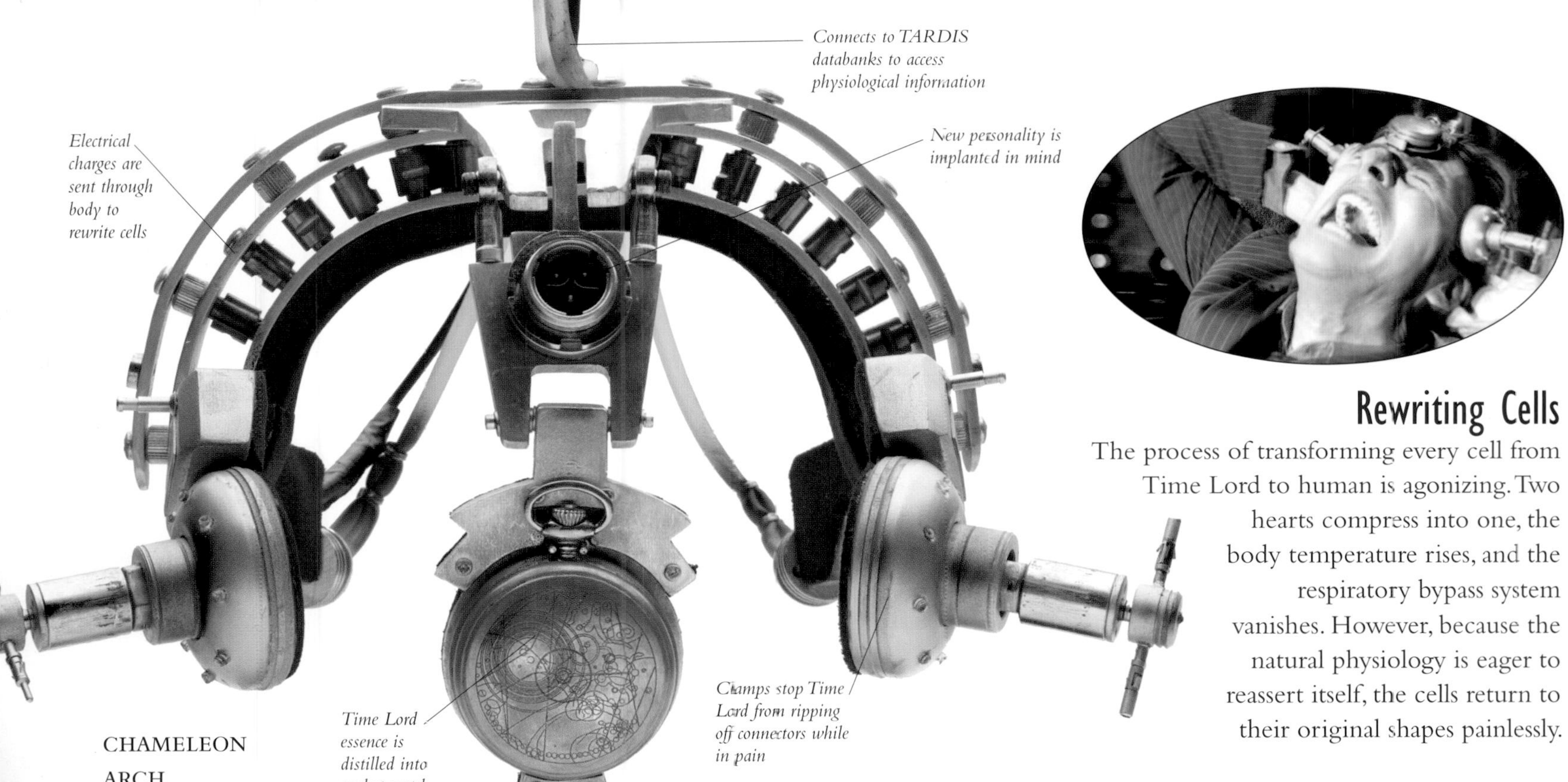

CHAMELEON ARCH

Rewriting Cells

The process of transforming every cell from Time Lord to human is agonizing. Two hearts compress into one, the body temperature rises, and the respiratory bypass system vanishes. However, because the natural physiology is eager to reassert itself, the cells return to their original shapes painlessly.

The Doctor in Love

Nurse Joan Redfern, a young war widow, is the Matron of Farringham School. Joan's unassuming but caring personality appeals to shy and insecure Smith. As an ordinary man, he can see the beauty in an ordinary woman. It is only natural that when two people are thrown together, a bond may develop—but falling in love is something the Doctor never allowed for in his plan.

Martha is the only one who knows the truth about John Smith. The Doctor has trusted her with his life, but in the meantime she has to endure the racism, sexism, and classism of the early 1910s—even from John Smith himself.

John Smith's Decision

When the Family's sense of smell tracks the Doctor down, Martha reveals his true identity to John Smith. But opening the pocket watch is not straightforward—it would mean the end of John Smith.

John Smith must choose which to follow: the life of a human, who loves and ages, or the eternal, lonely life of a Time Lord. Time energy from the pocket watch lets him see what could happen if he stays human. In 1915, he marries his true love, Joan Redfern.

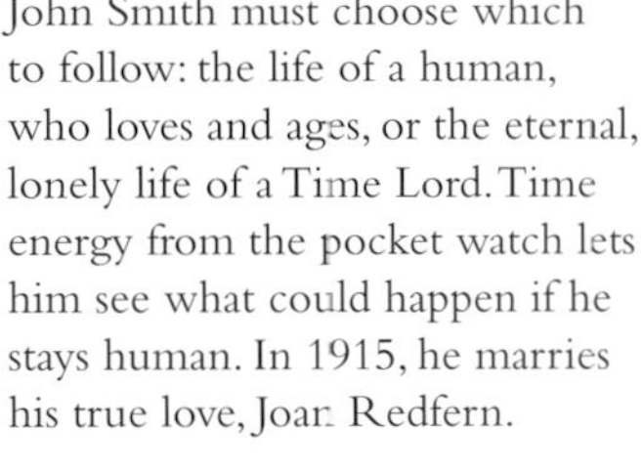

The next year, 1916, John experiences the overwhelming joy of holding his baby for the first time. He and Joan will have two daughters and a son.

Fifty years later, after a long and happy life, filled with love from his wife, children, and grandchildren, John breathes his last. The Doctor—virtually immortal—will never experience mortality like this.

John Smith cannot bear to give up his life, but he realizes he must sacrifice his chance of happiness for the greater good. Once back as the Doctor, however, he cannot imagine exchanging a Time Lord existence for a human one again!

Sarah Jane Smith

FEARLESS REPORTER Sarah Jane Smith traveled with the Doctor in his third and fourth incarnations. Together they confronted Daleks, Cybermen, android mummies, and many other strange creatures from the most distant parts of the universe. However, when the Doctor was suddenly recalled to Gallifrey he left Sarah Jane behind on Earth, without even saying goodbye. When the Doctor did not return for her, Sarah Jane assumed he was dead.

Thirty years later, Sarah Jane meets the Doctor when they both happen to be investigating strange events at a school. She doesn't recognize him in his tenth incarnation.

Sarah Jane Facts

- **Sarah Jane's adventures with the Doctor led her to pursue a career investigating occurences that were too strange or dangerous for other journalists to explore.**
- **When the Doctor builds a third version of his robot dog, K9, and sends it to Sarah Jane with his fondest regards, she realizes he hadn't forgotten her after all.**
- **Since settling back into life on Earth, Sarah Jane has never married or had any children.**

Friends Reunited

When she realizes that he really is the Doctor, Sarah Jane helps him outwit the deadly Krillitanes who are posing as teachers. This time, the Doctor says goodbye to Sarah Jane.

Mr. Smith

After traveling with the Doctor, Sarah Jane is aided in her adventures by supercomputer Mr. Smith. He was created through a union between her laptop and a Xylok crystal, which scans for alien threats from its attic hideaway. Mr. Smith can also link up with all the telephone exchanges in the world.

When Mr. Smith's Xylok side attempts to destroy the Earth, a virus wipes this objective from his memory banks and allows the talking computer to continue to help Sarah Jane.

Motherhood

An alien race called Bane created a boy from thousands of DNA samples, in a quest to find the archetypal human. He is rescued by Sarah Jane, who names him "Luke" and adopts him as her son.

Years later, Sarah Jane is reunited with the Doctor again. This time, to help defeat Davros and his Daleks.

K-9

LOYAL AND FEARLESS, boasting vast memory banks and highly sophisticated sensors, K-9 became indispensable to the Doctor during his fourth incarnation. He traveled everywhere with the Doctor and would defend him at all costs. When the Doctor's companion, Leela, decided to remain on Gallifrey, K-9 stayed with her. The Doctor then built a replacement, K-9 Mk II, and a third model was sent to Sarah Jane Smith. After K-9 Mk III is blown up defeating the Krillitane, the Doctor presents Sarah Jane with K-9 Mk IV.

Thirty years after the Doctor gave him to Sarah Jane, K-9 is in a bad way. The British climate and salted roads have taken their toll, but, fortunately, the Doctor is on hand to repair his old friend.

Old Friend

A brilliant doctor named Professor Marius created the first K-9 in the year 5000. Posted to a medical station near Titan, Marius needed a mobile computer and laboratory to assist him. Put together from available parts, Marius styled K-9 after his beloved pet dog on Earth.

Personality matrix

K-9 Facts

- **After the first K-9 helped the Doctor defeat a sentient virus, the robot's maker, Professor Marius, gave his creation to the Time Lord so he could assist him on his travels.**
- **According to the Doctor, K-9's design is the height of fashion in the year 5000.**

Sensor can analyze all known substances

DATA-COM PROBE (EXTENDED)

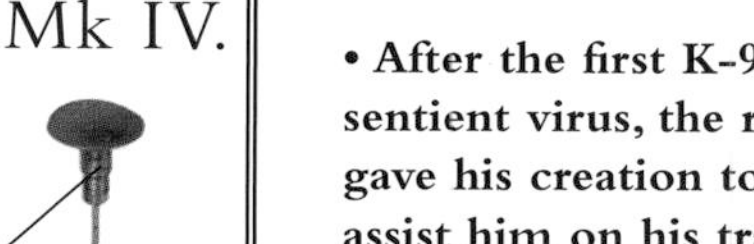

Tracking sensors

Gravitronic brain enables K-9's artificial intelligence

Multi wavelength optical spectrum sensor

Operator's manual console

Data-com probe (retracted)

Signal booster antenna

Storage for fully buffered deutronic battery

Removable cover to primary drives

Photon blaster

Name tag contains tracking beacon

Each model of K-9 has been equipped with a photon blaster in the snout. Like many human colonists, Professor Marius was wary of potential space threats.

All-terrain protective alignment buffer

Torchwood

Torchwood Facts

- **Security firm H. C. Clements acted as one of London Torchwood's many fronts for 23 years.**
- **Torchwood Three was charged by Queen Victoria with policing the Rift in Cardiff.**
- **There is a Torchwood Four, but no one, not even Captain Jack, knows its location.**
- **Torchwood is a top-secret organization—very few are supposed to know of its existence. Drugs are used to erase the memories of those who find out about it.**

IN 1879, QUEEN VICTORIA VISITED Torchwood House in Scotland, where she met the Doctor, and discovered the existence of aliens. Determined that the British Empire would be ready for its next extraterrestrial visitors, she founded the Torchwood Institute to protect Britain and its territories from aliens—but with the Doctor listed as enemy number one. Bases were established in London (Torchwood One), Glasgow (Torchwood Two), and Cardiff (Torchwood Three).

Over the years, the Torchwood Institute moved from defending against aliens to exploiting their technology, its motto being: "If it is alien, it is ours." Under Yvonne Hartman, this attitude led to a battle between Daleks and Cyberman at Canary Wharf and the destruction of the Torchwood Institute.

Torchwood Tower was built to reach a spatial breach 600 feet above sea level.

Captain Jack has worked at Torchwood for over a century

Hub may be entered via an invisible lift in Roald Dahl Plass, or a disused Tourist Information Center

Torchwood Three's HQ, the "Hub," is found under the Oval Basin in Cardiff's Bute Docks

Window was originally a marine outlet pump

Powerful and mysterious Rift Manipulator

The Hub has many levels, reaching deep underground

A New Torchwood

After the exploitative and aggressive Torchwood regime was destroyed in the Battle of Canary Wharf, Captain Jack reestablished Torchwood with a new ethos. Based in Cardiff, it returned to its original principles of defending the Earth.

Jack in Charge

Captain Jack recruited a new team to run Torchwood Three: Suzie Costello, Dr. Owen Harper, Toshiko Sato, and Ianto Jones. Costello was later replaced by police officer Gwen Cooper. Jack is fiercely loyal to his team, even to the point of turning down an opportunity to rejoin the Doctor to stay with them. He inspires loyalty in return, although his refusal to explain his past can cause resentment.

The Doctor puts aside his animosity toward Torchwood and asks for its help after the Earth is abducted by Daleks. Ianto and Gwen use the Rift to provide the power needed to tow the planet back home.

UNIT

THE UNIFIED INTELLIGENCE TASKFORCE (UNIT) was set up in the late twentieth century to deal with the alien menaces facing humankind. Although its remit is similar to Torchwood's, UNIT is a predominantly military organization. The Doctor spent several years as UNIT's scientific adviser after he was exiled to Earth by the Time Lords for meddling in the affairs of other planets.

The Valiant

UNIT's flagship is an aircraft carrier with a difference—it floats in the air, not on the sea! It was designed by evil Time Lord the Master while he was masquerading as Mr. Saxon and working for the Ministry of Defense, and he later made it his base of operations on Earth. After the Master's defeat, UNIT readopted the ship—but not before checking it thoroughly for any Time Lord tricks. Colonel Mace uses its strong engines to disperse the Sontarans' poisonous gas.

UNIT is based in Geneva but has branches worldwide. The British section (HQ: London) was headed for many years by the Doctor's friend Brigadier Lethbridge-Stewart; Colonel Mace is currently in charge. The US forces (HQ: New York) are commanded by General Sanchez.

UNIT Weaponry

After years of fighting aliens menaces, UNIT has amassed a stock of unusual weapons, each with a very specific purpose. Silver bullets are kept in case of a Werewolf attack, while anti-Dalek shells are troops' best hope of defeating Daleks. Gold-tipped bullets are reserved for Cybermen, and following recent intelligence, rad-steel coated bullets have been added to the arsenal to overcome Sontaran defenses.

Teleport operates when both cords are pulled

Technology salvaged from the Sontarans

Central panel conceals teleport base code

PROJECT INDIGO

UNIT's experimental teleport, Project Indigo, is untested, does not have coordinates, and is not stabilized—it is a possible death trap. But Martha uses it anyway because she is UNIT's only hope of finding the Doctor when Davros threatens the whole universe.

OSTERHAGEN KEY

Three Osterhagen stations must be online to use the Key

When the Earth faces destruction from Davros, Martha is sent by UNIT to prepare the Key for detonation

Twenty-five nuclear warheads have been placed at strategic locations under the Earth's crust, so that if the suffering of the human race reaches crisis point, they can be detonated by the holder of the Osterhagen Key.

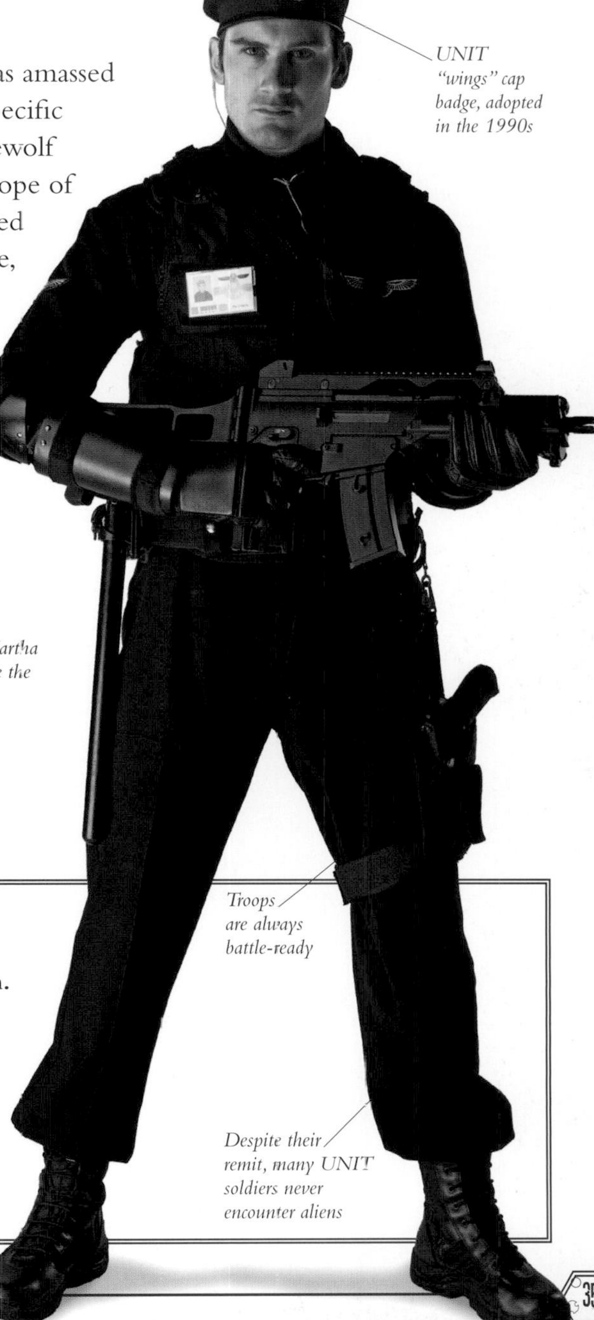

UNIT "wings" cap badge, adopted in the 1990s

Troops are always battle-ready

Despite their remit, many UNIT soldiers never encounter aliens

UNIT Facts

- **Martha Jones gets a job as a UNIT medical officer following the Doctor's recommendation.**
- **The Doctor is still officially a member of UNIT, never having resigned. However, he has never considered himself bound by the organization's rules and regulations.**
- **UNIT and Torchwood reluctantly share intelligence and resources, and staff are occasionally swapped between organizations.**

Platform One

WHEN ROSE CHOOSES the future for her first trip in the TARDIS, the Doctor shows off his time-traveling skills by taking her to the year 5.5/Apple/26, five billion years in the future. They arrive on *Platform One* half an hour before the Sun is due to engulf the Earth. The galaxy's rich and elite, which include the last-ever human, have assembled on the space station to witness the planet's demise.

The Steward is a blue-skinned humanoid
He wears a formal robe of welcome

The Steward

As the manager of *Platform One*, the Steward has many duties to perform. He acts as host, greeting and announcing visitors. At first, he thinks that the Doctor and Rose are intruders, but the Doctor uses his psychic paper to convince him he has an invitation. The Steward orders the TARDIS be towed away for illegal teleportation and issues the Doctor with a ticket to reclaim it later.

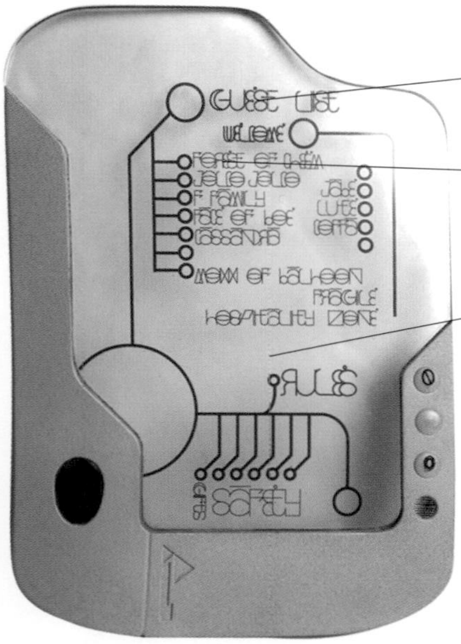

Guest list
Guests' names
Touch-sensitive screen

SPACE PANEL

This electronic device is used by the Steward to check the guest list for the Earth event. It connects with *Platform One*'s mainframe computer system, authenticating the guests' identification details.

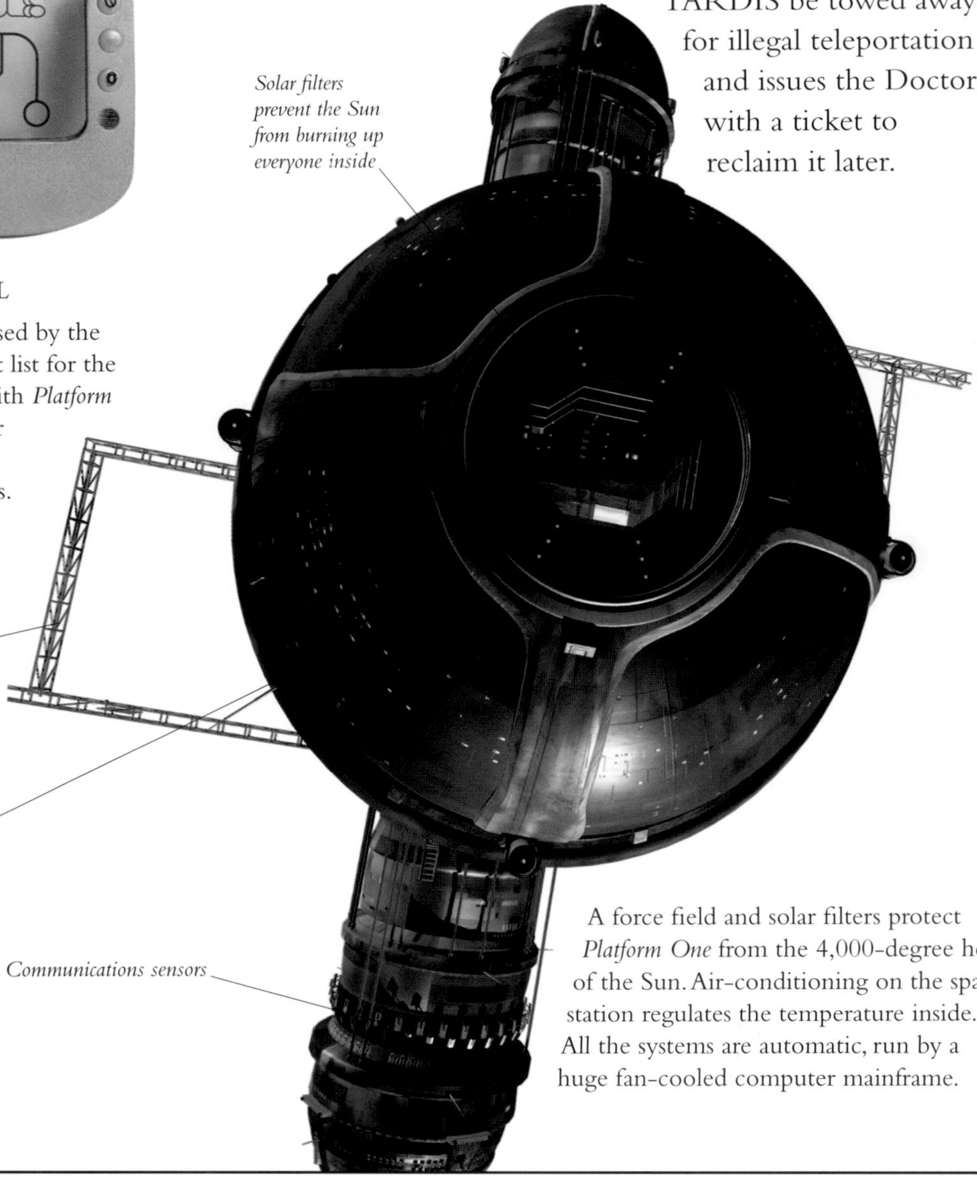

Solar filters prevent the Sun from burning up everyone inside
Maintenance girders
The marble-lined Greeting Hall and other formal rooms are situated in the disk-shaped hub
Communications sensors

A force field and solar filters protect *Platform One* from the 4,000-degree heat of the Sun. Air-conditioning on the space station regulates the temperature inside. All the systems are automatic, run by a huge fan-cooled computer mainframe.

Swept up "birds' nest" hairstyle is adorned with leaves

To show her status, Jabe wears a luxurious robe with a jewel-encrusted collar

Out of courtesy, Jabe keeps her liana, a vinelike appendage, out of sight

Rose sees the Earth from space for the first time

The Sun had been threatening to swallow the Earth for years, but the planet was saved by the National Trust. It used gravity satellites to stop the Sun's expansion and restored the planet to its former glory. But when the Trust's money ran out, the Earth was evacuated and left to die.

Helmet and visor for protection

Small blue-skinned aliens work as guards

PLATFORM GUARD

Thousands of blue-skinned humanoid aliens work on *Platform One*. One of them, a plumber named Raffalo, tells Rose that she is from Crespallion, which is part of the Jaggit Brocade, affiliated to the Scarlet Junction, in the Convex 56. This makes Rose realize how far away from home she is.

Dignitaries from the Forest of Cheem

Ceremonial armor of lacquered paper

Official robes, made of woven paper and gold thread

COFFA AND LUTE, JABE'S COMPANIONS

The Trees from the Forest of Cheem are an arboreal species descended from the tropical rain forests on Earth. They are highly intelligent and have deep respect for all life-forms. As the owners of vast amounts of land and forests on many planets, they have great wealth and influence.

Jabe, the Walking Tree

A seven-foot-tall alien, Jabe is the leader of the Trees, visitors from the Forest of Cheem. This noble, woody creature's full name is Jabe Ceth Ceth Jafe. Her scanning device reveals the Doctor's true identity, and she sympathizes with his plight as the last Time Lord.

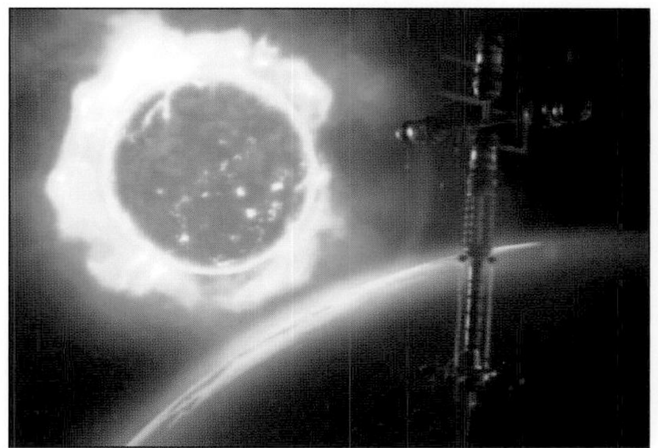

Platform One Facts

- **The station is an observation platform that travels between stars.**
- **The galaxy's elite pay to watch artistic events on the luxury space station.**
- **It is owned by a vast intergalactic corporation, which employs the Steward.**
- **Like many items on the station, the exo-glass in the viewscreen is capable of self-repair.**
- **Teleportation, religion, and all forms of weapons are forbidden on *Platform One*.**

Guests of *Platform One*

THE STRICTLY INVITATION-ONLY event on *Platform One* is reserved for the galaxy's wealthy elite. The honored guests, from many different worlds and a variety of races and species, have all come to pay their last respects to the Earth—and to network with the universe's most influential beings.

Chain of rank

THE ADHERENTS OF THE REPEATED MEME

The faceless, black-robed Adherents are greeted as guests on *Platform One*. But they are really remotely operated droids controlled by Lady Cassandra. Their gifts of metal spheres contain sabotaging robot spiders.

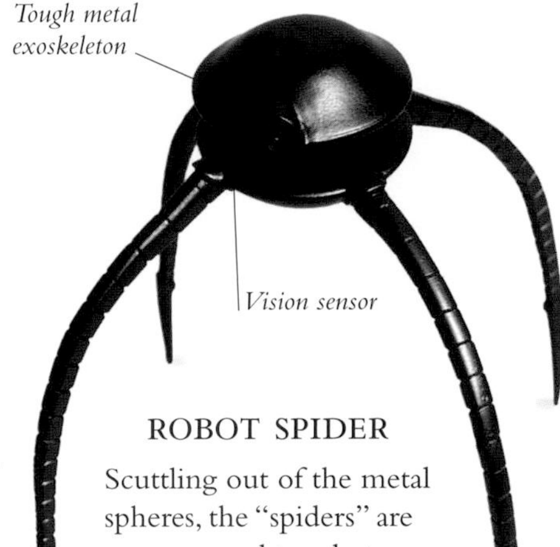

ROBOT SPIDER

Scuttling out of the metal spheres, the "spiders" are programmed to sabotage the *Platform One* computer, lift the sun filters, and destroy the space station.

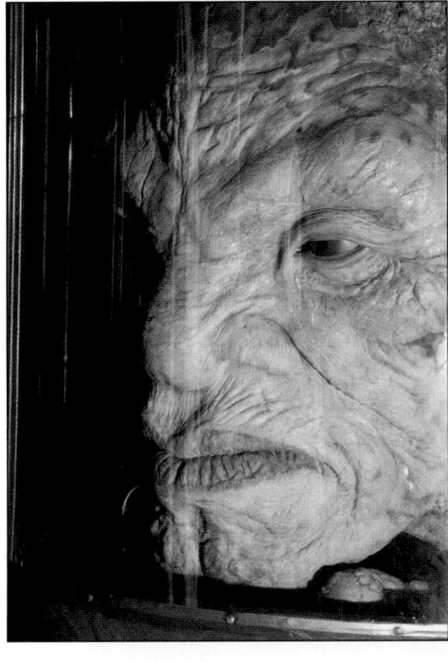

THE FACE OF BOE

The sponsor of the *Platform One* event is a huge humanoid head called the Face of Boe. He is the last of Boekind and, at millions of years old, the oldest being in the Isop galaxy. Boe's head is kept in a huge jar, and instead of hair, he has tendrils that end in small pods. This influential alien is one of the few survivors of the *Platform One* disaster.

THE BROTHERS HOP PYLEEN

These two wealthy lizard brothers are from the clifftops of Rex Vox. The pair made their fortune by inventing Hyposlip Travel Systems. They favor fur clothes, which keep their cold-blooded bodies warm.

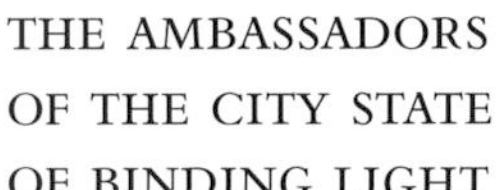

THE AMBASSADORS OF THE CITY STATE OF BINDING LIGHT

Due to their race's oxygen sensitivity, oxygen levels must be monitored strictly at all times in the Ambassadors' presence.

CAL 'SPARKPLUG'

The cybernetic hyperstar Cal "Sparkplug" MacNannovich arrives with his "plus-one."

MR. AND MRS. PAKOO

These birdlike creatures may be husband and wife but it is impossible to tell who is who. The pair have huge eyes and vicious-looking beaks. Their feathered heads give away their avian origins, although they walk like humans.

THE MOXX OF BALHOON

This goblinlike creature's legs are crippled by disease. He travels around on a speedy antigravity chair that contains a servo-motor. This device replaces his bodily fluids every 20 minutes because otherwise he sweats glaxic acid. The Moxx greets visitors with formal spitting.

Lady Cassandra

THE LAST "PURE" HUMAN, Lady Cassandra O'Brien Dot Delta Seventeen, is the only human who hasn't interbred with other species. Being incredibly beautiful in the past, Cassandra was adored by everyone. Now, her desire to keep thin and wrinkle-free means she is prepared to murder the guests on *Platform One* and cash in on the insurance money to pay for more operations.

Cassandra gives this rare ostrich egg to the Steward. It actually contains a teleportation field that Cassandra uses to escape, temporarily, from *Platform One*. She also secretly controls the Adherents of the Repeated Meme.

The ostrich is an extinct fire-breathing beast from Earth

CASSANDRA'S 'GIFT'

Lipstick and skin are all that are left of Cassandra's body

Without moisturization, her skin would dry out and disintegrate

Metal frame connects nerve fibers to Cassandra's brain

Brain kept in a jar of preserving solution

Lady Cassandra was thought to have died on *Platform One*, but her faithful servant, a forced-growth clone named Chip, hides her in a hospital on New Earth. With access to medicine and supplies, he cares for her while spider robots search for a new body.

Skin Deep

After 708 plastic surgery operations, Cassandra is finally as thin as she always wanted to be. Reduced to a translucent piece of skin with eyes and a mouth stretched across a frame, she is still obsessed with her looks. Rose is repulsed by her shallowness, calling her "the bitchy trampoline."

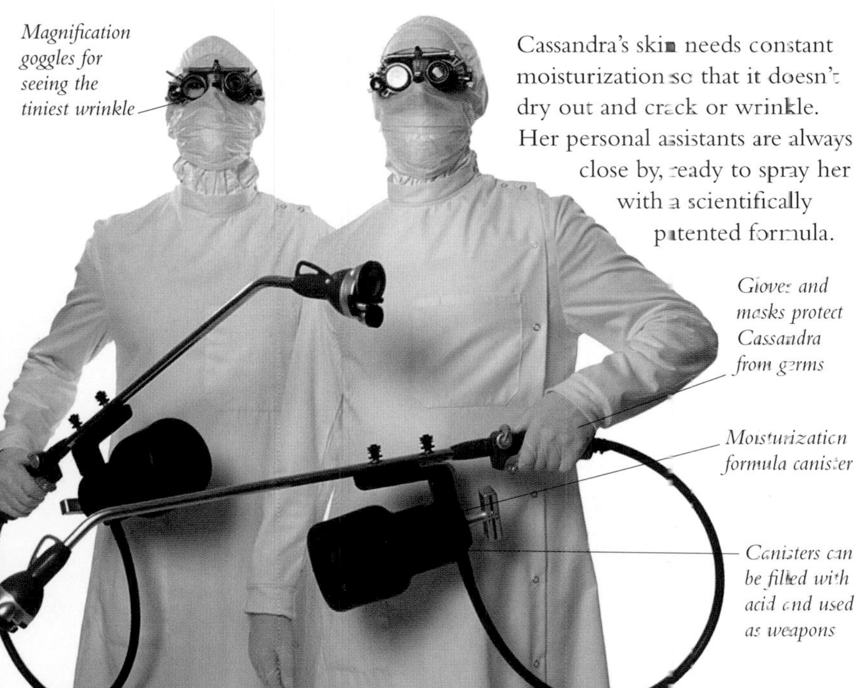

Magnification goggles for seeing the tiniest wrinkle

Cassandra's skin needs constant moisturization so that it doesn't dry out and crack or wrinkle. Her personal assistants are always close by, ready to spray her with a scientifically patented formula.

Gloves and masks protect Cassandra from germs

Moisturization formula canister

Canisters can be filled with acid and used as weapons

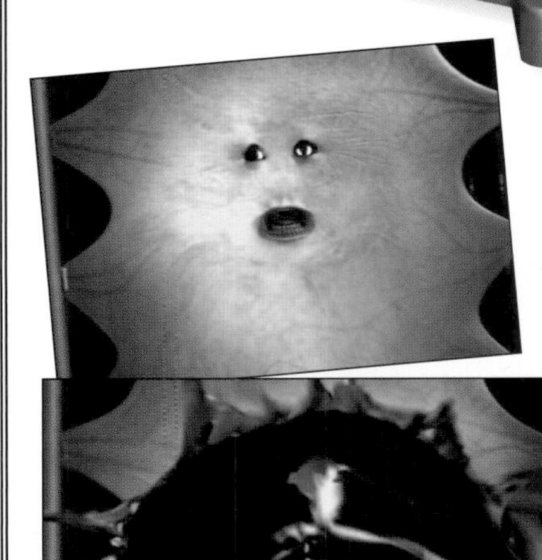

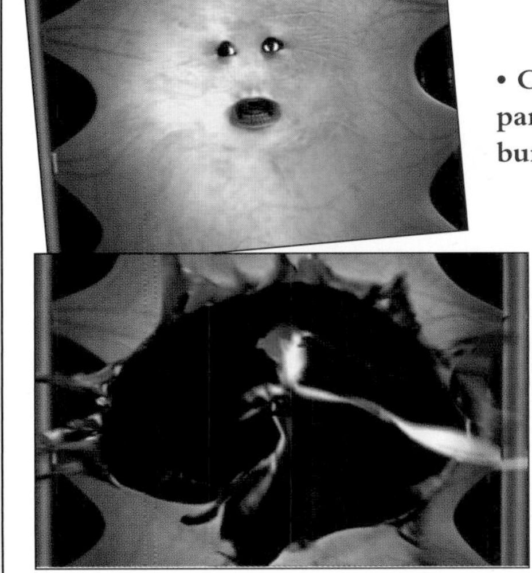

Cassandra Facts

- **Cassandra's "pure" human parents were the last to be buried in Earth's soil.**
- **She was born an American male but was transformed into an English woman.**
- **She has been married several times.**
- **Although her "body" was destroyed in the *Platform One* disaster, her brain survived.**

The Slitheen

The lush, abundant planet of Raxacoricofallapatorius, on the edge of the Milky Way, is home to a species of green-skinned, calcium-based bipedals. While most Raxacoricofallapatorians are peaceful and law-abiding, one particular family's criminality has given the entire species a bad reputation: the Slitheen clan. Banished from their own star system, the Slitheen now terrorize other worlds—including Earth.

Poisonous fingertips

Eyes blink from side to side

Compression field collar acquired through criminal contacts

Auxiliary tendons support long arms

Well-adapted Life-forms

Raxacoricofallapatorians are well suited to life on their own planet, using their powerful arms to swim from island to island in the great burgundy oceans and piercing through blizzards at the four poles with their large eyes.

Gas exchange during compression causes painful flatulence

The Slitheen family thinks nothing of profiting from planetary war. On Earth, family members stage the crash-landing of a spaceship in order to kick-start a nuclear war and turn the planet into radioactive waste—which can be sold in other galaxies as spaceship fuel.

Second Skins

As wanted criminals on many worlds, the Slitheen are often forced to work in disguise. Earth-based family members use compression field-generating neck collars to squeeze their huge bulks into the empty skin vessels of their human victims.

Excess skin folds tightly during compression process

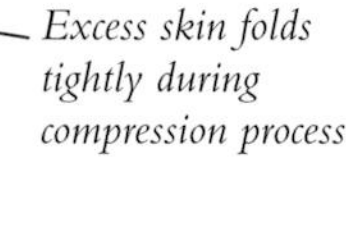

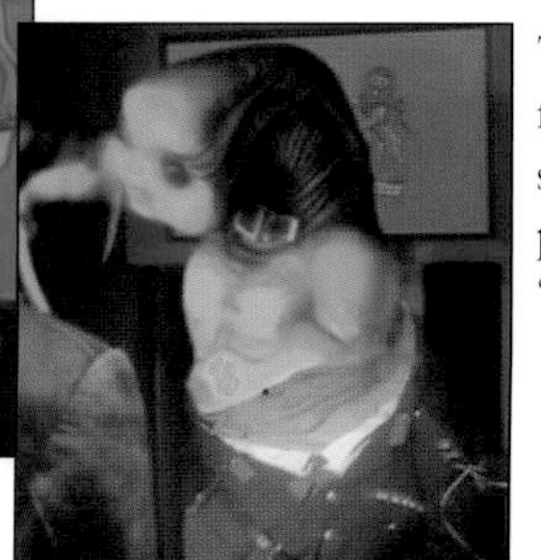

The Slitheen equipped their human costumes with zippers, hidden under hairlines or hats. Unzipping produces a burst of contained compression energy.

The Slitheen find human skins cramped, preferring their "naked" form.

Raxacoricofallapatorian Facts

- Raxacoricofallapatorian society is organized entirely around its large, powerful families. Family members use the species' extraordinary sense of smell to locate each other across vast distances and even to sense the death of loved ones.
- Raxacoricofallapatorian family names are a complex affair, with any number of hyphenations expressing the exact branch and sub-branch of complicated family trees.
- The Slitheen is one of the planet's oldest families, tracing its line back to the legendary Huspick Degenerate scion, who controlled an illegal spice-smuggling organization.
- Raxacoricofallapatorians hatch from eggs (*shown right*), using their powerful claws to break through the shell.

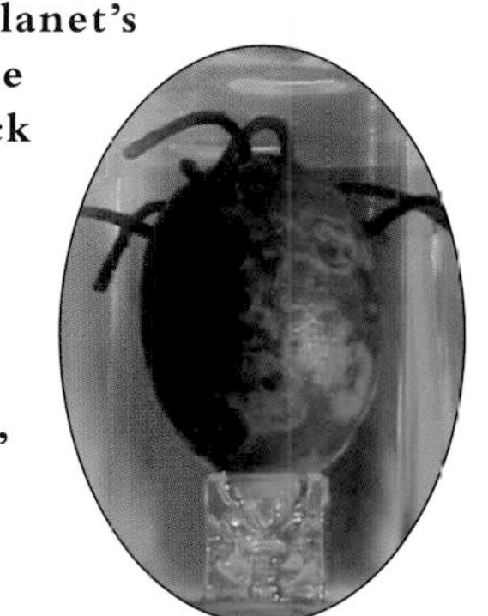

Faced with a murderous Slitheen on Earth, Jackie throws vinegar at it....

The acid in the vinegar reacts with the calcium in the Slitheen's body....

Fatal Weakness

Raxacoricofallapatorians' living-calcium structure is highly vulnerable to certain substances, most dangerously acetic acid, which causes an almost always fatal explosive reaction. On their home planet, the most heinous criminals were executed by being lowered into vats of acetic acid, ensuring a slow, painful death.

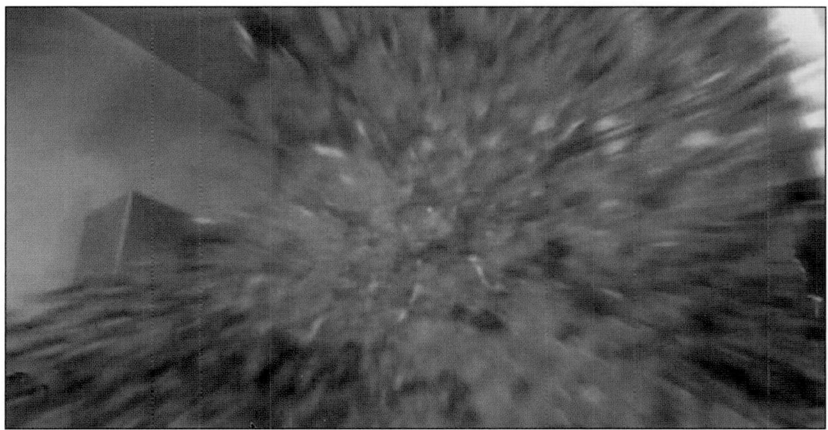

The resulting explosive reaction causes instant annihilation.

Unwitting Target

The closeness of the Slitheen clan is its undoing when all the Earth-based members hold a triumphant family gathering in 10 Downing Street. Given a single, reasonably contained target, the Doctor decides to risk launching a Harpoon missile.

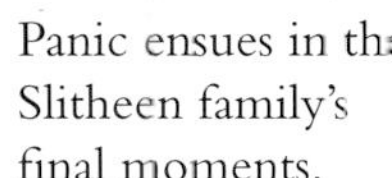

Panic ensues in the Slitheen family's final moments.

The Slitheen impersonating Margaret Blaine of M15 broke rank with the family and teleported away from the Downing Street blast using a teleporter device hidden in her earrings. She vowed revenge on the miserable human race.

The Abzorbaloff

Originating on Raxacoricofallapatorius' sister planet Clom, the creature known as the Abzorbaloff can absorb other creatures in order to steal their knowledge and consciousnesses. The process is highly unstable, however, and requires a limitation field device to keep the remnants of the most recently absorbed victims from pulling him apart from the inside.

Cane contains limitation field that stops Abzorbaloff from being absorbed himself by trapped consciousnesses
Faces of absorbed victims remain visible in flesh

The Vault

PORTRAIT OF VAN STATTEN

IN THE YEAR 2012, a highly secret and bizarrely exotic museum lies half a mile beneath the dusty soil of Utah, in the converted shell of a nuclear bunker. Containing a priceless collection of extraterrestrial exhibits, the Vault is privately owned by American billionaire Henry Van Statten. While he claims that his artifacts are harmless, Van Statten's one living exhibit is capable of obliterating humanity.

Henry Van Statten began his collection by buying extraterrestrial technology at auctions then using it to create new forms of technology that he sold for vast amounts of money.

The Metaltron

A secure cage within the compound contains Van Statten's one living exhibit: a single surviving Dalek from the Great Time War. Van Statten has no idea of the power of this artifact, which he calls the Metaltron. The Dalek has shielded itself, but is being tortured to make it speak.

Stabalizing pillars emitting passive light

Tensile steel chain

Battle scar dating from the Great Time War

Base contains antigravity engines

The Vault is located on the lowest floor of the 53-story underground compound. There, the preserved bodies of alien life-forms, fragments from alien spacecraft, and lumps of extraterrestrial rock are displayed in glass cabinets with individually controlled temperatures.

Museum Curator

Self-proclaimed genius Adam Mitchell was headhunted by Van Statten while he was still in college. Adam purchases new items for the collection without always knowing what they are and often pays exorbitant prices.

From his workshop, Adam shows Rose the museum's one live specimen. Rose is horrified that it is being tortured, and Adam takes her to the cage so Rose can try to save it.

Museum Highlights

Although part of Adam's job is to catalog all the artifacts, most of these labels are based on guesswork. For example, Adam thought that one piece of misshapen metal was part of a spaceship engine. It was actually a musical instrument.

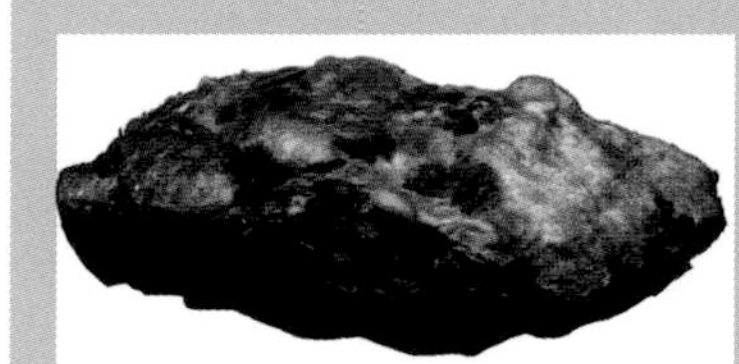

METEORITE
- **Date: 1993**
- **Martian meteorite recovered from New Mexico**
- **Rock contains structures similar to human bacteria**

ALIEN LIZARD
- **Date: unknown**
- **Extraterrestrial armored lizard**
- **Superdense bone structure would enable survival in intense atmospheric pressure, e.g., surface of Venus**

APE-MAN HEAD
- **Date: 2009**
- **Missing link between ape and man**
- **Recovered from ice in Northern Siberia**
- **Head has been thawed and preserved**

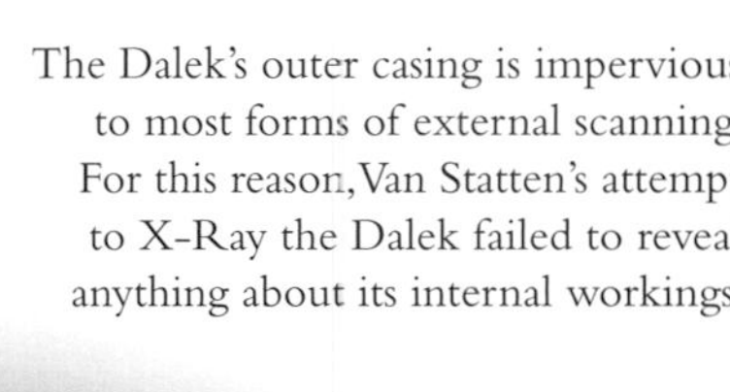

The Dalek's outer casing is impervious to most forms of external scanning. For this reason, Van Statten's attempt to X-Ray the Dalek failed to reveal anything about its internal workings.

DALEK SCAN

Simmons

Desperate to find out more about the mysterious Metaltron he has chained in the cage, Henry Van Statten hires a cold-blooded ex-security chief named Simmons to find ways of making the Dalek talk and reveal its secrets.

The last person to touch the Dalek without gloves burst into flames

Dial adjusts flow of air into suit

Airtight suit

Ex-Army issue footwear

Dalek Regenerated

A Dalek can draw vast energy simply by extrapolating the biomass of a time traveler. By tricking Rose into touching it, the Dalek absorbs her DNA and begins to regenerate.

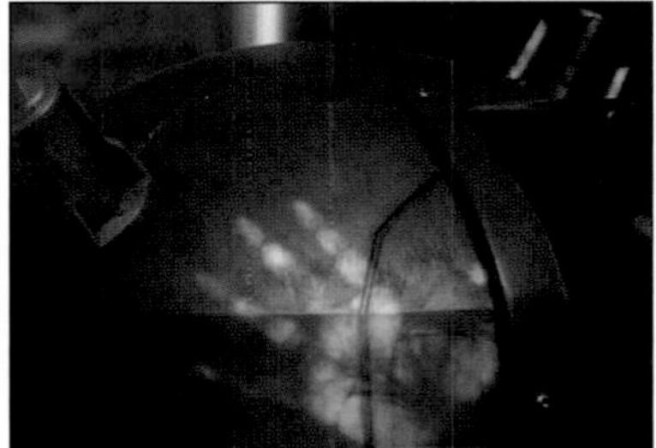

The Doctor searches Adam's workshop for a weapon capable of destroying the Dalek and discovers an alien warrior's blaster.

Self-repairing casing

Globes contain explosives

BLASTER

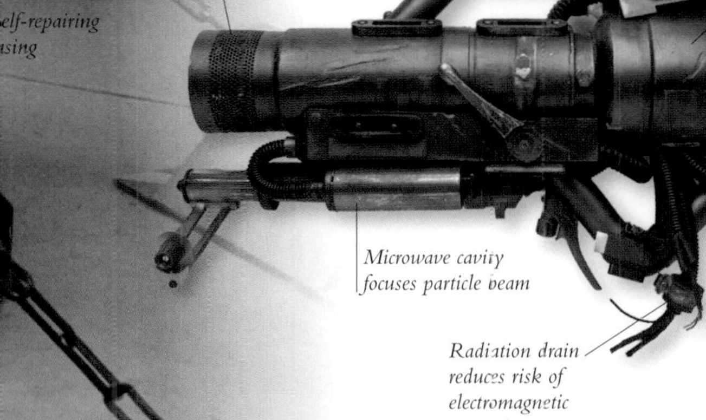

Large barrel allows massive energy discharge

Particle accelarator

Microwave cavity focuses particle beam

Radiation drain reduces risk of electromagnetic saturation

The regenerated Dalek kills hundreds of personnel then self-destructs. After such a massive mistake, Van Statten is mindwiped and dumped on a street.

ROSWELL MILOMETER
- **Date: 1947**
- **Navigation device from spacecraft**
- **Circuitry enables high-speed data transfer**
- **Recovered from Roswell, New Mexico**

REPTILLIAN HEAD
- **Date: 1972**
- **Head of Earth-bound bipedal reptile**
- **Specimen has suffered severe decay**
- **Recovered from British coastal waters**

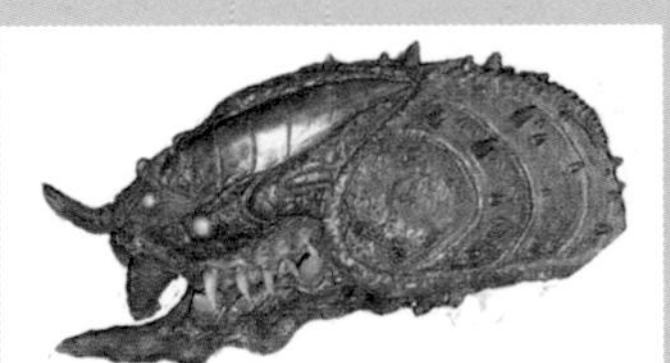

GIANT BEETLE
- **Date: 1922**
- **Colossal extraterrestrial insect**
- **Specimen thought to have survived entry through Earth's atmosphere**
- **Recovered from Brazilian rain forest**

CYBERMAN HEAD
- **Date: unknown**
- **Incomplete extraterrestrial cyborg specimen**
- **Recovered from United Kingdom**

Daleks

EXTERMINATE! EXTERMINATE! The battle cry of the Daleks, and the mindset it represents, has made them feared throughout the universe. Concealed inside armored life-support casings, the Daleks are ruthless conquerors, who believe only in the superiority of their own race and hold all other beings in contempt, suitable only for extermination. Across time, Dalek aggression has led to interstellar wars and encouraged alliances against them. The Time Lords became so fearful of the Daleks' potential for universal domination that they attempted to tamper with their creation, sparking the last Great Time War.

The Daleks originated on the planet Skaro, which was home to two races: the Kaleds and the Thals. After a thousand-year war fought with biological, chemical, and nuclear weapons, environmenatal contamination caused both races to mutate. The Thals mutated toward physical perfection, while the Kaleds degenerated into physically weak, tentacled creatures.

Creating a Deadly Army

The Kaled scientist, Davros, built armored traveling life-support systems to support the tentacled creatures and genetically engineered them, accelerating and manipulating the mutation. He instilled an overwhelming drive for survival and a hatred of all other species, while magnifying their intellect and stripping them of all "unnecessary" emotions. He named the perfect "killing machine" he had created... the Dalek.

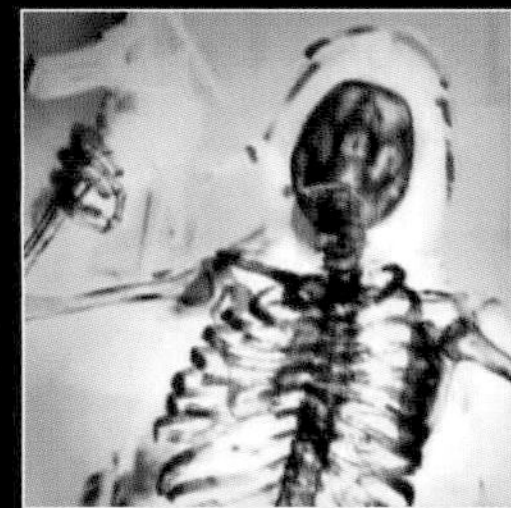
A Dalek's death ray gun uses a ray beam to destroy every cell in a human body.

A Dalek's arm is strong enough to crush a human skull, but it can also kill by extracting all brain waves.

Extermination Tools

Each warrior Dalek is equipped with a ray gun and a manipulator arm. The "death ray" is a directed energy weapon that can stun or kill. The manipulator arm can interface with computer systems or mimic hand movements with its "sucker" made of morphic material.

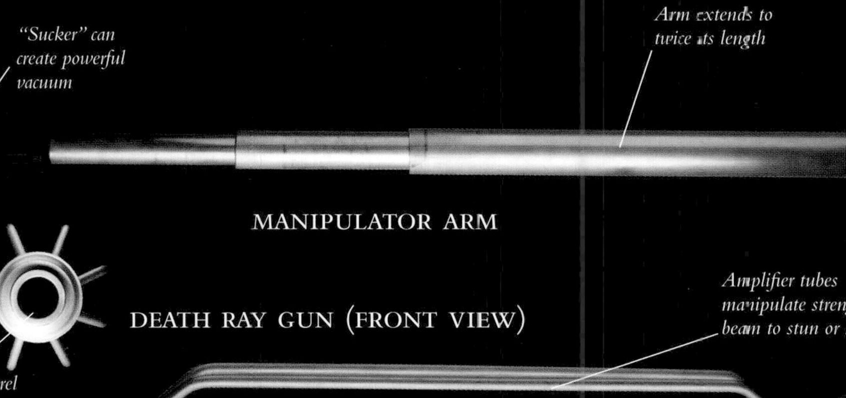

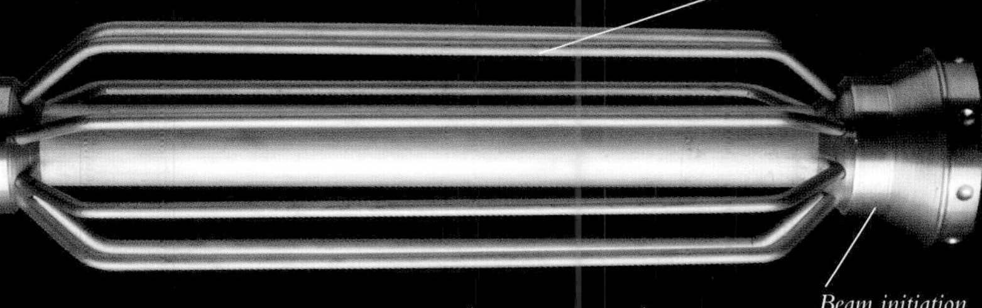

Dalek Point of View

The eyestalk of the Dalek battle armor provides enhanced vision in the natural colors of Dalek sight. Built-in multispectral sensors also allow the Dalek to see in infrared, X-ray, and ultraviolet modes. The single eyestalk is a Dalek's weakest point, since it has no backup system.

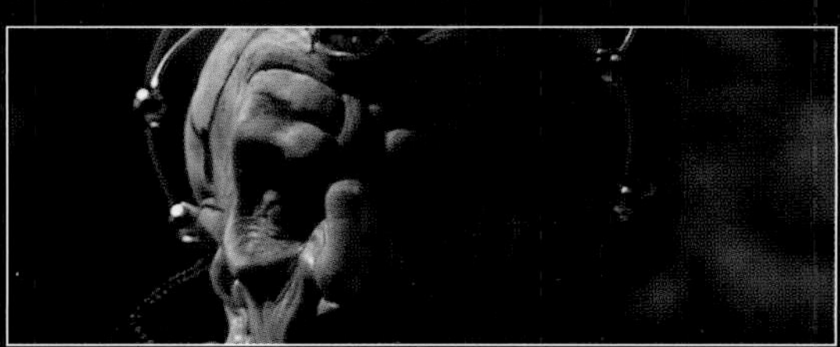
The brilliant and psychotic Davros created the Daleks.

On the Warpath

The Daleks have waged war across time and space since their creation, but the complexities of time travel, and the Time Lords' attempts to change Dalek history, make a comprehensive timeline of their battles and invasions difficult. Here are some of their attempts at conquest:

- **Generations after their initial creation, Daleks on Skaro were still battling the Thals, when they were first encountered by the Doctor in his first incarnation.**
- **While chasing the first Doctor through time, a Dalek execution squad fought, and was defeated by, the robot Mechanoids in the 23rd century. This was the beginning of a long war between the two races.**
- **The Daleks fought another long war, over many centuries, with the android Movellans from star system 4-X-Alpha-4, as both tried to expand their stellar empires. When that war came to a stalemate, the Daleks traveled through time to seek help from their ancient creator, Davros.**
- **Reviving Davros led to the development of factions within the Dalek hierarchy and a series of "civil wars" between different groups supporting and opposing Davros.**
- **In the 22nd century the Daleks twice invaded the Earth, the first time after the destruction of World War III and later, around the Earth year 2164, intending to turn it into a giant battleship to aid their wars of conquest.**
- **By the year 4000 the Daleks planned a master strike to conquer the galaxy with the aid of similarly power-hungry allies. When the Doctor defeated their plans, the alliance self-destructed and embroiled the Daleks in new conflicts.**
- **Learning of the Time Lords' attempts to thwart their creation, the Daleks attacked Gallifrey and the last Great Time War began.**
- **Although Gallifrey was destroyed in the attempt to wipe out the Daleks, the Cult of Skaro and the Emperor survived. By the year 200,100, the Dalek Emperor had rebuilt the Dalek race, but it was then destroyed by Rose Tyler.**

The Dalek's casing is made from dalekanium, an extremely robust bonded polycarbide material. It can be penetrated by bastic-tipped bullets, so the Daleks created an energy shield for additional protection.

Dalek battle armor is designed to open up, so that repairs, system enhancements, and medical treatments can be performed. Even without its weaponry, the Dalek is a dangerous creature and has been known to kill.

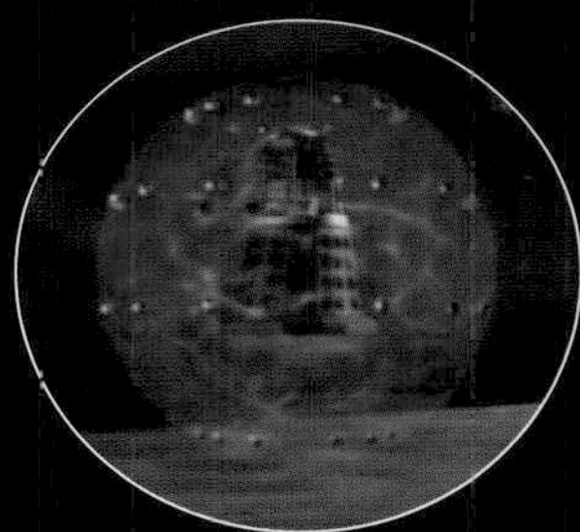
To avoid capture, or to atone for failing a mission, a Dalek is equipped with a self-destruct system for complete obliteration. The components of this system are mounted in the Dalek's sensor globes, which are capable of free flight.

Equipped with antigravity generators and gyroscopic stabilization systems, Daleks can glide across any terrain or hover over any obstacle—even a steep staircase is no hindrance.

Dalek Flagship

EMERGING FROM HIDING above Earth, the Dalek fleet is armed, dangerous, and all-powerfully gigantic. The massive Flagship that commands the fleet transports the Dalek Emperor, who is worshiped as a god by the rest of the Daleks. The Emperor is wired into the ship's systems, operating them by his mind, and from them to the rest of the fleet—allowing him total control.

Hidden Army

When it became clear that the Daleks were about to be wiped out in the Great Time War, a single ship managed to slip away into "the dark spaces." The badly hurt but functioning Dalek on board spent centuries in hiding. Slowly, it hatched a secret plan to harvest humans from Earth to supply the genetic material needed to rebuild an army of Daleks under his Imperial command.

Flagship Facts

- **The Flagship was used during the Great Time War between Daleks and Time Lords.**
- **The Dalek Emperor intends to create "Heaven on Earth" by bombing the planet until its landmasses are reduced to radioactive rubble.**

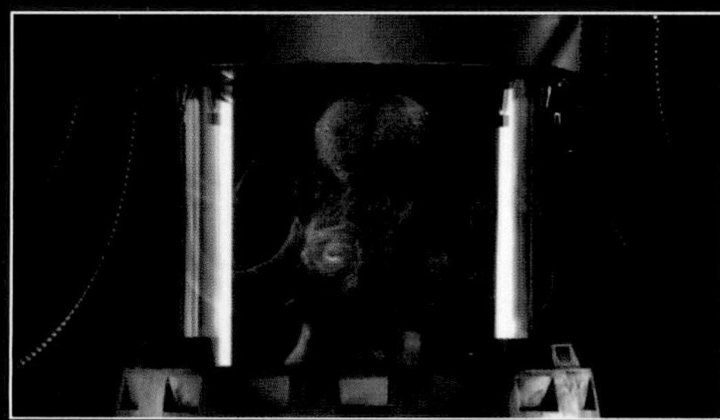

- **Rose utterly destroys the Dalek fleet when she gains godlike powers from looking into the time-space vortex at the heart of the TARDIS.**

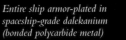

Hull strengthening plate

Entire ship armor-plated in spaceship-grade dalekanium (bonded polycarbide metal)

Hull damage from the Great Time War

Signal transmitter ring

Heavy polycarbide rivets

Ship energy-shielding pulses

Rotating dome and outer ring create spin that propels ship

Giant hangar openings located around the central disk allow millions of Daleks to emerge at once into the void of space, heading toward Earth.

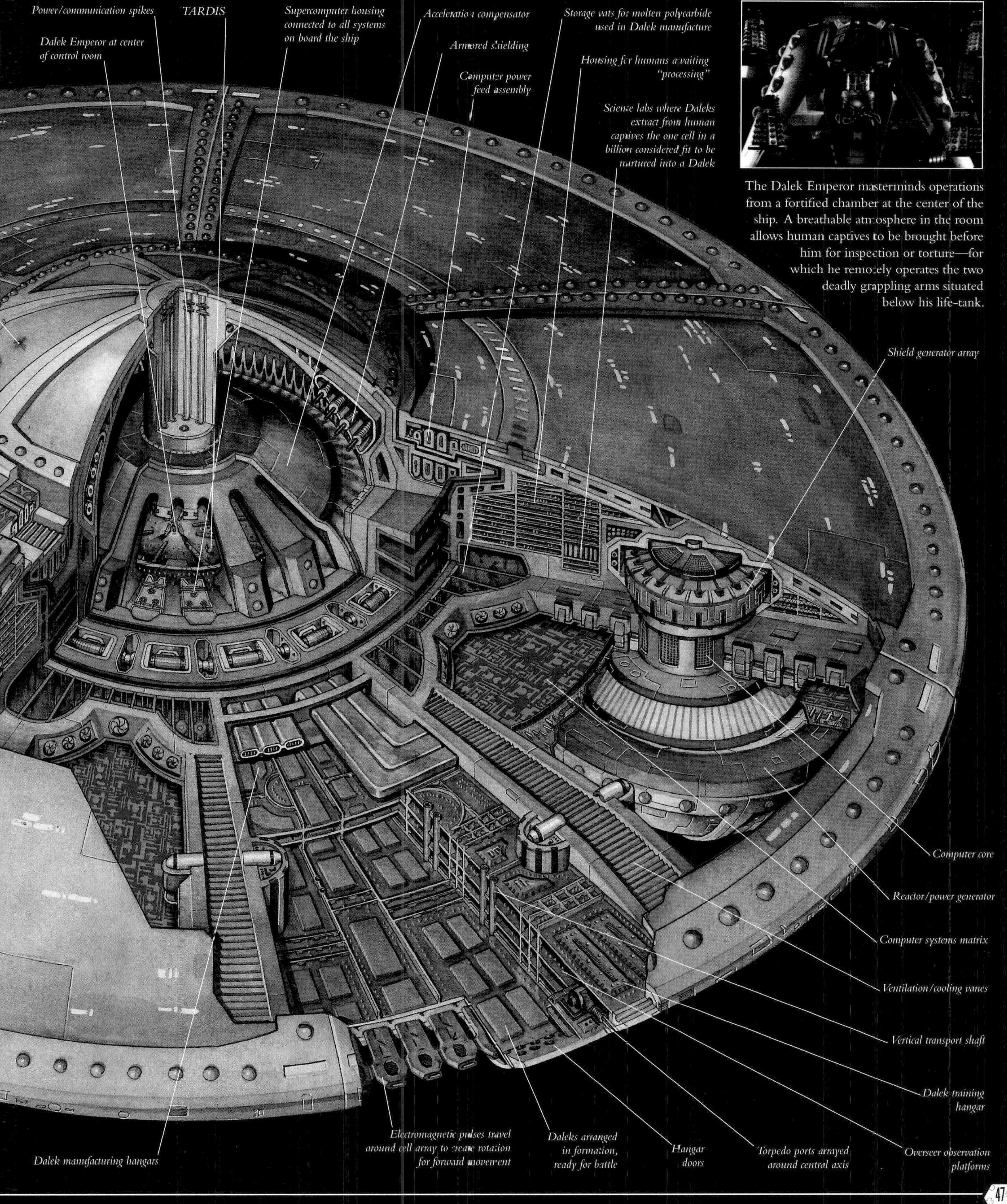

The Dalek Emperor masterminds operations from a fortified chamber at the center of the ship. A breathable atmosphere in the room allows human captives to be brought before him for inspection or torture—for which he remotely operates the two deadly grappling arms situated below his life-tank.

Satellite 5

ORBITING THE EARTH in the year 200,000, the Satellite 5 space station is the planet's largest media hub. Replacing all earlier broadcast satellites, it transmits news and entertainment throughout the Fourth Great and Bountiful Human Empire. The space station is also home to thousands of human employees, including journalists, who collect the news remotely via neural implants, and the Editor, who oversees them. Also on board is the Jagrafess, a gigantic sluglike alien, who secretly manipulates the news in order to turn humans into slaves.

In a media center on Satellite 5, journalists use the chips in their heads to gather news stories from across the Empire. They send the news via data hand plates to Cathica, a journalist implanted with an infospike. She lies on an infochair and processes the news before transmitting it to the Empire. However, unbeknownst to the journalists, the news is really going to the Jagrafess for editing before transmission.

The mysterious Editor manages the space station from Floor 500. Unseen and unknown, the Editor monitors the journalists' thoughts via the chips in their heads. He was appointed by a consortium of interstellar banks, who installed the Jagrafess to profit from humanity's enslavement. The Editor is a pale, softly spoken human and utterly ruthless.

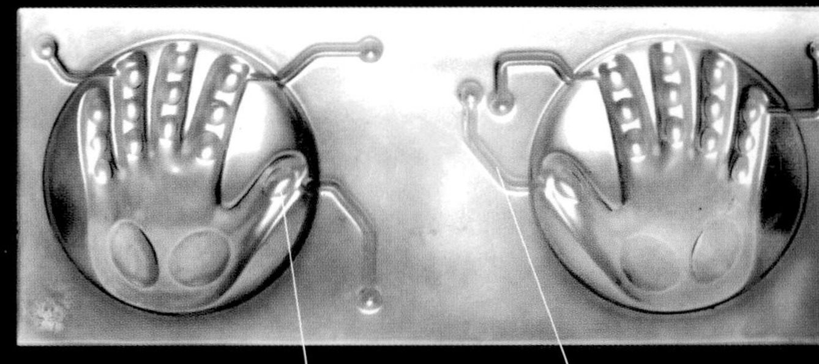

HAND PLATES

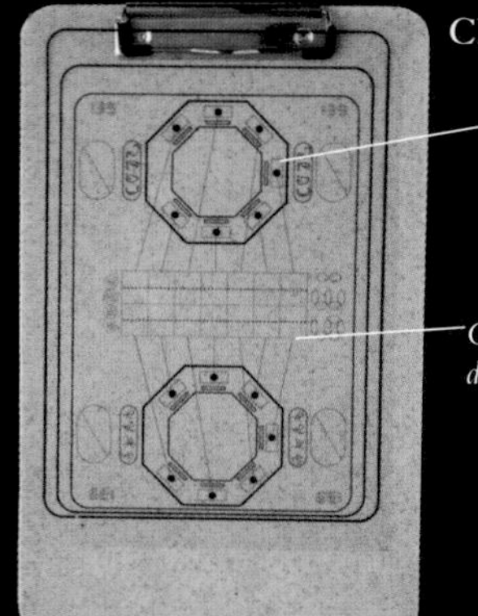
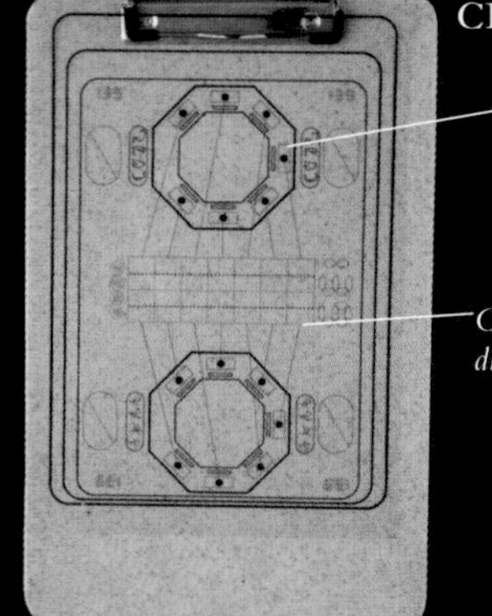

CLIPBOARD

Chip inside interfaces with pay stations

Stick is used like a credit card

Stick can be topped off with currency at credit terminals

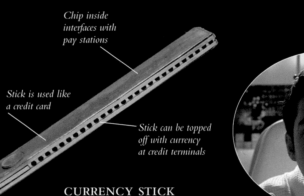

CURRENCY STICK

An infospike is a portal in the forehead that connects the brain to Satellite 5's computers. The infospike opens with a click of the fingers and connects to the computers via spheres of energy in the media centers. Using the currency stick the Doctor has given him, Adam pays to have an infospike installed.

The Freedom Foundation

The Freedom Foundation is a group of 15 humans who discovered Satellite 5's manipulation of humanity and were determined to stop it.

One by one, the 15 Freedom Foundation members have been eliminated. The last surviving member, Suki Macrae Cantrell, infiltrated Satellite 5. On Floor 500, she pulled a gun on the Editor, but she was killed by the station's real boss, the Jagrafess.

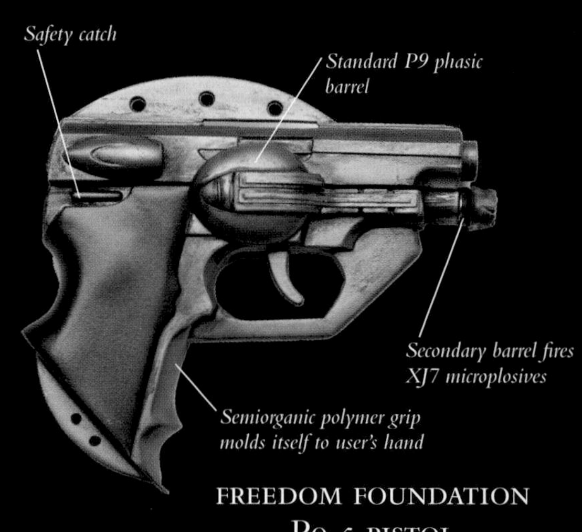

FREEDOM FOUNDATION P9 5 PISTOL

Freedom Foundation Manifesto

- Closure of Satellite 5
- Full investigation into Satellite 5's activities
- No individual to own more than 3 media outlets
- Freezing of the assets of Satellite 5's backers

Space Station

Satellite 5 functions as a regular working media hub—except for one section, which has been secretly modified to accommodate a highly unusual occupant: the Jagrafess. This gigantic creature lives on Floor 500, the topmost floor of the orbital platform. Since the Jagrafess's fast metabolism produces massive amounts of heat, a secondary ventilation system and auxiliary heat sinks were introduced to vent heat away from Floor 500. This has resulted in the top floor icing up like an Arctic winter, while the floors below are unbearably hot.

Excess heat vent

Medium range antenna

Fusion generators

Floor 500, occupied by the Jagrafess and the Editor

Floor 247 specializes in lifestyle programming

TARDIS lands on Floor 139 next to a fast-food joint

Main residential floors

Array of signal receivers

Docking ring

Floor 16, the non-emergency medical center

Main transmitter broadcasts 600 channels across the Empire

The Jagrafess's full name is the Mighty Jagrafess of the Holy Hadrojassic Maxarodenfoe. The Editor calls him Max for short. This monstrous, slimy alien with razor-sharp teeth is the true ruler of the Empire.

Employees on the hub are allowed access to specific zones only. Outside of these authorized areas, the space station is a mystery and the overall layout can only be speculative.

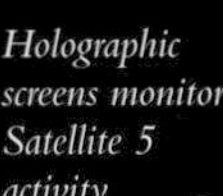

Holographic screens monitor Satellite 5 activity

Keyboard for manual entry

Chairs for the drones who operate the terminals

Floor 500 media center

Floor 500

Everyone who works on Satellite 5 wants to be promoted and transferred up to Floor 500. However, those who make it to the top floor don't live long. Killed by the Jagrafess, they work on as his drones—puppets controlled by the chip in their heads—until their bodies wear out. Floor 500 media center is the control room of Satellite 5, where the Editor and the drones monitor all human activity on the space station.

The Sycorax

The Sycorax adhere to traditions of honorable combat and will never turn down a challenge.

THESE SKINLESS HUMANOIDS inhabit a barren asteroid named the Fire Trap from the JX82 system. Consisting of many warlike tribes, the Sycorax fight with swords, whips, and their own school of magic spells and curses. To survive, these interstellar scavengers ransack other planets. One tribe, the Halvinor tribe, crash through Earth's atmosphere, planning to steal its land and minerals, but don't count on encountering the regenerating Doctor when he takes Rose home for Christmas.

Sycorax Ship Facts

• The Sycorax ship is an asteroid equipped with engines. When an alien ship collided with their asteroid, the Sycorax used the alien technology to add powerful engines.

• Many more asteroids have since been converted by the Sycorax, with each tribe claiming their own. These asteroid ships are used to raid other planets for food and resources.

• The Sycorax ship that attacked the Earth was driven by an All Speed Inter-System Type K engine.

Sycorax Great Hall

This enormous hall was hollowed out of the Fire Trap's core many centuries ago. Its primitive structure is combined with space-age technology such as a teleporter to travel on and off the ship. The hall is used for tribal meetings and the hole in the roof allows solar and lunar light for ancient Sycorax rituals.

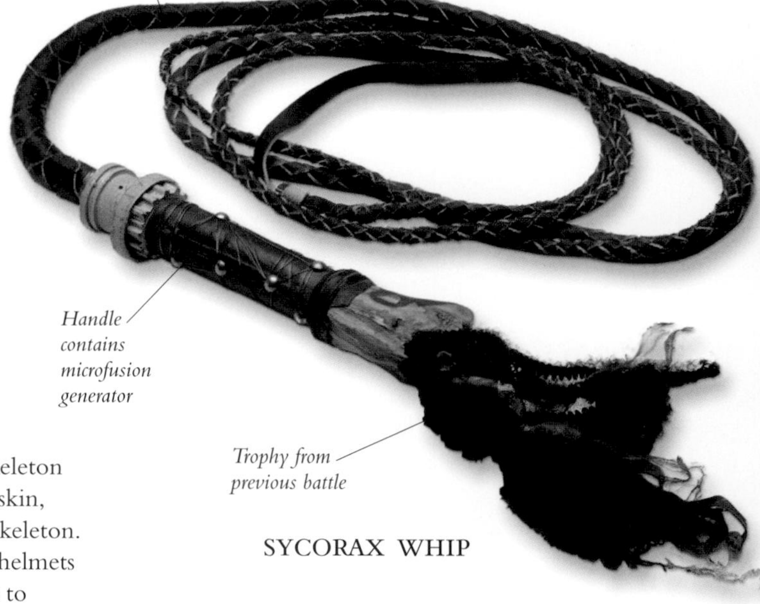

SYCORAX WHIP

Part of the Sycorax skeleton is located outside the skin, forming a partial exoskeleton. Their fearsome bone helmets are worn over the top to protect the vulnerable raw skin and muscle underneath.

The Sycorax whip, when used on a human body, instantly destroys all the atoms of human flesh, so that only a pile of charred bones remains. This devastating effect is seen on the prime minister's aide, scientist Daniel Llewelyn.

Sycorax Leader

Sycorax live for 400 years and it took two and half centuries for the Sycorax Leader to become head of his people—the Halvinor tribe. He rose through the ranks by various trials of strength and combat.

The Sycorax will conquer a world by any means. When an Earth probe containing A+ human blood crashes into their ship, they feed it into a control matrix and enslave everyone on Earth who has A+ blood.

The Doctor challenges the Sycorax Leader to single combat for the fate of Earth. Honor bound to accept, he is defeated by the Time Lord and the Sycorax agree to leave humanity alone.

New Earth

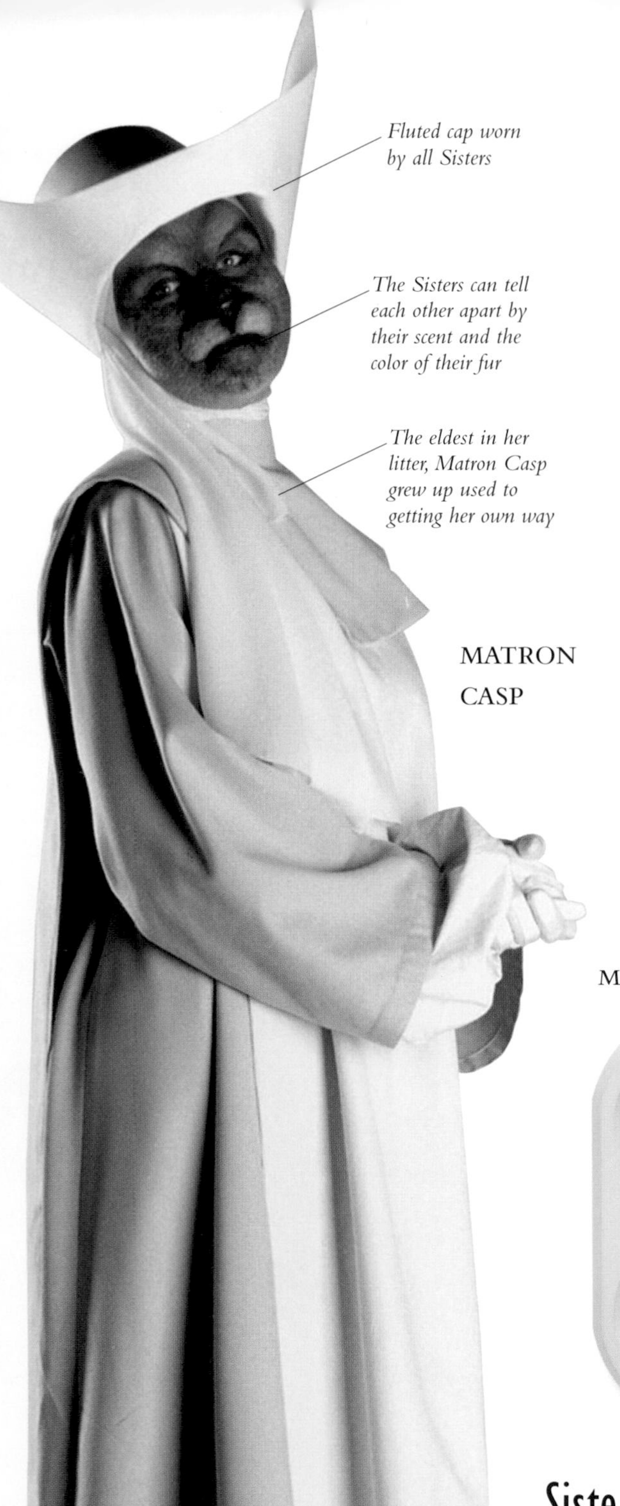

MATRON CASP

STANDING ON *PLATFORM ONE* in the year five billion, the Doctor and Rose had watched the Sun expand and obliterate the Earth. However, Earth's destruction inspired revivalists to search for a similar world. Twenty years later and 50,000 light-years away in galaxy M87, the ideal place was found and named New Earth. The Doctor takes Rose there in the year 5,000,000,023, and visits again with Martha 30 years later.

Dazzling New New York—the fifteenth since the United States' original—is New Earth's major city. It is ruled by the Senate, who live in the gleaming Overcity, while the poorer citizens live in the grim Undercity below.

MEDICAL SCANNER

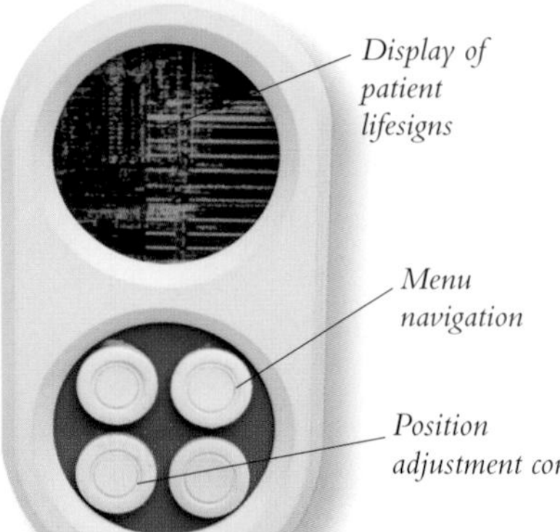

Prestigious Hospital

In 5,000,000,023, a hospital commands an imposing coastal position on New Earth. Its gleaming, sterile wards are sealed from the outside air to prevent contamination. Visitors to the wards are automatically disinfected when they enter the building's elevators.

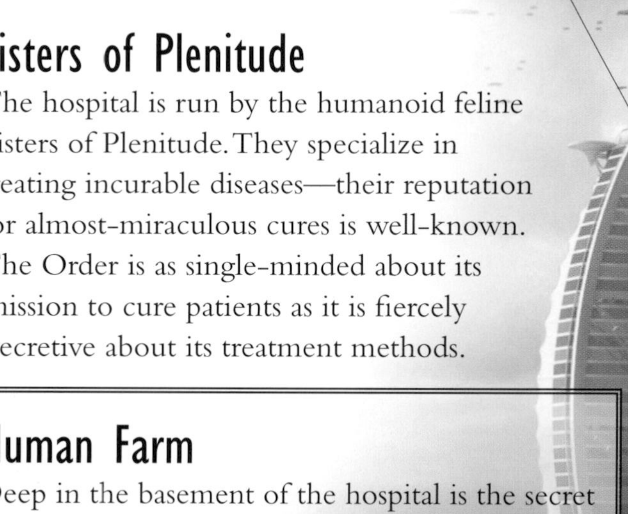

Sisters of Plenitude

The hospital is run by the humanoid feline Sisters of Plenitude. They specialize in treating incurable diseases—their reputation for almost-miraculous cures is well-known. The Order is as single-minded about its mission to cure patients as it is fiercely secretive about its treatment methods.

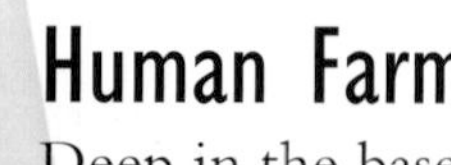

Human Farm

Deep in the basement of the hospital is the secret of the Sisters' healing powers. Human clones are infected with every known disease and experimented on to find new cures. When the Doctor and Rose discover the clones are sentient they free them, and a new human species is born.

Life on the Motorway

By the time the Doctor returns in 5,000,000,053, life in New New York has drastically changed. Many denizens of the Undercity have set off on the Motorway dreaming of a better life higher up. On this highway, 20 lanes across and 50 lanes deep, traffic moves five miles every 12 years, but is going nowhere because the exit has been sealed to protect it from danger above.

Fur is turning gray with age

Self-replicating fuel, muscle stimulants for exercise, and waste products recycled as food mean no one has to leave their car. Even babies are born on board—Valerie and Thomas Kincade Brannigan's litter of kittens are Children of the Motorway, and have never known any other way of life.

Kitten nursery, equipped for the babies' every need

Communicator used to call cars on the driver's Friends List

Novice Hame

Catperson Novice Hame nurses the Face of Boe as penance for the clone experiments. When a virus kills everyone in the Overcity, the Face of Boe hastily seals the Undercity, and uses his life-force to keep it running for 24 lonely years. When the Doctor arrives, he rescues the Undercity population, so they can reinhabit New New York.

Teleportation device, also controls external lights

NOVICE HAME'S BRACELET

Holographic presenter Sally Calypso's fabricated broadcasts convince the Motorway residents that all is normal in New New York.

Carries gun in case of Motorway pirates

Macra

The giant, crablike Macra were once the scourge of galaxy M87. They forced humans to mine the poisonous gas they fed on. Over billions of years they devolved into simple beasts and were kept in the New New York zoo. Escaped specimens have bred and thrive beneath the smog-shrouded Motorway, hunting its travelers.

The airborne virus that killed everyone in the Overcity mutated from the popular mood-changing drug, Bliss.

NOVICE HAME

The Werewolf

QUEEN VICTORIA suffered several attempts on her life, but none so bizarre as that of a power-hungry alien parasite that sought to infect her body in order to take over England for its own ends—perhaps even to steal Victorian technology to carve out its own vast steam-powered empire in space! Able to change into werewolf form, this alien life-form has bewitched the monks of a remote, Scottish monastery—and plans to use them to hatch its deadly plot against the Queen.

The Torchwood Estate is a place of legend and mystery, its very name said to derive from the wood of a lightning-struck gallows—torched wood—used in its construction. Wild rumors were further stoked in the 1800s when the house's eccentric owner, Sir George MacLeish, built a gigantic rooptop observatory.

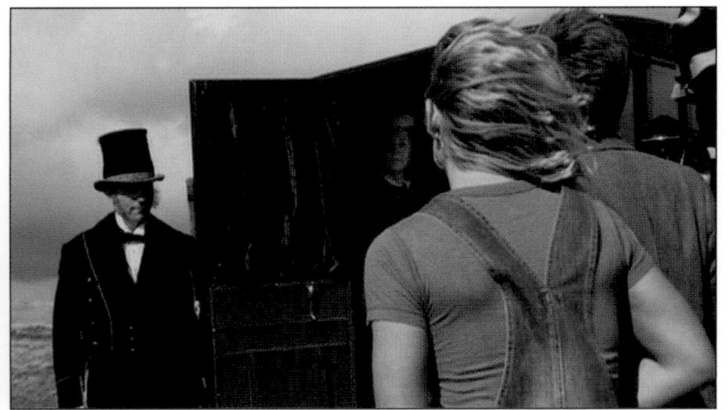

Chance Encounter

Landing in Scotland in 1879, the Doctor meets Queen Victoria on her way to Balmoral Castle. Unable to resist the opportunity to make the acquaintance of an English monarch, the Doctor uses his psychic paper to supply him with credentials to tag along to Torchwood House, where the Queen intends to spend the night.

Fighting staff made of a rare wood that grows in the area

Mistletoe worn around neck under robe

Habit conceals orange fighting robes

Bedeviled Brethren

Near Torchwood stands the monastery of St. Catherine's Glen. The monks, led by the crazed Father Angelo, are guardians of a powerful secret—they have begun worshiping an alien being that fell to Earth close to their monastery in the 1500s. The alien survives by infecting human hosts.

Before the Queen and the Doctor arrive at Torchwood, the monks take over the house, overpowering the staff with unnaturally fast fighting techniques.

Informed of Queen Victoria's movements by the monks, and desperate to infect itself into a being of real power, the alien commands the monks to transport it—in its human host—to Torchwood House. Now, all it needs is for the full Moon to provide the power to transform it to its werewolf form.

Sharp claws rip prey apart

To a seasoned space-time traveler like Rose, the young prisoner's eyes betray the unmistakable presence of a life-form that is not from Earth.

Mistletoe headbands used to ward off the werewolf

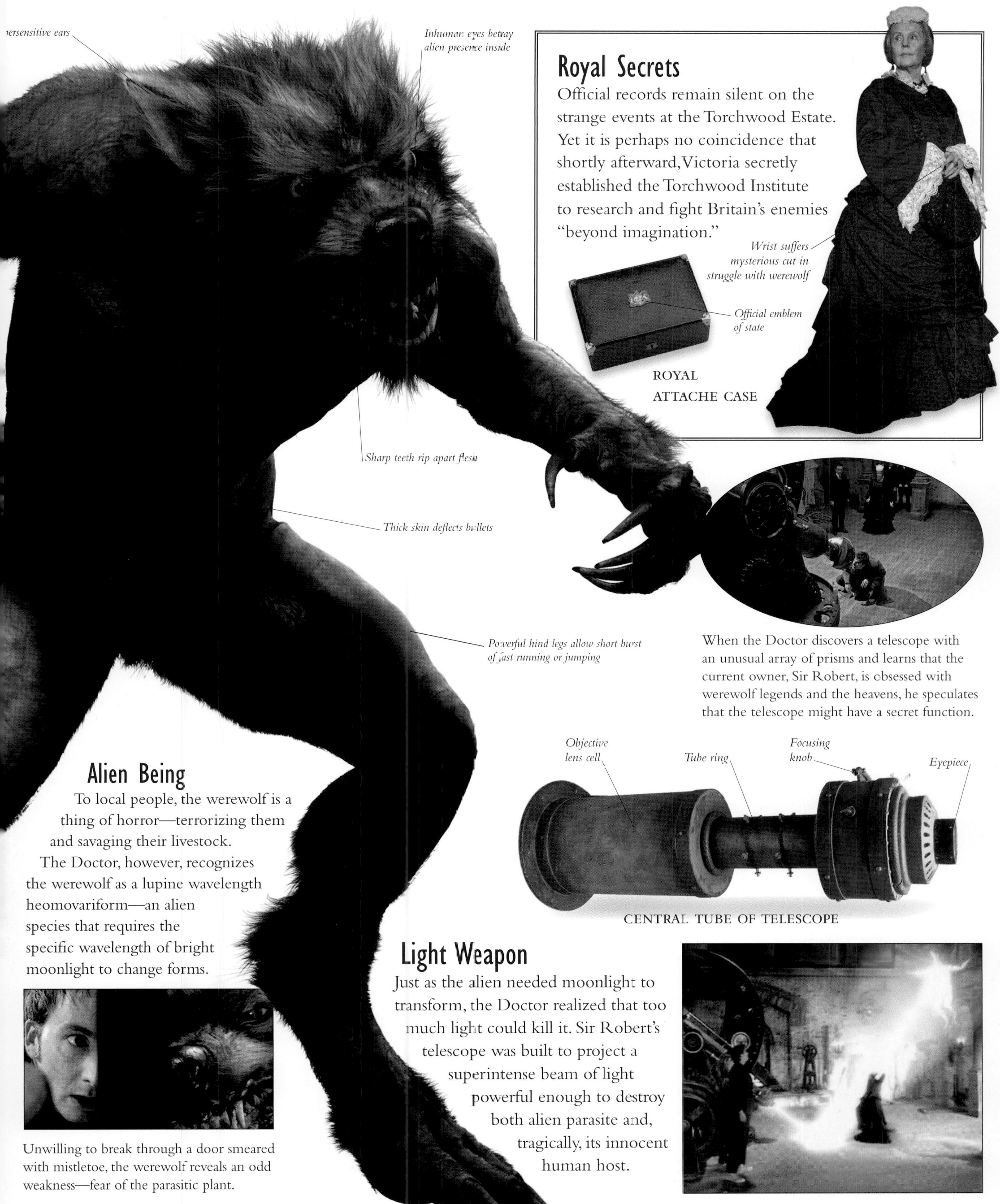

Royal Secrets

Official records remain silent on the strange events at the Torchwood Estate. Yet it is perhaps no coincidence that shortly afterward, Victoria secretly established the Torchwood Institute to research and fight Britain's enemies "beyond imagination."

ROYAL ATTACHE CASE

When the Doctor discovers a telescope with an unusual array of prisms and learns that the current owner, Sir Robert, is obsessed with werewolf legends and the heavens, he speculates that the telescope might have a secret function.

CENTRAL TUBE OF TELESCOPE

Alien Being

To local people, the werewolf is a thing of horror—terrorizing them and savaging their livestock. The Doctor, however, recognizes the werewolf as a lupine wavelength heomovariform—an alien species that requires the specific wavelength of bright moonlight to change forms.

Unwilling to break through a door smeared with mistletoe, the werewolf reveals an odd weakness—fear of the parasitic plant.

Light Weapon

Just as the alien needed moonlight to transform, the Doctor realized that too much light could kill it. Sir Robert's telescope was built to project a superintense beam of light powerful enough to destroy both alien parasite and, tragically, its innocent human host.

Gelth

PITY THE GELTH! These formless creatures have been trapped in a gaseous state ever since the Time War, but they long to have physical existence again. An advance party of Gelth make their way to 19th-century Cardiff, Wales, where they ask a young girl for help. But there are more than three or four Gelth left, there are billions, and they are killers!

Blue eyes turn red once the Gelth are through the Rift

The Rift

The city of Cardiff is the location of a weak point in space and time. Known as the Rift, it is where connections are formed with other eras and places and is the cause of the many ghost stories circulating in the area. Having grown up on the center of the Rift, servant girl Gwyneth has become part of it. It has given her "the sight"—the ability to read minds.

The Rift is weakest at 7 Temperance Court, home to Sneed and Co. undertakers. Here, the Doctor communicates with the Gelth via psychic Gwyneth. He allows them use of the corpses, just until he can find them a new home.

The Dead Walk

Decomposing human bodies at the funeral parlor produce gas, which forms the perfect home for the gaseous Gelth. They plan to kill the whole human race and use their gas-producing bodies as vessels.

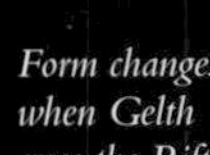

Form changes when Gelth cross the Rift

Gelth Facts

- **The Gelth need a gaseous atmosphere to survive—19th-century gas pipes provide an ideal environment.**
- **It takes three months of hijacking Sneed's corpses before the Gelth manage to communicate their request to Gwyneth at a seance.**

- **Without a proper bridge across the Rift, the weakened Gelth are only able to inhabit corpses for short periods of time.**
- **When the gaseous Gelth animate cadavers, they stimulate the human's dead brain so the corpse becomes aware of details of its former life.**

Bridge Between Worlds

When the truth is revealed—that there are billions of Gelth and they plan to take over Earth—Gwyneth, who is their link across the Rift, sacrifices herself by blowing up the room full of gas.

Krillitanes

WHEN THE DOCTOR first met the Krillitanes, they appeared human, aside from having very long necks. But the next time he encounters them, they have become batlike! A composite race, the Krillitanes pick the best physical elements from the creatures they conquer and incorporate them to create an improved form.

Wings can lift considerable weight
Claws can rip flesh
Jaws ideal for eating children
Prefers human form of head teacher Mr. Finch to batlike body

The Krillitanes have had wings for nearly ten generations, ever since they invaded the planet Bessan, where they made a million widows in one day.

Substitute Teachers

If they crack the Skasas Paradigm—otherwise known as the God Maker, the Universal Theory—the Krillitanes will be able to shape reality and control time, space, and matter! They need the brains and imagination of children, enhanced by Krillitane oil, so they pose as staff at Deffry Vale High School and set the pupils to work.

A simple morphic illusion cloaks the Krillitanes in human form. However, it barely takes a moment to shrug off their disguise, should they need to use their Krillitane abilities.

Bat Beings

The Krillitanes take after bats in more ways than just the wings. They sleep hanging upside down and have very sensitive hearing. This means that they dislike loud noises.

Krillitane Facts

- **When there is no fresh flesh to feed on, the Krillitanes sustain themselves with vacuum-packed rats.**
- **The Krillitanes are extremely strong and can move very fast.**
- **The creatures have changed their physiology so often that the oil they use to make the children more intelligent has become toxic to them.**
- **In addition to physical attributes, the Krillitanes steal technology from other races, such as the means to create a deadlock seal.**

BROTHER LASSAR

SS Madame de Pompadour

THE SS *MADAME de Pompadour* is one of the great energy trawlers of the 51st century. It was originally crewed by humans assisted by wind-up repair robots; however, when the TARDIS arrives on board, the robots are the only life-form. Rose and Mickey make the grim discovery that, programmed to repair the ship at all costs, the robots used parts of the crew to fix the ship when it was damaged in an ion storm.

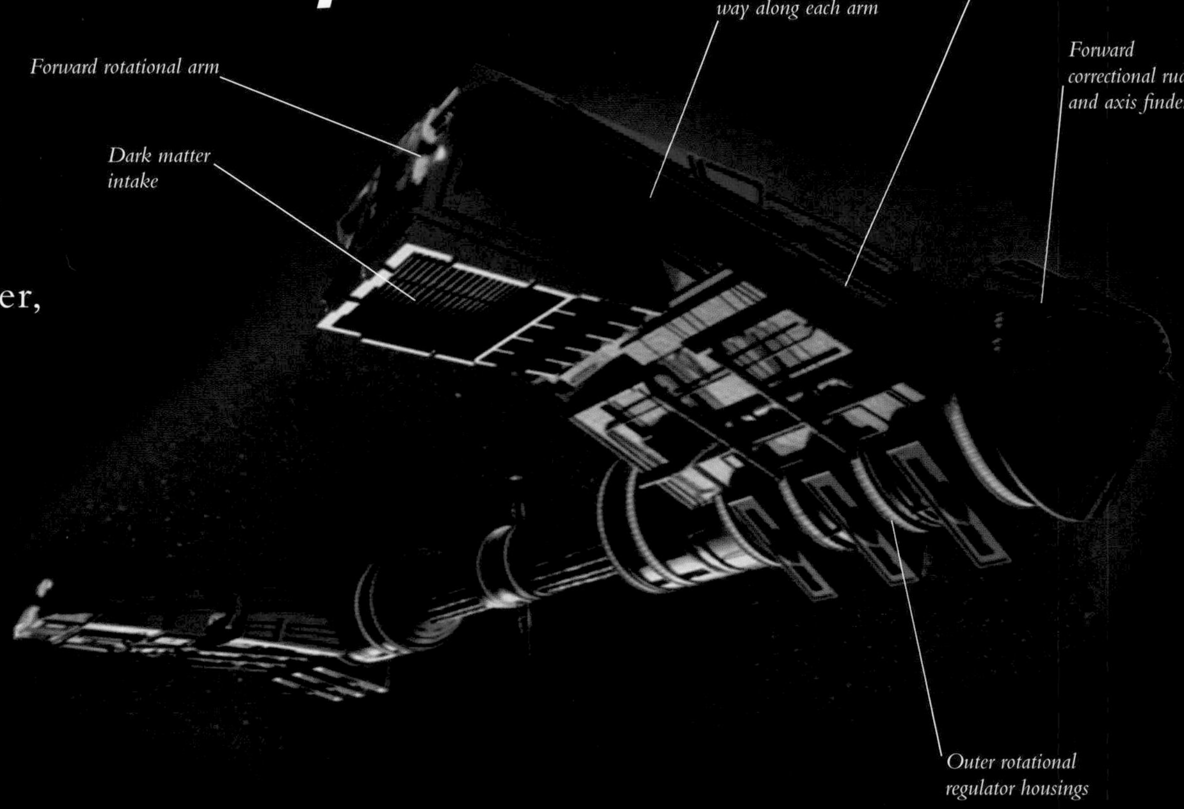

SS *Madame de Pompadour* Facts

• In the 51st century, humans were dependent on dark matter to fulfil their energy needs. Dark matter is an invisible form of energy that is only identified by its gravitational effects. Rotating arms on the ship scoop up dark matter, which is then stored in the ship's central hub.

• These arms also generate an artificial gravity field, as well as a negative magma field that drives the ship forward.

• The ship boasts antiquated sigmus-style warp engines in case its other power sources fail. The warp engines are powerful enough to punch holes in the universe and create time windows.

To repair the ship's computer, the robots need the brain of Madame de Pompadour, the ship's 18th century namesake. Using their warp drives they punch holes in the universe to create portals to 18th century France. The robots are searching for a window that will lead them to Reinette's 37th birthday, when she will be the same age as the ship.

Spare Part Surgery

With the SS *Madame de Pompadour* suffering severe damage in an ion storm, the robots do what they can to repair it. However, when they run out of mechanical spare parts, the only way to fix the ship is to use the living parts of the human crew.

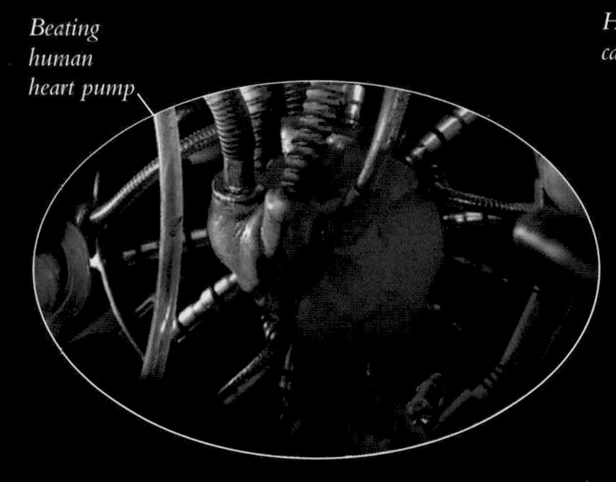

POWER FEED

SECURITY CAMERA

When the repair robots anesthetized Rose and Mickey and strapped them to surgical gurneys, it looked like they, too, would be integrated into the ship's systems.

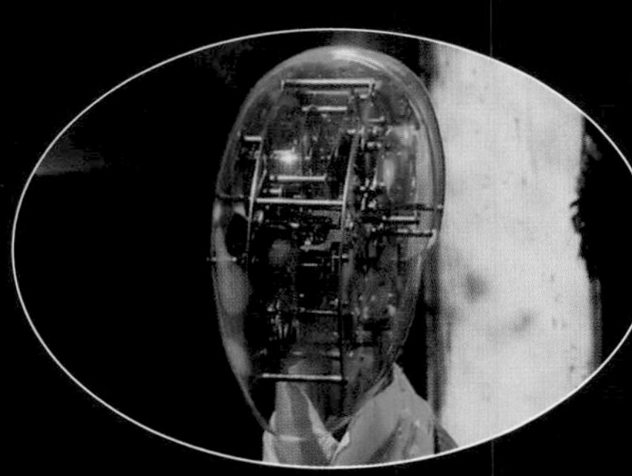

The repair robots are made from 51st-century clockwork technology. Old-fashioned and reliable Swiss clockwork techniques are integrated with sophisticated space-age computer chips. The robots are also able to teleport short distances.

Repair Robots

Although their costumes and masks give them the appearance of French courtiers, a loud ticking noise gives them away. Each deadly robot has a sharp blade hidden in its sleeve and can read humans' minds.

Wig typical of French court

Mask conceals clockwork head

Sharp, retractable blade

Silk stockings cover mechanical legs

REPAIR ROBOT

The Man in the Fireplace

Using the fireplace portal, the Doctor first meets Reinette as a child and saves her from the clockwork "monster." When he accesses the portal again a few minutes later he surprised to discover that Reinette is a beautiful young woman.

The repair robots are able to scan Reinette's mind to figure out when her brain is "complete." The Doctor uses telepathy to find out what the robots are looking for but he is shocked when Reinette is also able to read his mind and discover the secrets of his lonely childhood.

Necklace is a gift from the King

Madame de Pompadour Facts

- **Born Jeanne-Antoinette Poisson, in Paris in 1721, Madame de Pompadour was commonly known as Reinette.**
- **At a ball in 1745, Reinette caught the eye of the French King and became his official mistress.**
- **Reinette's title of Madame de Pompadour came from the Paris residence of Pompadour, given to her by the king.**

Cybermen

THEIR INVENTOR, John Lumic, believes Cybermen are the next stage of human evolution. He created these cybernetic creatures by bonding human brains within a strong steel shell. Cybermen are practically immortal, immensely strong, and without emotion. With one mind, they form a vast silver army that marches relentlessly on, chanting, "Delete, delete, delete!"

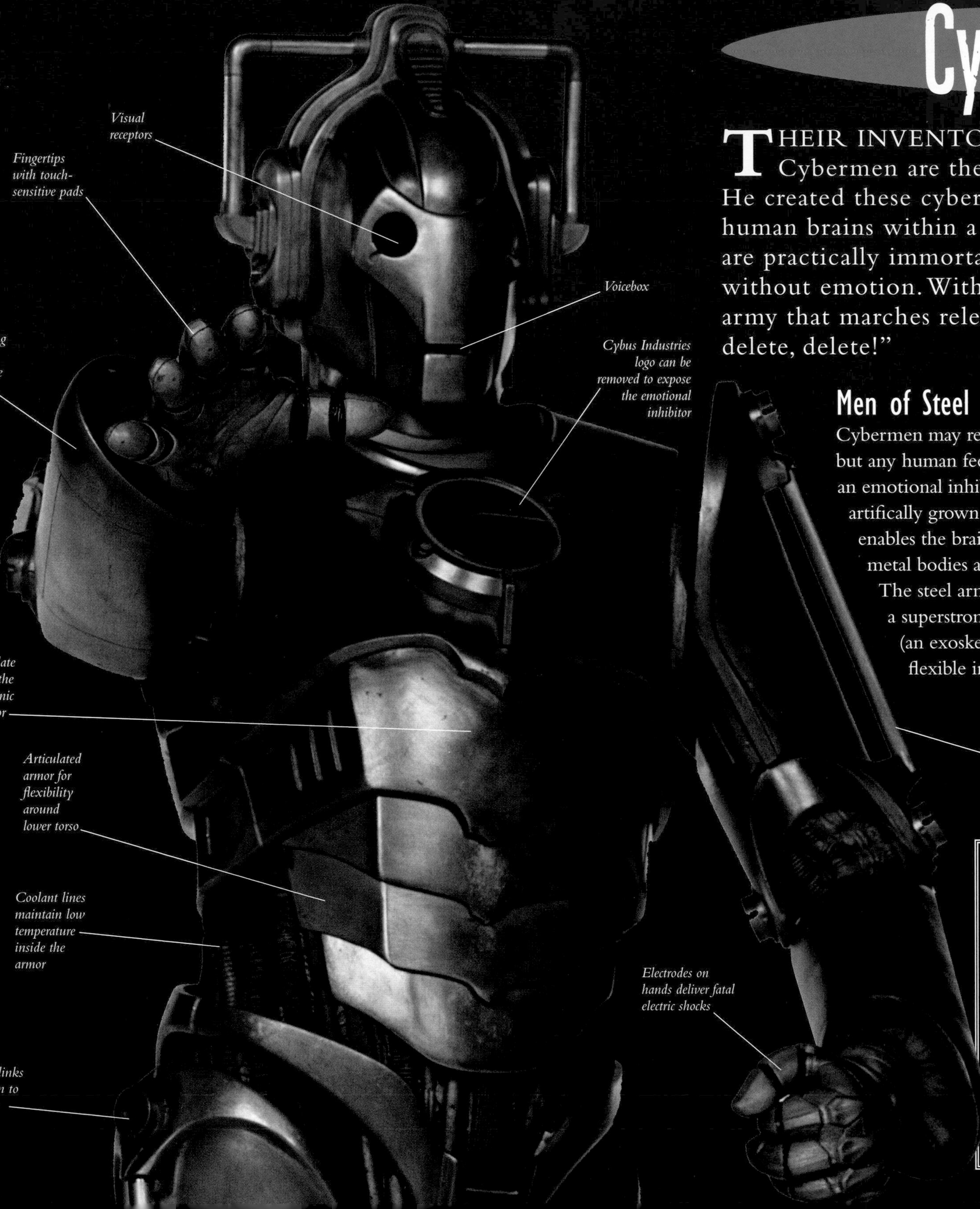

Visual receptors

Fingertips with touch-sensitive pads

Superstrong armor protects the forearms

Voicebox

Cybus Industries logo can be removed to expose the emotional inhibitor

Chestplate shields the thermionic generator

Articulated armor for flexibility around lower torso

Coolant lines maintain low temperature inside the armor

Hip joint links exoskeleton to core armor

Electrodes on hands deliver fatal electric shocks

Exoskeleton increases upper body strength

Men of Steel

Cybermen may retain their human brains, but any human feelings are suppressed with an emotional inhibitor. They have an artifically grown nervous system that enables the brain to control their metal bodies and electronic parts. The steel armor is made up of a superstrong exterior shell (an exoskeleton) and a more flexible interior casing.

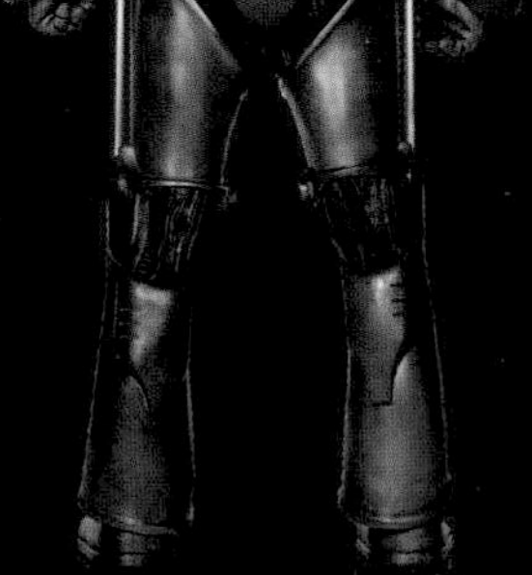

BACK VIEW

Cyberman Facts

- **The Cybermen's armor is made from an extremely strong manganese-steel alloy.**
- **All Cybermen's brains are linked to form a single collective consciousness.**
- **The human brain inside the Cyber-armor is stored at 43 degrees Fahrenheit in a patented protein solution.**
- **Each Cyberman is powered by a thermionic generator.**

CYBUS INDUSTRIES LOGO

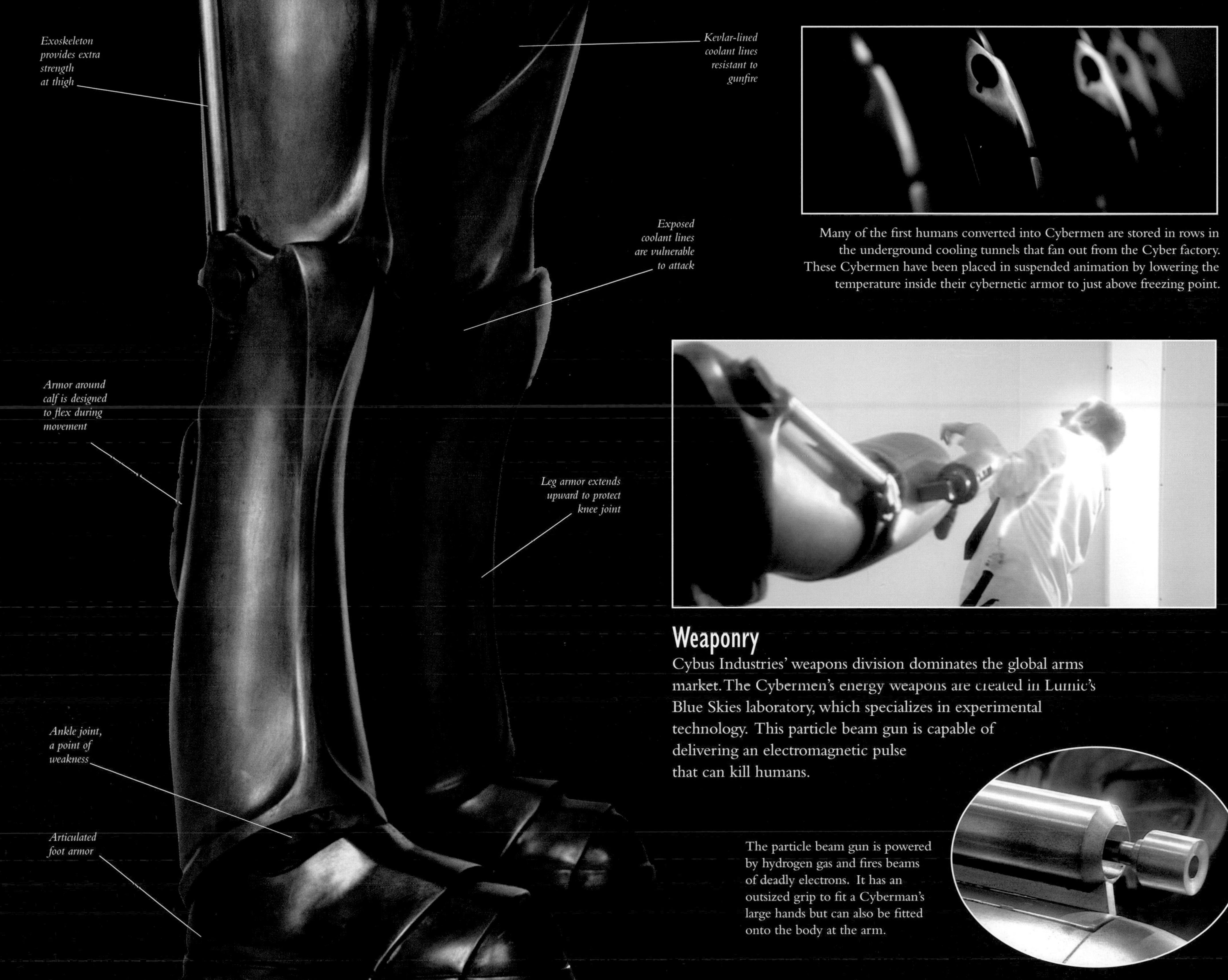
Exoskeleton provides extra strength at thigh
Kevlar-lined coolant lines resistant to gunfire
Exposed coolant lines are vulnerable to attack
Armor around calf is designed to flex during movement
Leg armor extends upward to protect knee joint
Ankle joint, a point of weakness
Articulated foot armor

Many of the first humans converted into Cybermen are stored in rows in the underground cooling tunnels that fan out from the Cyber factory. These Cybermen have been placed in suspended animation by lowering the temperature inside their cybernetic armor to just above freezing point.

Weaponry

Cybus Industries' weapons division dominates the global arms market. The Cybermen's energy weapons are created in Lumic's Blue Skies laboratory, which specializes in experimental technology. This particle beam gun is capable of delivering an electromagnetic pulse that can kill humans.

The particle beam gun is powered by hydrogen gas and fires beams of deadly electrons. It has an outsized grip to fit a Cyberman's large hands but can also be fitted onto the body at the arm.

Cybus Industries

WHEN THE TARDIS crashes on a parallel Earth, the Doctor and his companions find a world similar to their own but dominated by one organization, Cybus Industries. This massive business empire controls the world's media, finance, property, communications, and technology. Its mega-rich but dying leader, John Lumic, has secretly spent years and millions of dollars researching an end to mortality. His plan is to "upgrade" humanity, turning it into a race of immortal Cybermen.

Air Ship

With crime rampant on the streets of Britain and a night-time curfew in place, Britain's wealthy elite have taken to living in giant air ships floating above London. The zeppelins are manufactured by Cybus Industries, whose leader, John Lumic, has his own luxury model. He can send signals to people's EarPods via a transmitter on his ship.

EarPod transmitter

Bow reinforced to withstand headwinds

Satellite transmitter

Rigid hull, made from a light aluminum alloy

Spotlights, used when landing the airship in darkness

Bridge at front of gondola

Horizontal fin for stability

Gondola with accommodation and facilities for passengers and crew

Starboard propeller

Port propeller for forward thrust

Ventral fin

John Lumic

The founder of Cybus Industries, John Lumic, is a scientific genius whose inventions have made him the most powerful man on Earth. But he suffers from a terrible wasting disease that has confined him to a wheelchair and will ultimately kill him. Power and a fear of death have turned him into an insane megalomanic who sees mortality as the ultimate enemy. To him, humanity and individuality are expendable in the search for an end to death.

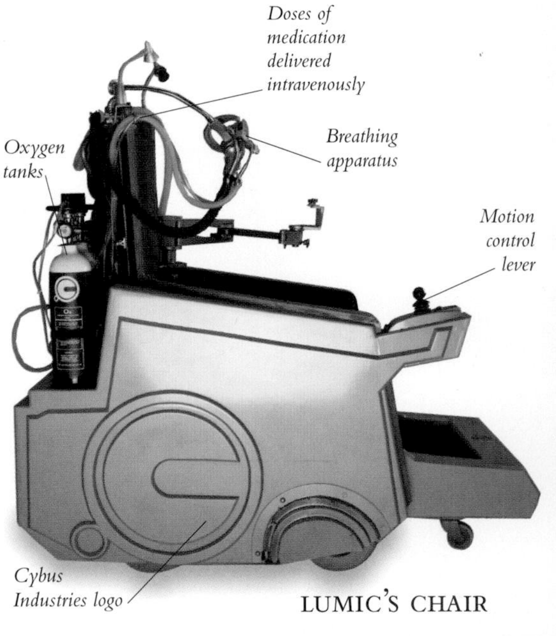

LUMIC'S CHAIR

On this parallel Earth, everyone wears an EarPod. Developed by Cybus Industries, these sophisticated communications devices download news and entertainment directly into the user's brain and exert a form of mind control.

EARPOD

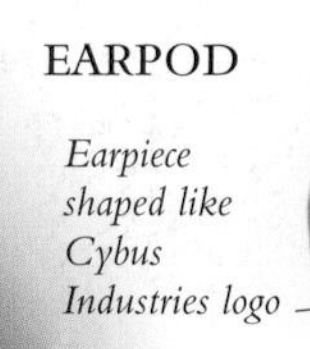

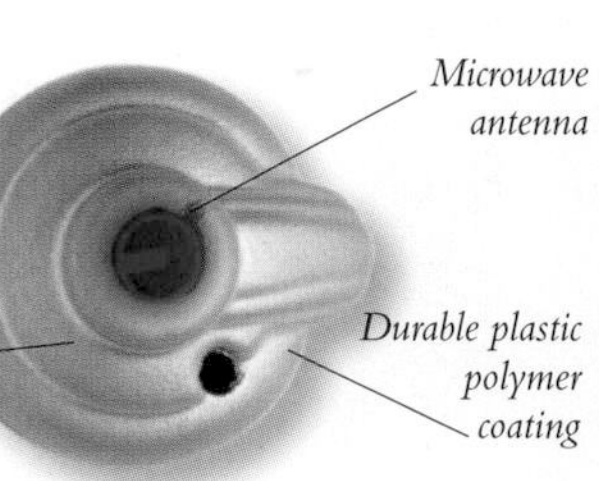

The Cybus Factory

Lumic secretly converted the disused buildings at Battersea Power Station in London into a factory for creating Cybermen. It is just one of many similar factories across the world. As Lumic attempted to perfect his cyber-conversion techniques, many of London's homeless people were abducted and experimented on. Inside the factory, there are hundreds of cylindrical conversion chambers. Each chamber is designed to transform a human into a Cyberman in less than a minute. The factory is capable of converting thousands of people a day into emotionless Cybermen.

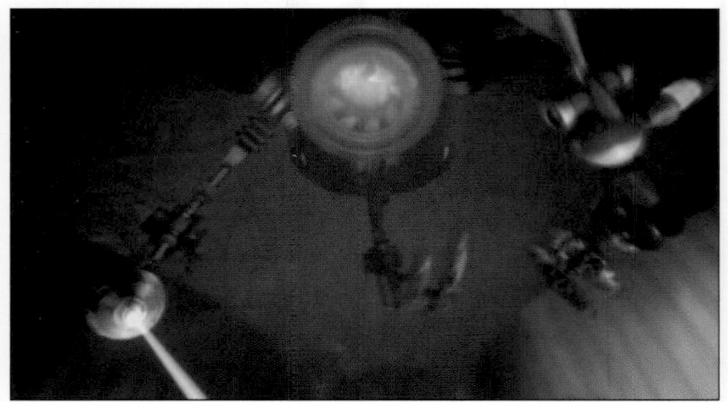

The brain is the only part of a human that survives inside a Cyberman. Lumic had to find a way to remove the human brain without killing it. He realized that speed was key. With pain receptors in the brain deactivated by EarPods, the powerful cutting gear cuts open the human skull, carves out the brain, and transfers it into its new metal home in seconds. The remaining body is simply incinerated.

A Cyberman's human brain is housed in its steel helmet. Once in place, the brain is flooded with a chilled protein solution that preserves and nurtures it, eliminating cellular decay.

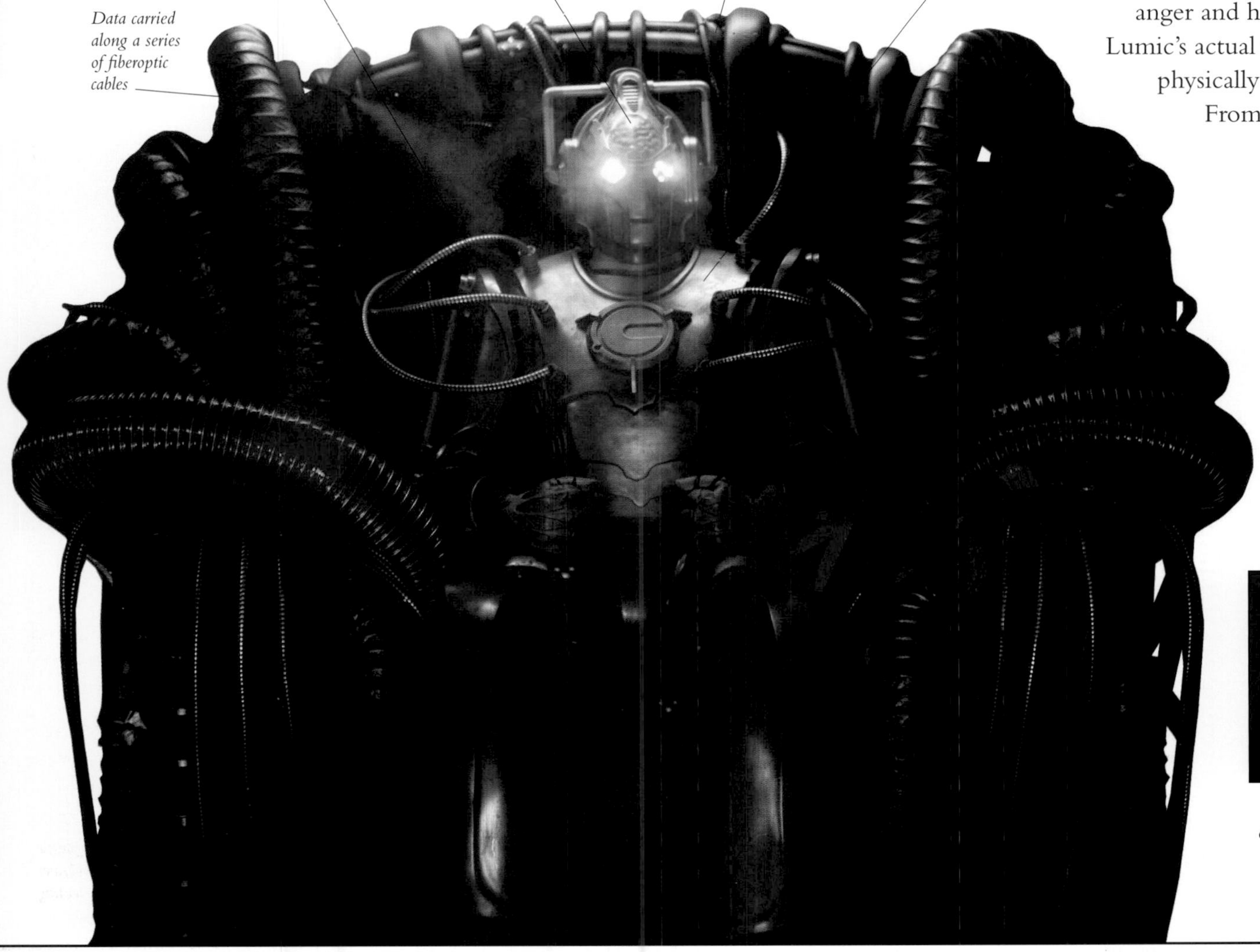

Data carried along a series of fiberoptic cables

Coolant fed into Cyber Controller's body

Transparent brain-case

Throne constructed from titanium alloy

Steel body armor

The Cyber Controller

When John Lumic is transformed into the Cyber Controller, he retains the emotions of anger and hatred, and his voicebox mimics Lumic's actual voice. The Cyber Controller is physically connected to a Cyber Throne. From there, he is able to control the activity of all the Cybermen.

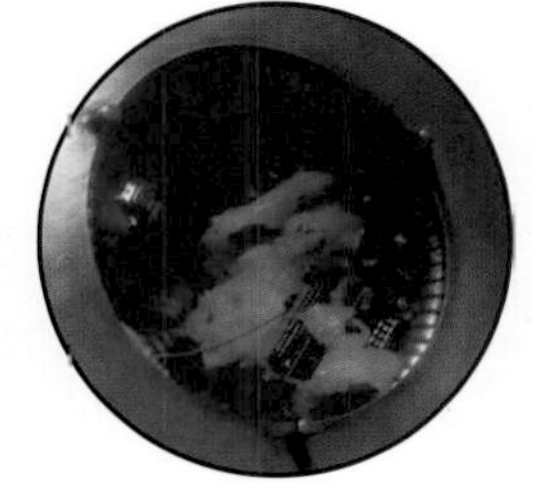

The emotional inhibitor removes a Cyberman's human feelings. Without it, the Cyberman would go insane.

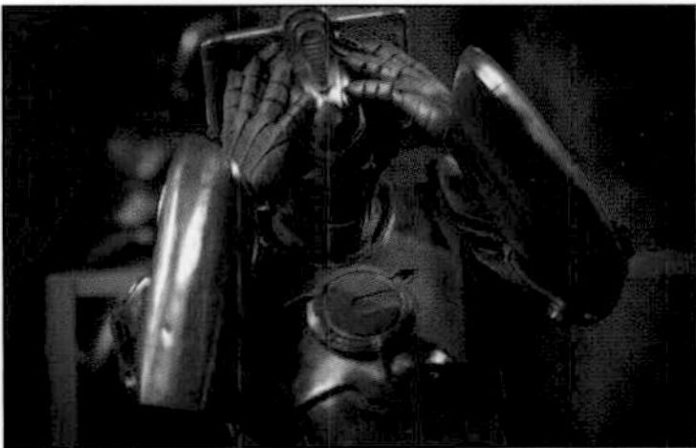

When the emotional inhibitors are deactivated, the Cybermen are killed by the mental trauma.

The Ood

IN THE 42ND CENTURY, HUMANITY is led to believe that the Ood have only one purpose—to serve people. In fact, the Ood are not naturally subservient at all. A humanoid herd species, with squidlike tentacles, they lived in telepathic harmony on their planet, the Ood-Sphere, until the arrival of the entrepreneurial Halpen family. The tycoons enslaved the peaceful Ood and sold them throughout the Human Empire.

Bred to Serve

Ood Operations sets up breeding farms to produce the hundreds of thousands of Ood needed for the domestic and military markets. The company lobotomizes the Ood into servitude and convinces their customers that the Ood's only goal is to receive orders and that without tasks to perform they would die.

Destroy the evidence! When the Ood regain the ability to think for themselves, ruthless company CEO Halpen is prepared to wipe out every captive Ood in his factory complex in order to protect his reputation.

Brainy Aliens

Natural Ood do not have just one brain, but two! Mostly they use the brains in their heads, but memory and emotions are processed by the hind-brain, which is held in the peaceful Ood's hands. The Company replaces the hind-brain with a translator, which limits the Ood's telepathic ability and cuts them off from their communal Center Brain.

The Center Brain

The telepathic Center Brain connected the Ood in beautiful song for millennia, until Halpen's ancestors discovered it beneath the Ood-Sphere's Northern Glacier. It has been kept in captivity for 200 years.

Color of eyes indicates level of telepathic activity
Eyes turn red with telepathic ability
Front lobe houses telepathy sensors
Coleoid tentacles for feeding
Variety package for translator ball provides different voices
Translation sphere connects to nervous system and enables the Ood to speak

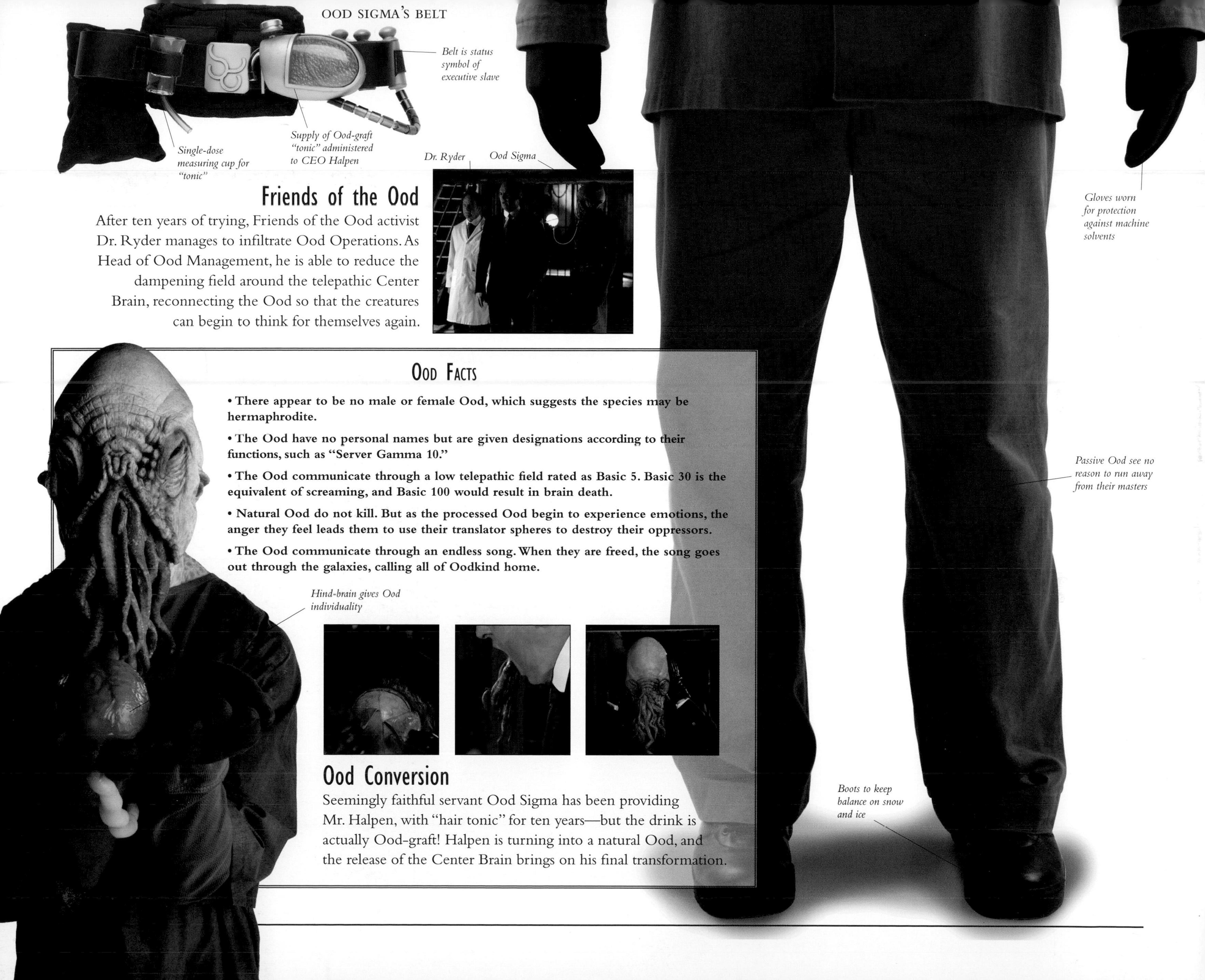
OOD SIGMA'S BELT
Belt is status symbol of executive slave
Supply of Ood-graft "tonic" administered to CEO Halpen
Single-dose measuring cup for "tonic"
Dr. Ryder
Ood Sigma
Gloves worn for protection against machine solvents
Passive Ood see no reason to run away from their masters
Hind-brain gives Ood individuality
Boots to keep balance on snow and ice

Friends of the Ood

After ten years of trying, Friends of the Ood activist Dr. Ryder manages to infiltrate Ood Operations. As Head of Ood Management, he is able to reduce the dampening field around the telepathic Center Brain, reconnecting the Ood so that the creatures can begin to think for themselves again.

Ood Facts

- **There appear to be no male or female Ood, which suggests the species may be hermaphrodite.**
- **The Ood have no personal names but are given designations according to their functions, such as "Server Gamma 10."**
- **The Ood communicate through a low telepathic field rated as Basic 5. Basic 30 is the equivalent of screaming, and Basic 100 would result in brain death.**
- **Natural Ood do not kill. But as the processed Ood begin to experience emotions, the anger they feel leads them to use their translator spheres to destroy their oppressors.**
- **The Ood communicate through an endless song. When they are freed, the song goes out through the galaxies, calling all of Oodkind home.**

Ood Conversion

Seemingly faithful servant Ood Sigma has been providing Mr. Halpen, with "hair tonic" for ten years—but the drink is actually Ood-graft! Halpen is turning into a natural Ood, and the release of the Center Brain brings on his final transformation.

The Beast

WHEN THE TARDIS materializes in a planetary exploration base it is soon clear that all is not quite right. Scripture from a prehuman civilization marks the walls, and the planet is orbiting a black hole—which goes against the laws of physics. The base's crew is drilling to the center of the planet to harness the mysterious power that keeps it in orbit. But as they mine, an ancient evil trapped in its core begins to stir.

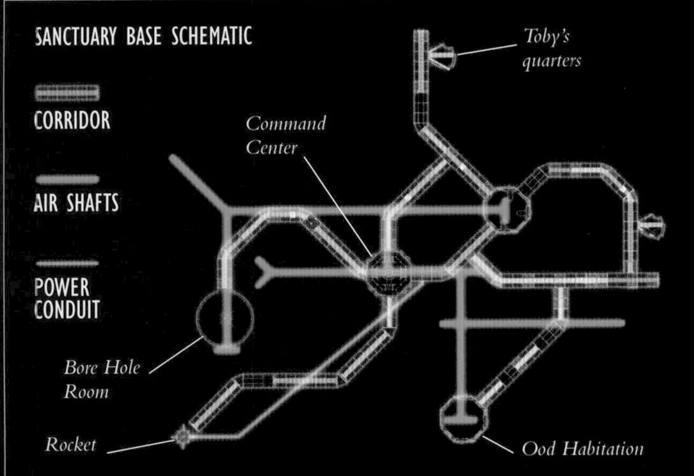

Base Floorplan

One of many identical bases used in deep space exploration, Sanctuary Base is constructed from prefabricated kits. Separate segments allow the oxygen field to be contained in different parts of the base, and areas can be sealed off in the event of a hull breach. This enables the team to enact "Strategy 9"—sheltering in a locked-down safe area and opening the base's airlocks, sucking invaders into space.

Somehow, the planet is generating enough power to keep it in perpetual geostationary orbit around black hole K37 Gem 5. The Doctor calculates that such a power would need an inverted self-extrapolating reflex of 6 to the power of 6 every 6 seconds—a theoretically impossible figure.

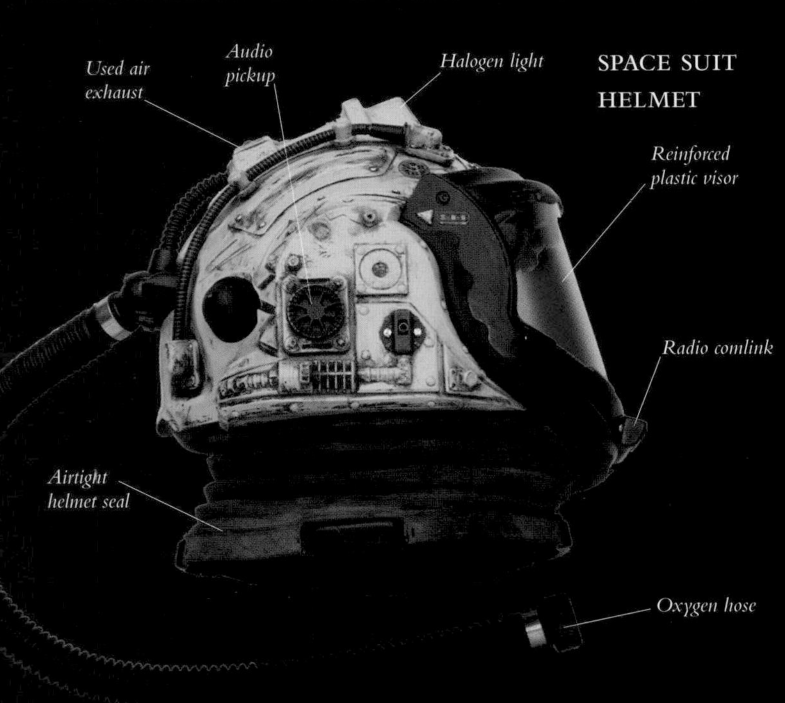

SPACE SUIT HELMET

Command Center

The central desk of the command center controls all the base's essential functions, including the oxygen field, internal gravity system, and rocket link. From here the captain tracks everyone's location from their biochip signals. Overhead shields can be opened to monitor black hole activity.

Surface Work

Protective space suits must be worn on the surface since the planet lacks atmosphere and gravity. The drills are shut down at night by the maintenance trainee and the base's computer shuts off access to the surface.

Drilling Platform

The planet's solid-rock crust is excavated with robot drills and the base crew painstakingly cut a mineshaft 10 miles (16 km) beneath the surface in a bid to reach the planet's mysterious energy source—an energy giving readings of over 90 Statts on the Blazen scale. The enslaved race, the Ood, do all the dangerous maintenance work on the drilling platform.

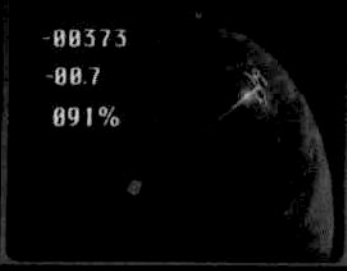

Screens monitor the capsule's rate of descent into the mineshaft.

Black hole
Sanctuary Base 6
Drilling platform
Capsule
Drilled mineshaft
Gravity globe
Carved monolith of demon
Seal
Starlight shines through pothole
The Doctor
TARDIS

When the Doctor and Officer Ida Scott investigate the source of the mysterious power, they discover a vast cavern beneath Sanctuary Base that is the prison home of the Beast, an ancient creature akin to the devil. Two stone monoliths stand guard before a great circular seal set into the floor, which the Doctor guesses is a trap door.

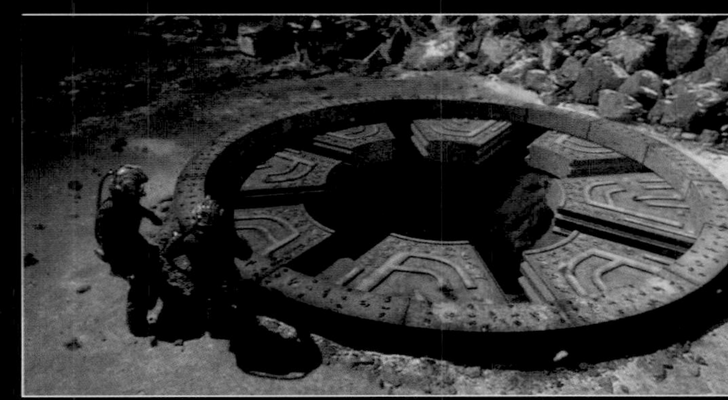

Going Deeper

The Doctor, wearing protective clothing, ponders the strange seal, unable to read the alien writing on it. Sensors indicate that the power source lies beneath. Without warning, the cavern shakes as the trap door's segments slide back to reveal a deep, black chasm. A voice booms from darkness "The pit is open and I am free!"

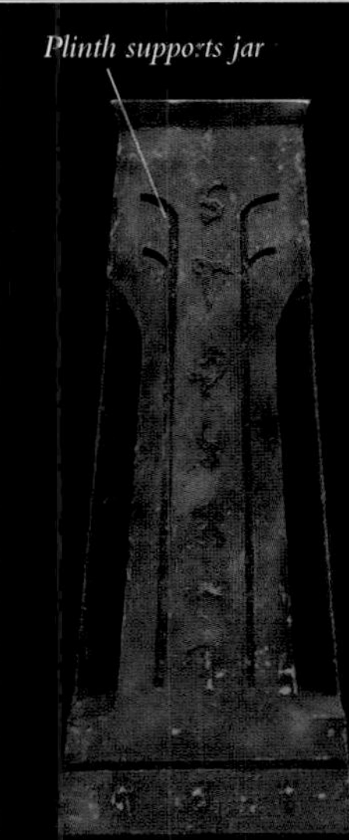

ANCIENT REACTOR

Ancient Civilization

The voice of the Beast tells the Doctor of a people called the Disciples of Light who rose up against him in a time before the universe was created—something the Doctor finds impossible to believe. As if in confirmation of the Devil's words, the Doctor finds cave drawings recording a victory over the Beast and his imprisonment in the pit.

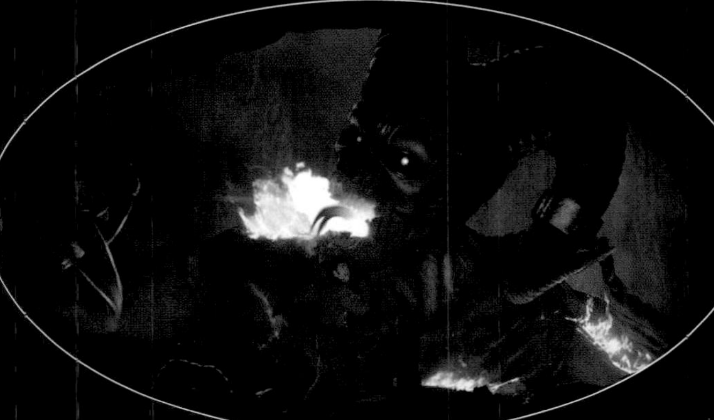

The Perfect Prison

The Doctor realizes that the planet is an ingenious prison. If the Beast escapes from the pit, the energy source keeping the planet in orbit will collapse, and the planet will be sucked into the black hole. The air in the pit was supplied by the ancient gaolers so a traveler could stop the Beast's escape by smashing the power source.

The monster before the Doctor is the empty body of the Beast—whose mind has fled by possessing one of the crew. The Doctor has only seconds to destroy the planet and foil the Beast's escape.

The Genesis Ark

WHEN THE SECRETIVE Torchwood Institute Two attempts to harness energy from a spatial disturbance over London, they unwittingly break through the wall between dimensions. A sinister metal sphere emerges through the breach, which the Doctor instantly recognizes as a Void Ship. Knowing that nothing good can be inside it, the Doctor urges Torchwood to send it back through the Rift.

Torchwood

The Torchwood Institute's mission is to acquire and analyze alien hardware and use it for the good of the British Empire. Torchwood One has its headquarters in Canary Wharf, in the Docklands area of London.

Torchwood originally discovered a dimensional breach when it appeared as a radar black spot, 600 feet (180 meters) above the ground. The breach was opened when particle engines were fired at the spot.

The Void Ship

This hypothetical craft was designed to exist outside space and time, traveling between dimensions. The sphere fills all who near it with foreboding. In theory it does not exist because it lacks both radiation and atomic mass.

When the Void Ship activates, the lab screens go wild. Suddenly, the object has height, mass, and an electromagnetic field. The Sphere Chamber doors immediately seal shut to put the area in automatic quarantine.

Inside the Sphere

A sinister casket is concealed inside the Void Ship. Known as the Genesis Ark, it has dimensionally transcendental Time Lord technology similar to the TARDIS, and was used during the Great Time War for the sole purpose of imprisoning the armies of the Time Lords' deadliest enemy—the Daleks.

FRONT VIEW

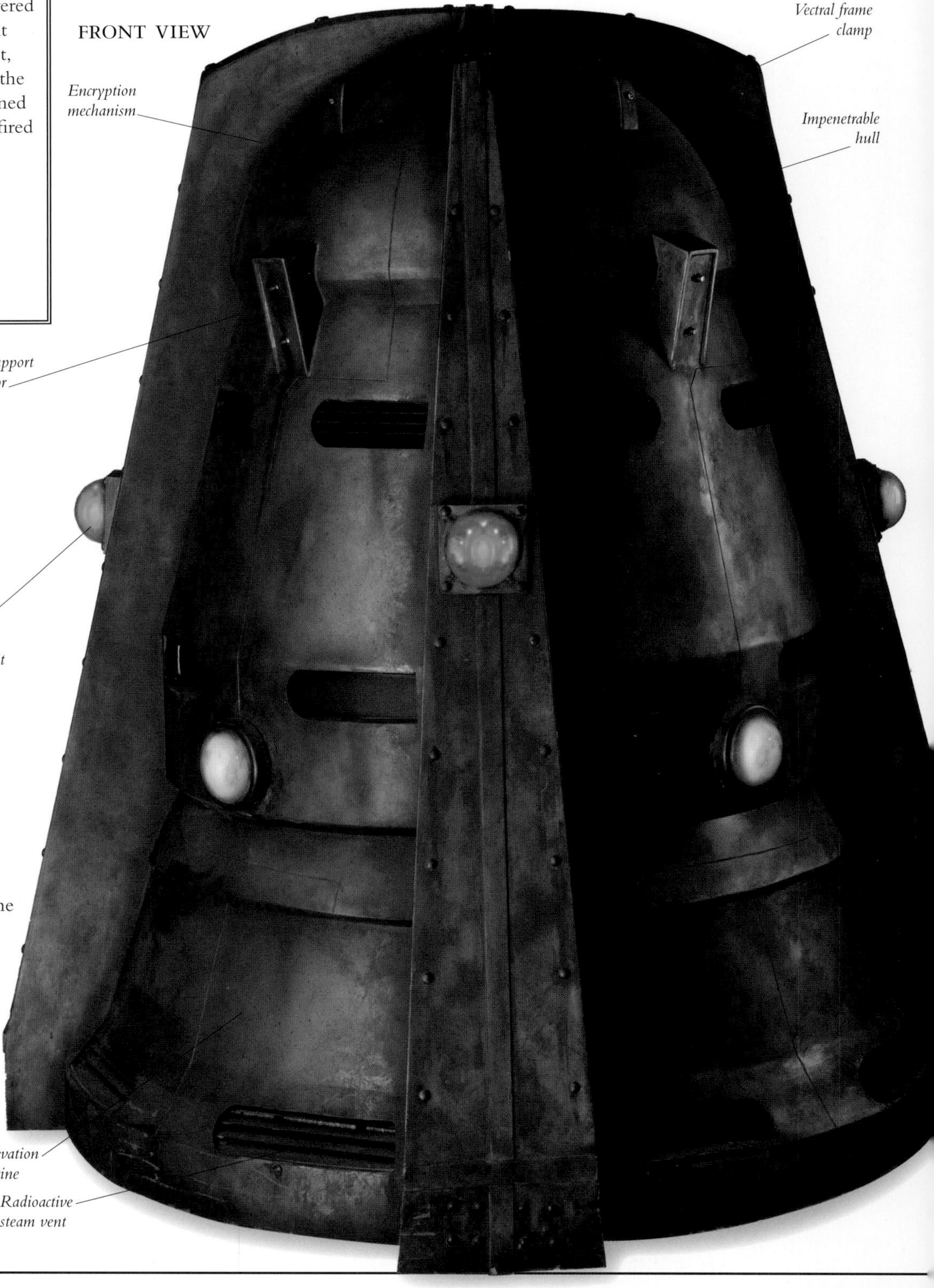

Vectral frame clamp

Encryption mechanism

Impenetrable hull

Life support monitor

Sensor processing unit

Elevation engine

Radioactive steam vent

The Key to the Ark

Rose and Mickey witness the Genesis Ark and four Daleks, the Cult of Skaro, emerging from the Void Ship. The Daleks must keep Rose and Mickey alive because a time-traveler's touch is the key that opens the Ark. As humanoid time-travelers, Rose and Mickey soak up the universe's background radiation—the power source for the Ark. When fighting rages between Daleks and Cybermen in the sphere chamber, Mickey is shoved against the Ark and touches it, causing it to prime.

Internal power drive activated

Handprint radiation primes mechanisms

Life support system powers up

Priming console activated

The lab doctor, Dr. Singh, volunteers information to the Daleks, but, in a sickening display of brutality, each attach their suckers to his head and extract his brain waves. Dr. Singh collapses on the floor as a withered husk.

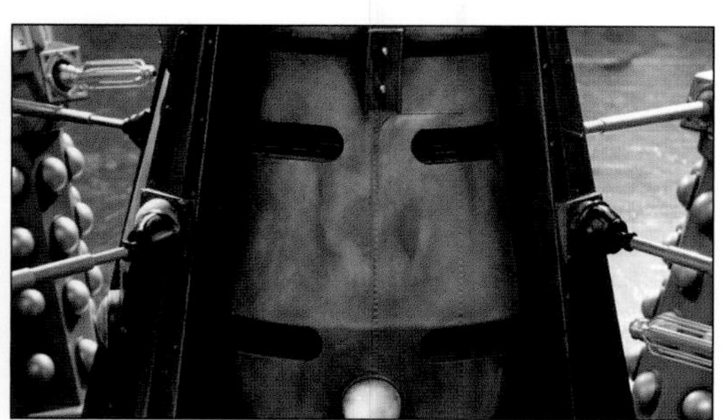

The Cult of Skaro circles the Ark at intervals, beginning the awakening process by attaching their suckers to the four priming consoles on each side of the casket. Rose asks the Black Dalek, Sec, what is inside. It replies, "the future!"

The Ark's Purpose

As the Ark is activated in the sky above London the Doctor finally understands what the Daleks meant by "Time Lord science." Like the TARDIS, the Ark is much larger on the inside than on the outside, and was used as a prison ship for the millions of the Daleks captured during the Great Time War.

The Black Dalek overrides the roof mechanism of the Torchwood hangar area, elevating the Ark the 18 square miles (48 square kilometers) needed for activation.

High over London the Doctor and his companions watch in horror as the Ark disgorges its evil cargo—millions of Daleks come shooting out in all directions, intent on extermination.

Doomsday Ghosts

Comms device is connected to brain tissue

WHEN THE VOID SHIP bursts through the breach in time and space, it is followed by a small army of humanoid, ghostly figures. Torchwood learns how to open and close the breach and allow the ghosts into their dimension. Every day at noon, Torchwood runs a "ghost shift." For a few minutes they open the breach a fraction and more ghosts enter. The Doctor warns that the sphere must be sent back and the ghost shifts stopped.

Cyberghosts

People welcome the humanoid ghostly entities, believing them to be departed loved ones. When the breach is finally forced open to 100 percent, the true nature of the "ghosts" is revealed—as millions of Cybermen materialize, and the steel soldiers commence their invasion.

Although the Torchwood CEO cancels the ghost shifts after the Doctor's warning, some staff ignore her orders and begin opening the breach. The Doctor sees that they are being controlled through cyber earpieces. Using his sonic screwdriver, he disrupts the signal and the staff collapse on their desks, dead.

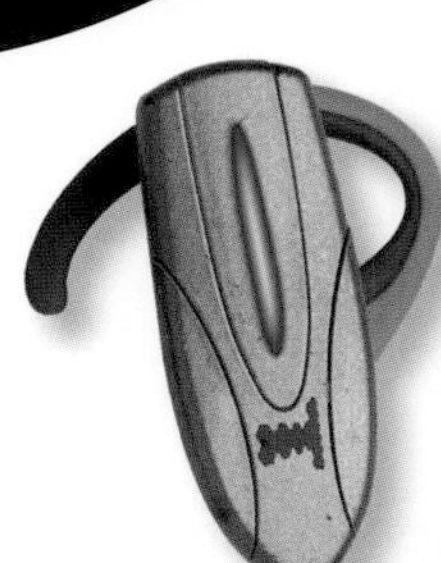

CYBER EAR-PIECE

Rival Races

As soon as the Void Ship opens, Daleks and Cybermen detect each other's presence. Both sides send envoys to investigate and the Cyber Leader addresses the Daleks on screen, beginning an historic exchange between the rival races.

Dalek and Cybermen Facts

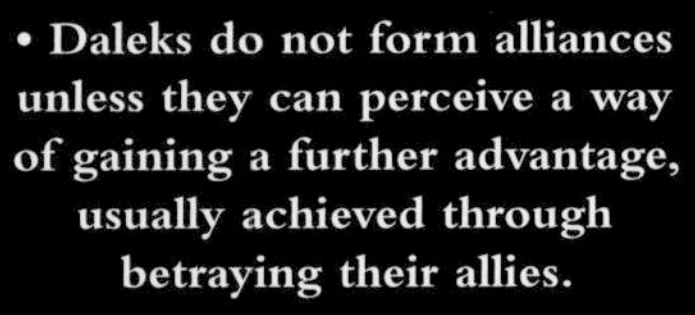

- **Daleks do not form alliances unless they can perceive a way of gaining a further advantage, usually achieved through betraying their allies.**
- **Daleks are confident of beating five million Cybermen, even with a single Dalek. They regard this not as war, but as "pest control."**
- **Dalek force fields absorb Cybermen laser blasts, rendering them ineffective. Cybermen have no such force field and can be instantly exterminated.**
- **Daleks measure time in "rels." Ordering the recording of the Cyber Leader's message to be rewound 9 rels, they identify a Dalek enemy on the screen, standing behind the Cyber Leader. Rose confirms that they have seen the Doctor.**
- **Daleks and Cybermen have never encountered each other before. Communication opens with both sides refusing to identify themselves first to the other.**

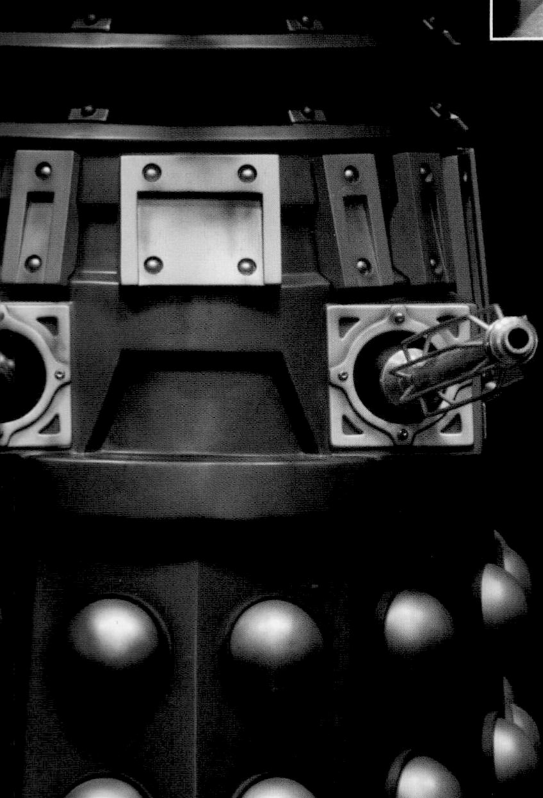

Parallel Worlds

A squad of humans from a parallel Earth materialize into the Torchwood Institute and blast the nearby Cybermen. By infiltrating their parallel Earth's Torchwood, the humans obtained a Parallel-World Transporter that allows them to cross between worlds. The Cybermen have escaped from their parallel Earth into this one.

BLASTER

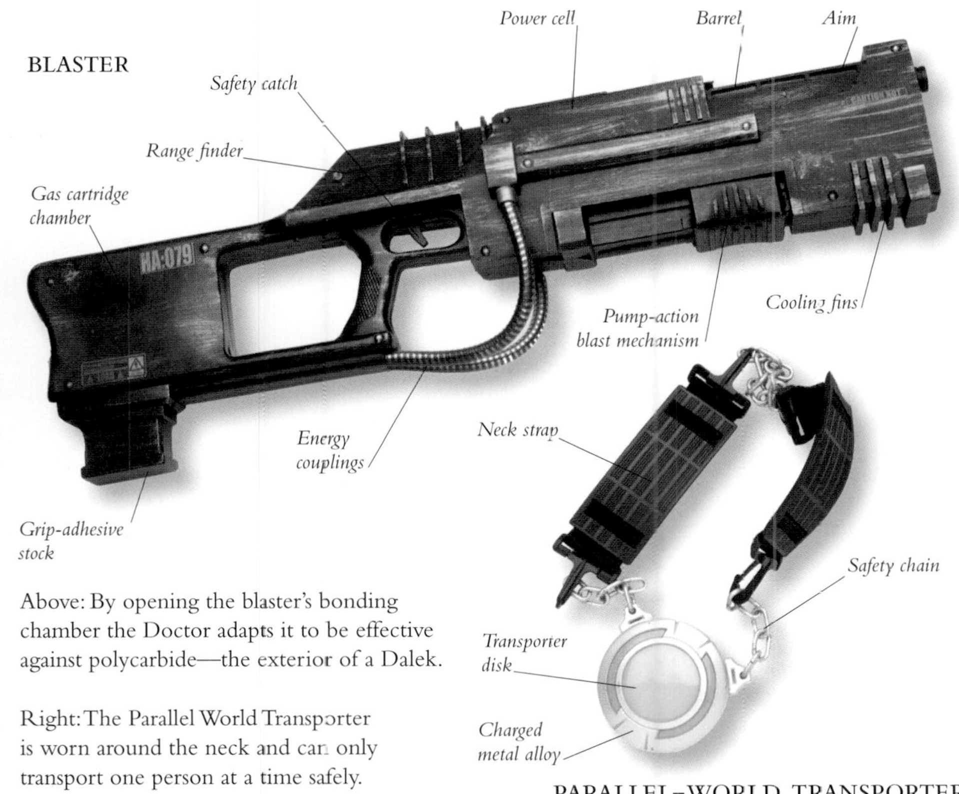

Above: By opening the blaster's bonding chamber the Doctor adapts it to be effective against polycarbide—the exterior of a Dalek.

Right: The Parallel World Transporter is worn around the neck and can only transport one person at a time safely.

PARALLEL-WORLD TRANSPORTER

The Battle of the Sphere Chamber

In a temporary alliance with the Cybermen, the parallel-world humans storm the Sphere Chamber after the Doctor blows its doors open with his sonic screwdriver. Caught off-guard, the Daleks' casings are impaired by the energy blasts and it is some moments before they can adapt their weaponry. In the chaos of the battle, the Doctor rescues Rose and Mickey.

As the scale of the Dalek threat becomes clear, the Cyber Leader declares an emergency and calls all units to converge on Torchwood. Immediately, the Cybermen abandon guard over their human captives and march in formation to meet the Dalek army.

The Battle of Canary Wharf

Dalek legions emerge from the Genesis Ark and begin a spectacular battle with the Cybermen. Dalek Sec orders his airborne forces to exterminate all life-forms below, sending terrified people diving for cover. But the Dalek supremacy is short-lived. The Doctor opens the breach once more, sucking almost every Dalek and Cyberman back into the void.

The Cybermen stand in formation to fire laser volleys at the Dalek legions overhead. A squadron of battle Daleks breaks off and swoops down to attack.

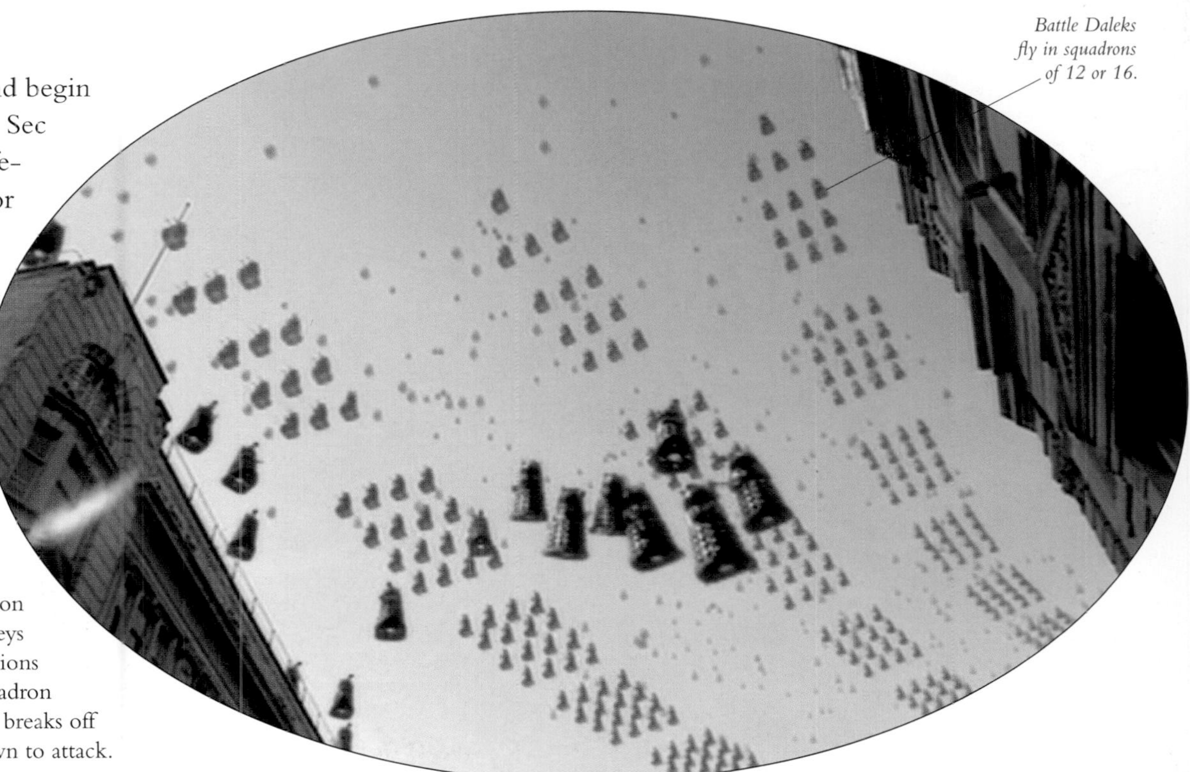

Battle Daleks fly in squadrons of 12 or 16.

The Cult of Skaro

A SECRET ORDER of Daleks, the Cult of Skaro, consists of four members. Their role is to think like the enemies of the Daleks in order to find new ways of exterminating them. They exist outside the normal Dalek hierarchy, above even the Emperor. To emphasize their special status, they even have individual names.

Dalek Sec

The utterly ruthless Dalek Sec is the Black Dalek leader of the Cult of Skaro, guiding the research of his colleagues. To escape the failure of the Genesis Ark plan, Sec transports the four members of the Cult away, using an emergency temporal shift.

Swiveling eyestalk and rotating dome provide almost spherical field of vision

Luminosity discharge valve dissipates excess energy from Dalek's cells, through light and sound emission

Dalek is equipped with automatic distress call if casing is breached or forced open

Sensor grid louvers allow waste heat exhaust

Force field broadcast antennae. Each flat panel broadcasts an overlapping field for complete coverage around the Dalek

Manipulator arm's telescopic tube and swivel mount provide tremendous reach

Rotating midsection gives Dalek 360° range of fire

"Sucker" tool, made of morphic material that can assume various useful shapes

Death ray beam is a focused electrical discharge of immense power

The Cult members escaped the destruction of the Dalek race at the end of the Great Time War by fleeing in a Void Ship with the captured Genesis Ark. Their ship used a spatial disturbance to break through to Earth.

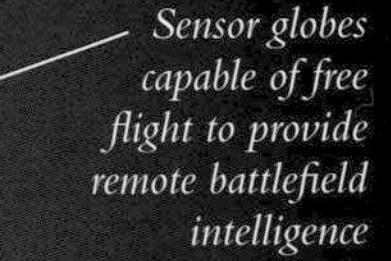

Sensor globes capable of free flight to provide remote battlefield intelligence

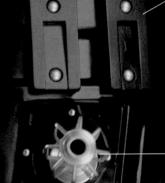

Dalekanium outer casing. Lightweight, yet incredibly strong and able to resist energy weapons

Cult of Skaro Facts

- The Cult of Skaro consists of four members, led by Dalek Sec. This small number can be strategically useful, but they are too few to be a military threat to the Emperor.
- The Cult is named after the Dalek homeworld Skaro, which was devastated by the supernova generated by the seventh Doctor's subterfuge with the Hand of Omega. It was finally obliterated during the Great Time War.
- In order to "think like the enemy," the Cult Daleks are encouraged to develop their imaginations.
- Unlike ordinary Daleks, Cult members do have limited emotions, which mimic those of other life-forms. They also have a sense of self-preservation not found in Dalek warriors.
- The Cult's existence was kept so secret by the Daleks that even the Doctor thought they were a legend.

with anti-gravity generators enables Dalek to hover and fly

DALEK SEC

DALEK THAY

DALEK JAST

DALEK CAAN

The Genesis Ark is actually a captured Time Lord prison ship, containing millions of Daleks.

Special Training

The Cult of Skaro members have a strong bond of loyalty to each other, and are fanatically driven by the need to use their special training to extend the Dalek Empire throughout space and time. Under the leadership of the Black Dalek, the Cult dedicates its existence to finding new ways to exterminate the Daleks' adversaries, by thinking creatively in "non-Dalek" ways. Like their leader, each Dalek is assigned its own name and personality, in the belief that understanding and mimicking the individuality of many of their enemies will allow them to discover new and more terrifying ways to overcome them.

Webstar of wonder! The Empress's ship flies over the Thames River on Christmas Eve night, but it is not bringing season's greetings. Bolts of deadly electricity arc from its tips, spreading terror on London's streets. It contains the Racnoss Empress, who has come to rescue the many Racnoss trapped in the Webstar that is at the core of the Earth.

Racnoss

THE ARACHNID RACNOSS are born starving and will devour everything, from people to planets. In the Dark Times, near the beginning of the universe, the Fledgeling Empires went to war against the ravenous Racnoss, wiping them out—or so it was thought. One Racnoss Webstar spaceship, hiding from the war, began to attract rocks toward it, creating a planet. Gradually, Earth was formed around the ship!

Blood-red color inspires fear in prey

Tough outer skin is shed when outgrown

The Empress

The Racnoss Empress is on a mission to rescue her children. Long ago, the Time Lords destroyed the Huon energy that forms the source of the Racnoss's power, and the Webstar at the center of Earth was immobilized. The Racnoss have been sleeping for billions of years when the Empress arrives with a plan to rebuild the Huon particles. She will mix them inside the living test tube of human bride-to-be Donna Noble. The energy will give her access to the ship so she can free her children, who will satisfy their hunger with human flesh!

Pedicle enables free movement of thorax

Racnoss Facts

- **Each Racnoss can produce miles of strong, thick protein strands that are used to form webs and bind prey.**
- **The Racnoss can hibernate without sustenance for billions of years, but when they stir, they are ravenous.**
- **The Racnoss have mastered teleportation, so do not need to land their Webstars on Earth.**
- **When the Empress refuses the Doctor's offer of a new home, she condemns her entire race to extinction—every Racnoss is wiped out.**

Robotic Mercenaries

These killer roboforms act as scavengers, trailing in the wake of alien invasions, or work as mercenaries, hired and controlled remotely by an offworld employer. The roboforms disguise themselves to blend in on their target planets—and on Earth at Christmas there is no better costume than Santa Claus.

In operations, robot mercenaries can operate undercover as backup to front-line troops, lying in wait to seal off escape routes for their targets. A specialized roboform with driving protocols in its programming poses as a taxi driver to bring Donna Noble—the key to creating Huon particles—to the Racnoss Empress.

P227 JVP
"Crownlike" bone structure denotes imperial Racnoss
Eight eyes allow wide field of vision
Fangs for tearing flesh
Bladelike arms slice through prey
Hairs on legs pick up vibrations
Spinnerets at base of abdomen produce web strands
Eight jointed legs keep heavy body stable
Removable mask conceals golden metal robot head
Polybonded casing husk
Signal emitter/receiver
Visual readout screen
Signal booster
Power unit
Movement control
Thermal vents

SANTA MASK

ROBOFORM REMOTE CONTROL

Plasmavores

PLASMAVORES ARE AN alien species who live off the vital life-juices of other creatures. While necessary to their survival, bloodsucking is also an addictive pleasure, and many Plasmavores travel the universe searching for rare species to sample. This mania for blood can lead to psychosis and a severe disregard for the lives of others.

To medical specialist Dr. Stoker, Mrs. Finnegan is just another elderly patient

Plasmavore in Hiding

Plasmavores are shape-changers: they can assimiliate the genetic material of any species whose life juice they drink. One such Plasmavore has taken on the persona of frail 70-year-old Florence Finnegan in order to hide on Earth, in the Royal Hope Hospital. "Florence," wanted for murder, is on the run from intergalactic law enforcers, the Judoon.

Drone Bodyguards

The Plasmavore calling itself Florence Finnegan is guarded by two Slab henchmen disguised as motorcycle couriers. These basic slave drones are genetically reared for combat and strong-arm work.

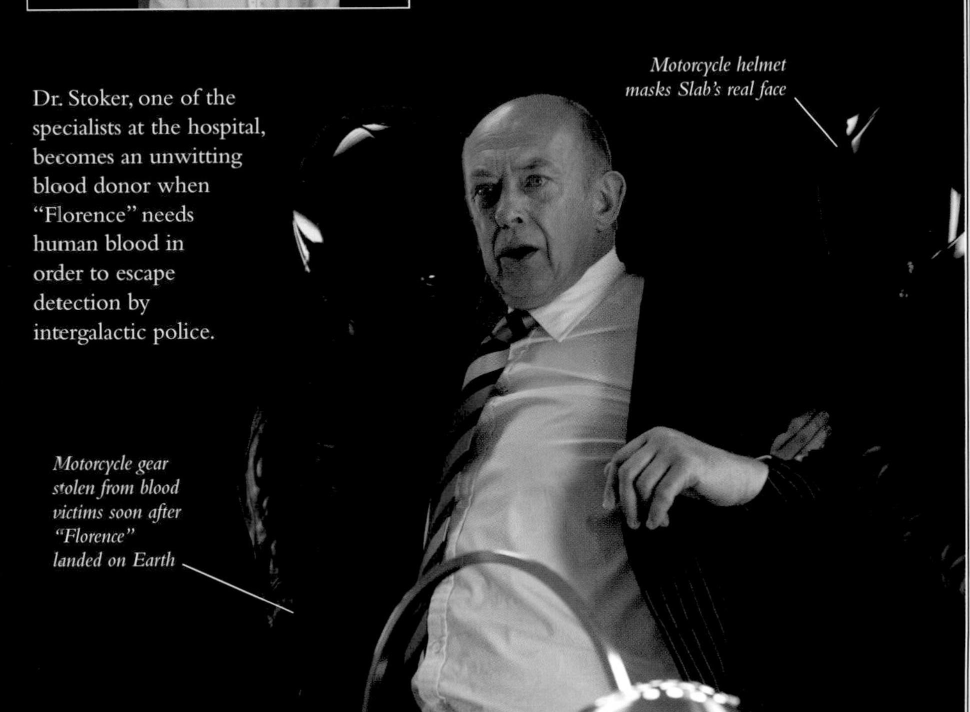

Dr. Stoker, one of the specialists at the hospital, becomes an unwitting blood donor when "Florence" needs human blood in order to escape detection by intergalactic police.

Motorcycle helmet masks Slab's real face

Motorcycle gear stolen from blood victims soon after "Florence" landed on Earth

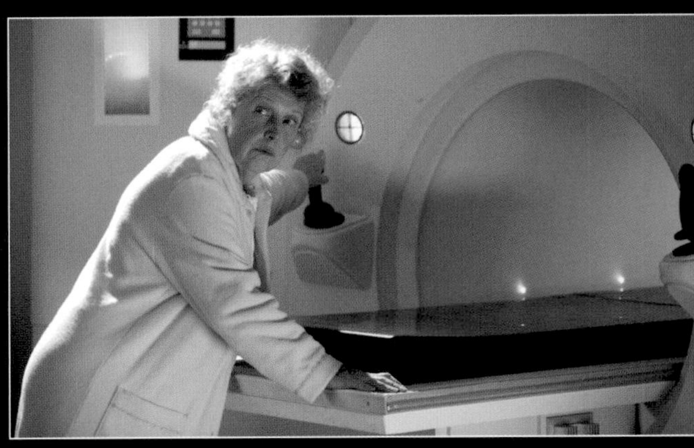

Faced with capture by interplanetary police, "Florence" uses her criminal know-how to turn an MRI scanner into a lethal weapon. She resets the machine's magnet to 50,000 tesla to send out a massive magnetic pulse that will fry the brainstems of all living things within a 200 to 50,000 mile (320 to 80,000 kilometer) radius—leaving her unharmed in the room.

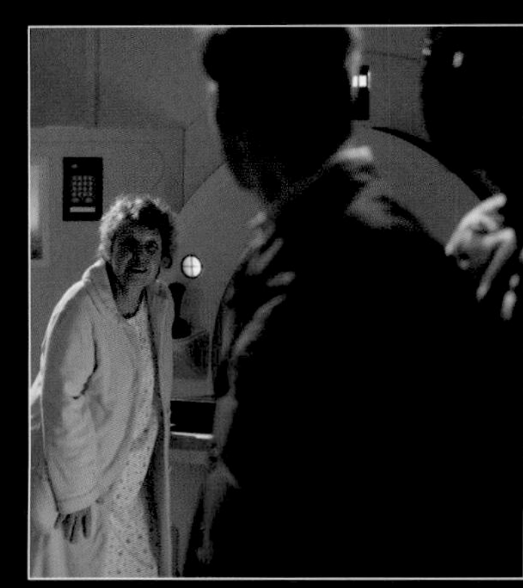

The Doctor, impersonating a human patient, draws out the Plasmavore. She reveals her plans to wipe out everyone so she can escape in the ships belonging to the Judoon police agents.

Plasmavore Facts

• The Plasmavore known as Florence Finnegan randomly landed on Earth while on the run from Judoon—galactic hired police. Her crime: murdering the Child Princess of Padrivole Regency Nine on a whim.

• "Florence" quickly identified the large amounts of blood stored in the Royal Hope Hospital as perfect for "midnight snacks."

• When assimilating blood, Plasmavores generate an exotic plasma energy that attuned individuals like the Doctor can detect. In fact, the Doctor's presence in the hospital can be attributed to him noticing plasma coils surrounding the entire building.

When desperate for blood, Plasmavores will use any ingestion method available at the time. On Earth, the renegade Plasmavore finds a simple straw suitable for its needs.

The Judoon

THROUGHOUT THE UNIVERSE, police authorities come in many shapes, sizes, and species. One of the most feared is the private paramilitary security force organized by the thick-skinned, twin-horned species called the Judoon. Each Judoon police officer has the power to administer swift justice: he can charge, judge, sentence, and execute a suspect in a matter of seconds.

Hired Thugs

Judoon police have a reputation as little more than hired thugs. Their methods are certainly brutal and authoritarian, but carried out without emotion. They focus only on their objective, and let nothing stand in the way of justice being done. As they say, "justice is swift." Among other clients, the Judoon enforce laws for the intergalatic regulatory body, the Shadow Proclamation.

Battle helmet with breathing equipment

One-way viewing slit

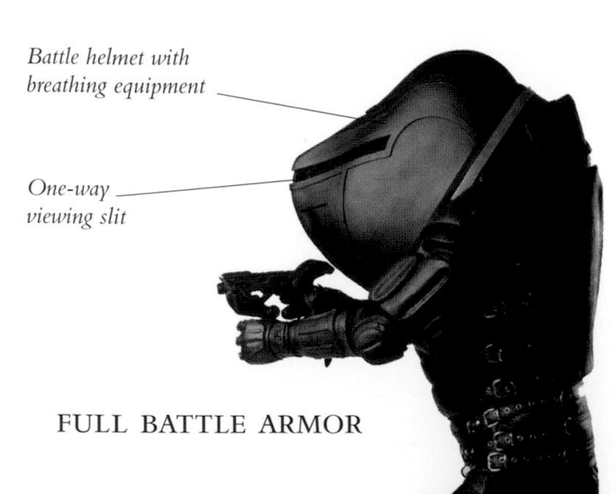

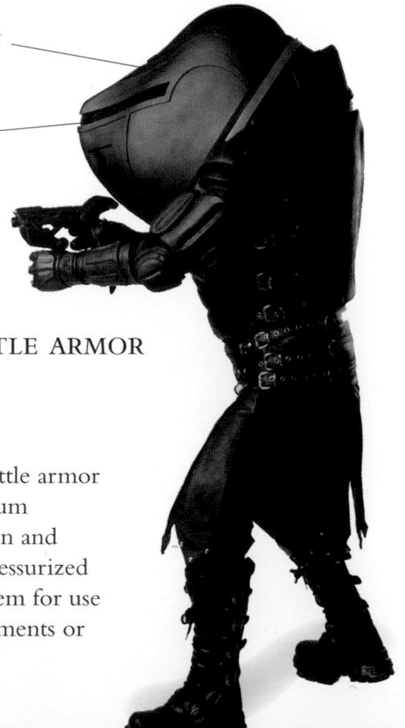

FULL BATTLE ARMOR

The Judoon's battle armor provides maximum impact protection and functions as a pressurized life-support system for use in toxic environments or on planets with nonbreathable atmospheres.

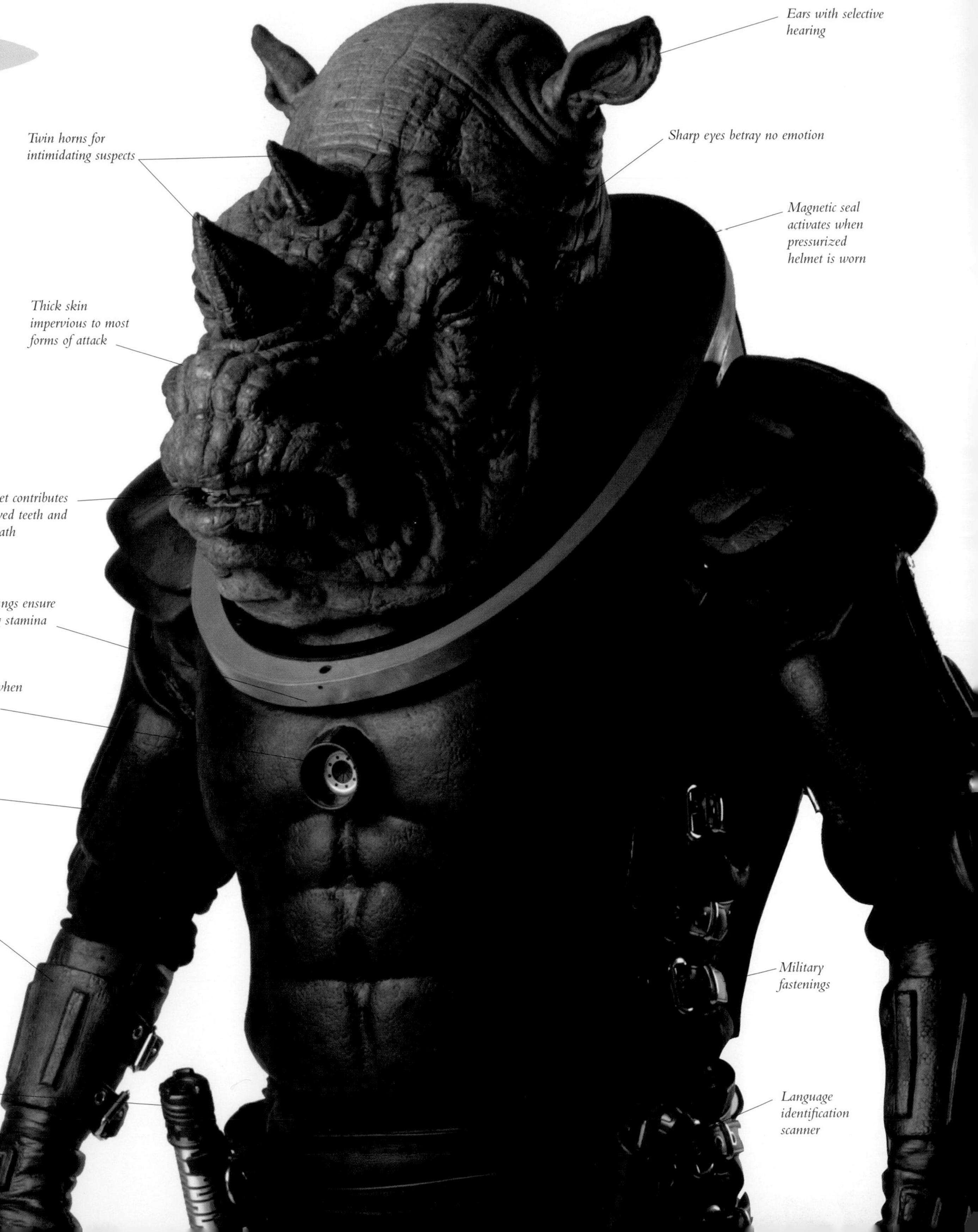

Ears with selective hearing

Sharp eyes betray no emotion

Twin horns for intimidating suspects

Magnetic seal activates when pressurized helmet is worn

Thick skin impervious to most forms of attack

Poor diet contributes to decayed teeth and bad breath

Powerful lungs ensure long-lasting stamina

Voice emitter for use when battle helmet is worn

Bulletproof armor padding

Armored wrist guard

Military fastenings

Variety of weapons and equipment can be slung on utility belt

Language identification scanner

JUDOON BLASTER
Blaster gas cartridge chamber
Muzzle guard
Igniter pin
Cooling unit
Grip for Judoon hand
Trigger
Power cell housing
SPECIES SCANNER
DNA scan emitter
Indelible branding tip
LANGUAGE IDENTIFICATION SCANNER
Memory chips hold most known languages
Holster for blaster
In Judoon culture, the studded kilt is a symbol of a warrior
Reinforced knee guard used offensively and defensively in combat
Elaborate military boots
Boots reinforced with bioengineered metal plates to add extra power to bone-shattering kicks
Distinctive boot fastenings—Judoon are said to sleep with their boots on as a sign of their dedication to the job
Thick soles provide protection on uncertain terrain, including toxic spills

Police Equipment

Judoon police carry high-powered blasters, which they are empowered to fire at their own discretion. A single blast of the deadly energy beam can obliterate a person in a flash. Judoon also carry various scanners that allow them to identify and catalog suspects by species. Another scanner can sample and assimilate the language of most known species—so that their orders will be clearly understood.

Judoon Facts

- **The Judoon travel in gigantic tube-shaped spaceships. Originally built as military battle ships, the Judoon chose these intimidating vehicles for their ability to strike fear in others.**
- **Although the Judoon have no official jurisdiction over Earth, this does not stop them from attemping to capture a Plasmavore suspect known to be hiding on the planet. They use an H_2O scoop to suck an entire Earth building onto the surface of the Moon, where they have authority.**
- **The Judoon are organized along military lines, with troops led by commanders.**

The Carrionites

MOTHER BLOODTIDE LILITH

Eldest Carrionite

Can transform into beautiful human

AT THE BEGINNING OF the universe, foul witchlike creatures known as the Carrionites flew the skies of the Rexel Planetary System, using the power of words to manipulate the universe. When the infinitely powerful Eternals discovered the word that would control the Carrionites, they banished them to the Deep Darkness. The Carrionites remained trapped in their prison for millions of years.

Spread "wings" of cloak help witch float in the air

The Grief of a Genius

The Carrionites want to take over the world and they plan to use William Shakespeare to do it. When the famous wordsmith loses his son, his uncontrolled grief and near madness act as a key to the Carrionites' prison. Three escape, and are drawn to Shakespeare on Earth.

The Carrionites act like witches, but they use science not magic. They are planning to create a new empire on Earth, but unlike the numerical equations used in Earth's sciences, the Carrionites use formulae made out of significant shapes and words.

Carrionite Facts

- **Carrionites are all female. They try to keep their names secret because a person's name is the most powerful spell of all. However, it can only be used once.**
- **When a Carrionite forges a connection with a victim's mind, it allows them to sense his or her location and see through his or her eyes.**
- **Carrionites kill with words, a touch to the heart, or the use of dolls. The fumes from their witches' brew can control a man's actions, while his mind is oblivious.**
- **Until the Carrionites appeared on Earth in 1599, many races—even the Time Lords—thought they were a myth.**

The cauldron is used to communicate, to view the past, and to brew potions.

A broomstick aids a Carrionite in her flight, although she is able to fly without one.

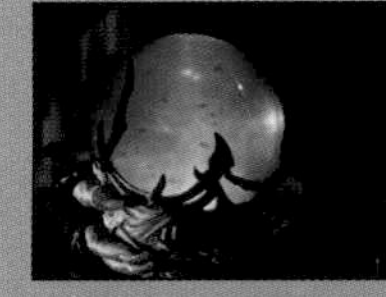

The Deep Darkness in which the rest of the Carrionites are trapped is shown as a crystal ball.

MOTHER DOOMFINGER

Able to materialize instantly by victim's side

Finger can kill with a touch to the heart

Billowing black robes resemble a crow in flight

DNA Replication Module

The Carrionites can replicate a person's DNA and control them simply by attaching a lock of hair to a doll. They use a doll to make Shakespeare add an extra paragraph to his new play, *Love's Labour's Won.*

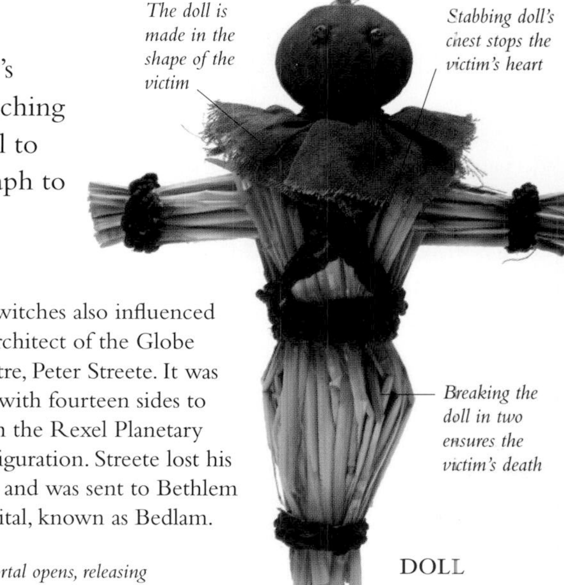

The doll is made in the shape of the victim

Stabbing doll's chest stops the victim's heart

Breaking the doll in two ensures the victim's death

DOLL

The witches also influenced the architect of the Globe Theatre, Peter Streete. It was built with fourteen sides to match the Rexel Planetary Configuration. Streete lost his mind and was sent to Bethlem Hospital, known as Bedlam.

Portal opens, releasing Carrionites into the Globe Theatre

The Hour of Woven Words

When the last lines of *Love's Labour's Won* are spoken, the Globe acts as an energy converter, opening a portal to the Deep Darkness and releasing the Carrionites from their prison. Only Shakespeare—with a little help from Martha—can find the words to close the portal and send the Carrionites back to their eternal prison.

Shakespeare Facts

- **William Shakespeare was born in Stratford-upon-Avon in 1564. He started out as an actor, but turned to writing toward the end of the 1580s. He died in 1616 and is now considered the greatest playwright ever.**
- **Shakespeare married Anne Hathaway and had two daughters, Susanna and Judith, and a son, Hamnet, who died aged 11 in August 1596.**
- **When Shakespeare closes the portal, all copies of *Love's Labour's Won* are lost with the Carrionites. The world is left to wonder what happened to Shakespeare's mysterious lost play.**

The Doctor has met Shakespeare before but the playwright does not recognize him because he has regenerated.

The Family of Blood

The TARDIS chooses to hide the Doctor in 1913 among the pupils of Farringham School. The boys are being prepared for war, but when the Family comes, they take up arms earlier than expected.

THE FAMILY OF BLOOD ARE HUNTERS with an acute sense of smell, but their life span is only three months. In their natural form they are merely balls of gas, but they are able to take the bodies of other intelligent beings and gain their strength and physical abilities. However, these feeble forms are soon expended, so they want the Doctor's body, which will give one of their number the many lives of a Time Lord.

SON OF MINE

MOTHER OF MINE

Gaseous form enters human through eyes

Pupil's body allows access to Farringham school

Family of Mine

The Family's bond is strong and the nameless aliens refer to themselves only in terms of kinship: Father of Mine, Mother of Mine, Son (or Brother) of Mine, Daughter (or Sister) of Mine. Son of Mine is the natural leader and favored child—he is the one for whom the Family seeks immortality.

Body Snatchers

When their hunt for the Doctor brings them to England each Family member takes on a human shape. The mind of each victim is entirely consumed—memory traces may survive, but not enough to enable the Family to pass as their assumed species without arousing suspicion.

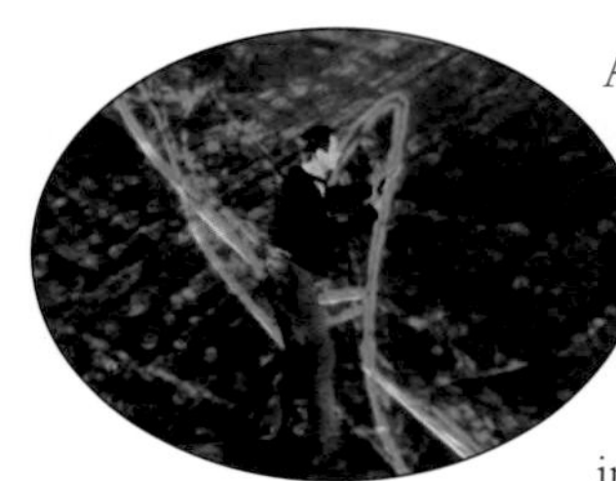

A Vortex Manipulator stolen from a Time Agent allows the Family to track the Doctor. Once on Earth, their spaceship is concealed by an invisibility shield.

Schoolboy Jeremy Baines is getting illicit beer from Blackdown Woods when he stumbles across the Family. Upon investigating, his body is taken over by Son of Mine.

Martha suspects something is wrong with maid Jenny when she agrees to share a teapot of gravy. Jenny was snatched by the Family's scarecrow soldiers and has been consumed by Mother of Mine.

The Family Facts

- **The Family's strong sense of smell is just as keen within their human bodies.**
- **Their sense of smell can be fooled by olfactory misdirection, or "ventriloquism of the nose," an elementary trick for the Doctor.**
- **Family members communicate with each other telepathically. In moments of extreme trauma, they feel each other's pain.**
- **The laser gun is the Family's weapon of choice. It shoots energy bolts that disintegrate its targets instantly.**

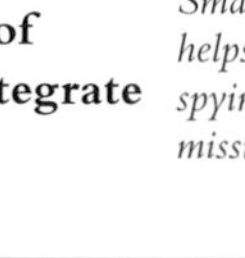

Small size helps in spying missions

The scarecrows, who were turned by the Family into moving soldiers, are sent to locate a body for Father of Mine. They find Farmer Clark in his field at Oakham Farm.

Little Lucy Cartwright is happily walking along with her balloon when the scarecrows take her. Her parents soon realize Daughter of Mine is not their child and so are swiftly killed.

DAUGHTER OF MINE

Childlike appearance disarms foes

Olfactory abilities are concentrated in human nose
FATHER OF MINE
Respectable appearance helps in human society
Quickly masters control of human body

Scarecrow Soldiers

Scarecrows are not uncommon in rural Herefordshire—but these ones scare more than just crows. Son of Mine creates this scarecrow army. He fashions rough humanoid shapes out of inanimate materials and gives them basic motor and sensory abilities using the process of molecular fringe animation.

"Eyes" allow limited vision
Clothes keep straw in humanoid shape
Straw filling provides bulk of scarecrow
Shoes provide firm base for straw-filled legs

Following the Family's orders, the scarecrow foot soldiers march inexorably toward the schoolboys' guns. Straw men feel no pain but they are unable to mend themselves if they lose their humanoid form.

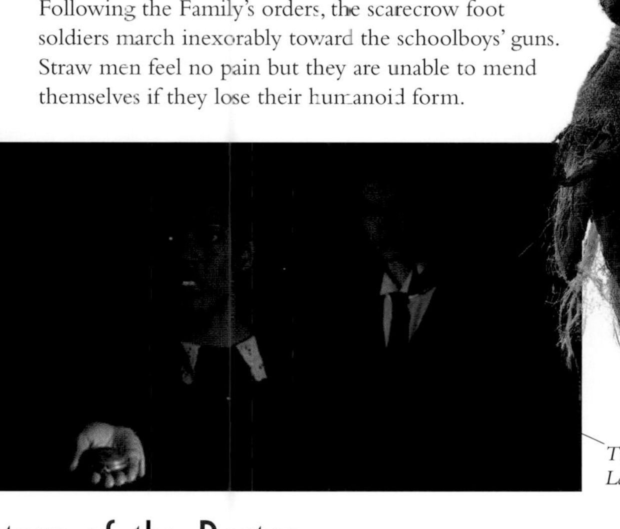
Tim Latimer

Return of the Doctor

The Doctor goes to great lengths to make himself human to hide from the Family, not just for his sake, but also to protect them from punishment at his hands. But in the end, Martha—helped by psychic schoolboy Tim Latimer—has to bring the Time Lord back before the Family destroys everything.

Eternal Life

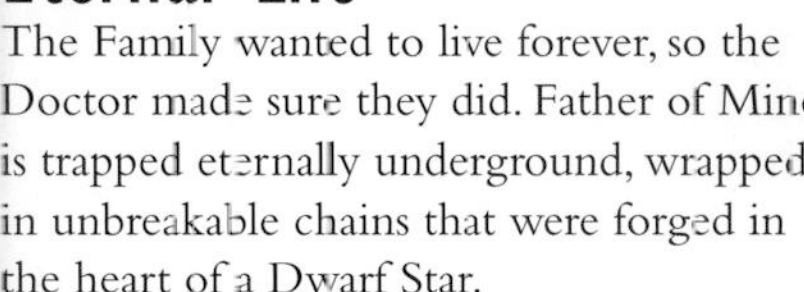

The Family wanted to live forever, so the Doctor made sure they did. Father of Mine is trapped eternally underground, wrapped in unbreakable chains that were forged in the heart of a Dwarf Star.

Inside every mirror, occasionally glimpsed but rarely fully seen, is Daughter of Mine. She can never leave her looking-glass prison, where the Doctor visits her once a year.

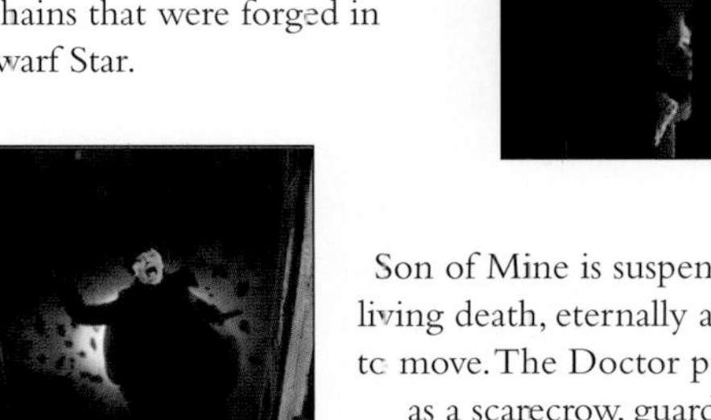

The Doctor tricks Mother of Mine into the event horizon of a collapsing galaxy. She is drawn irresistibly into an inescapable black hole, through which she will fall, screaming, for all eternity.

Son of Mine is suspended in time in a living death, eternally aware but unable to move. The Doctor puts him to work as a scarecrow, guarding the fields of England forever.

Weeping Angels

The moment a Weeping Angel is seen, it turns into harmless stone.

WEEPING ANGELS are almost as old as the universe itself. They feed off potential energy by sending people into the past. Confined to history, their victims live out their lives, but in the present they are dead and the Angels feast on the days they might have had. The deadly Angels are quantum locked—they only exist when no one can see them—and so they can never be killed.

Hands hide eyes, not tears

Angelic appearance disguises a killer

Sally Sparrow

When photographer Sally Sparrow breaks into the creepy old house Wester Drumlins to take some atmospheric pictures, she discovers the Weeping Angels. Many people have disappeared near Wester Drumlins, having fallen prey to the Angels. One of their victims is the Doctor, who is stranded in 1969 with Martha Jones.

Sally peels back the wallpaper to reveal a message from the Doctor—addressed to her! She's freaked out, but it takes more messages before she is ready to believe that someone is speaking to her from the past.

Kathy Nightingale

This is not the first time Sally has dragged her best friend, Kathy, into one of her schemes. Beneath her cheerful exterior, Kathy was actually lonely and longed for a new start. She gets her wish when she is zapped back to 1920, where she finds happiness with a new life in Hull and a husband named Ben.

The Grandson Paradox

Before Kathy died in 1987, she made her grandson Malcolm promise to deliver a letter to Sally at Wester Drumlins in 2007, explaining her disappearance. While he is doing so, the young Kathy is snatched out of time by the Angels—the event that will lead, ultimately, to Malcolm's birth.

Aged with time

KATHY'S LETTER

Weeping Angel Facts

- **Because they are quantum locked, no one knows what Weeping Angels look like in their natural, unfrozen state.**
- **The Angels are harmless while they are frozen in stone, but if their victim so much as blinks, they are set free to attack.**
- **The potential energy of the TARDIS could feed the Angels forever, but the power released would be enough to destroy the Sun.**
- **The Angels move incredibly fast—they can cross a room in the blink of an eye, and that's only about 250 milliseconds!**

The Angel's touch is deadly

The Angels are known as the Lonely Assassins—if an Angel ever looks at another of its kind, it will freeze, and if an Angel touches another, it will vanish into the past!

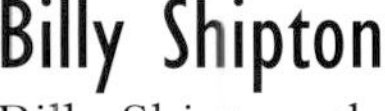

Billy Shipton

Billy Shipton, the policeman investigating the mysterious disappearances at Wester Drumlins, also falls prey to the Weeping Angels and finds himself in 1969, where the Doctor tracks him down. Billy then waits 38 years to deliver a message in person to Sally about the Doctor's plight.

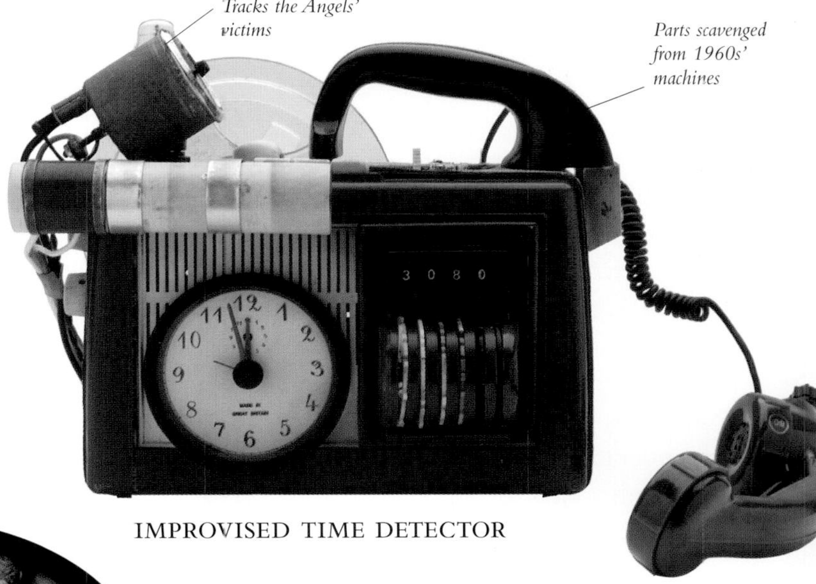

Tracks the Angels' victims

Parts scavenged from 1960s' machines

IMPROVISED TIME DETECTOR

Easter Eggs

In his new life in the past, Billy Shipton goes into DVD publishing and puts hidden tracks—Easter Eggs—on 17 DVDs. The recorded messages are for Sally and enable her to have a conversation with the Doctor across time.

The Doctor tricks the Angels. As the creatures surround the TARDIS, it dematerializes, leaving them staring at each other. Constantly observed, the Angels will remain stone forever.

With the help of Kathy's brother, Larry, Sally compiles a folder of information for the Doctor. This completes the link so that, in his future, he will be able to communicate with her from the past.

The Master

THE MASTER WAS one of the Doctor's oldest friends, but he became his most bitter enemy. They attended the Time Lord Academy together, but eventually both tired of Gallifreyan life and became exiles. The Master's evil schemes were frequently foiled by the Doctor, and he met his final end when he was sucked into the Eye of Harmony—or so the Doctor thought.

Has powers of hypnosis
Respectable appearance conceals a psychopath
Weapon of choice was the Tissue Compression Eliminator; now it's the Laser Screwdriver
The Master has inhabited at least 17 bodies

Hidden in Time and Space

The Master was resurrected by the Time Lords to fight in the Time War but, scared, he ran away, turning himself into a human and hiding at the end of the universe. He was found as a human child on the coast of the Silver Devastation and eventually reached the planet Malcassairo where, as Professor Yana, he tried to help the last humans find a way to Utopia.

Aged eight, Gallifreyan children must stare into the Untempered Schism, a gap in the fabric of reality. The sight made the Master go insane, filling his head forever with the pounding sound of drums.

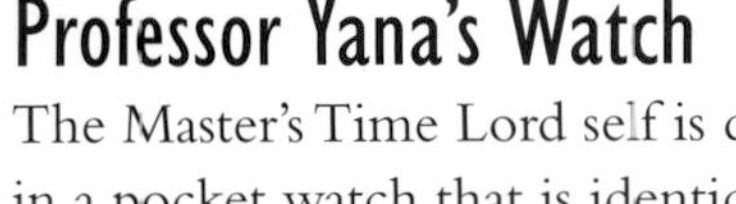

Professor Yana's Watch

The Master's Time Lord self is contained in a pocket watch that is identical to the one the Doctor used when he became human to escape the Family of Blood. Martha recognizes the watch and brings it to Yana's attention, overcoming the perception filter that had kept Yana from really noticing it.

On opening the pocket watch, the Time Lord's biology, personality, and memory return. One heart becomes two, the body temperature lowers, and the respiratory bypass system is restored.

You Are Not Alone

Professor Yana opens the pocket watch and becomes the Master again, revealing the meaning of the Face of Boe's message "You are not alone"; the Doctor is not the last of his kind. The restored Time Lord is shot by his erstwhile assistant, Chantho, but regenerates and escapes to Earth in the Doctor's TARDIS.

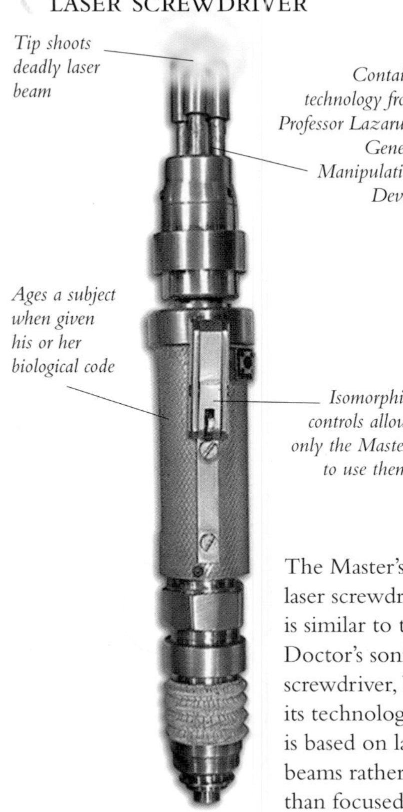
LASER SCREWDRIVER
Tip shoots deadly laser beam
Contains technology from Professor Lazarus's Genetic Manipulation Device
Ages a subject when given his or her biological code
Isomorphic controls allow only the Master to use them

The Master's laser screwdriver is similar to the Doctor's sonic screwdriver, but its technology is based on laser beams rather than focused sound waves.

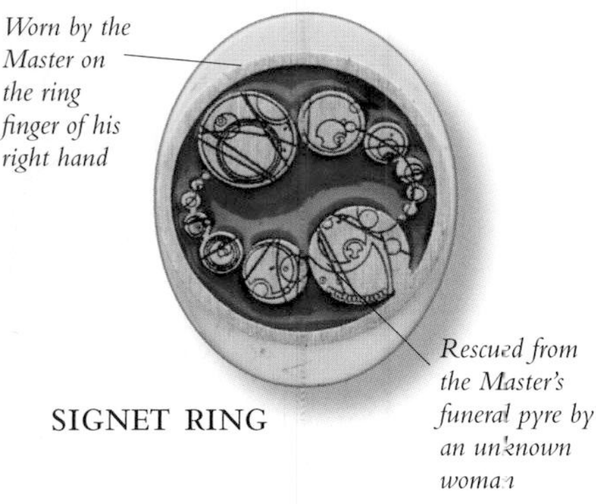
Worn by the Master on the ring finger of his right hand
Rescued from the Master's funeral pyre by an unknown woman
SIGNET RING

Elected to Power

After his release from the pocket watch, the Master arrives on present-day Earth, where he assumes the identity of "Harold Saxon." He convinces the world that he is a Cambridge University graduate and a novelist who became Minister of Defense and rose to prominence after shooting down the alien Racnoss. He is then is elected Prime Minister of Great Britain.

Prep-school-educated Lucy Saxon appears to be the Master's devoted wife and companion, but his cruel treatment slowly destroys her, and she is the one who finally shoots him dead.

The Archangel Network

Harold Saxon launches the Archangel Network. This worldwide cell-phone network, carried by fifteen satellites, transmits a rhythm that gives the Master hypnotic control over the entire population. But the system backfires on him when Martha uses it to feed power to the Doctor, who is imprisoned by the Master.

Each rocket contains a Black Hole Converter

The entire south coast of England is turned into a rocket shipyard. The rockets are built out of scrap metal by a slave labor force, in preparation for the day that the Master declares war on the universe.

The Master Facts

• The Master has used up his 13 regenerations, but has stolen several bodies to stay alive, including those of Consul Tremas of Traken and an ambulance driver named Bruce.

• In addition to "Professor Yana" and "Harold Saxon," the Master's aliases have included Reverend Magister (a country vicar), Professor Thascales (a time-meddling scientist), and Sir Gilles Estram (a thirteenth-century French knight).

• Yana—"You Are Not Alone"—is not the only clue left for the Doctor: "Magister" and "Thascales" both translate as "Master," and "Estram" is an anagram!

The Last of the Time Lords

When the Master is defeated, the Doctor will not let him be executed, but he knows that the Master cannot be allowed to go free. As the only other Time Lord in existence, the Master is his responsibility—the Doctor will keep him in the TARDIS and care for him. But Lucy shoots the Master and he refuses to regenerate, preferring death to eternal imprisonment with the Doctor. Despite the Doctor's pleading, the Master dies in his arms, leaving the grief-stricken Doctor as the last of the Time Lords once again.

The distraught Doctor takes the Master's body to a deserted beach and reverently places it on a funeral pyre.

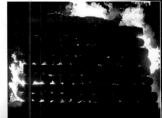

The Toclafane

When the human race is faced with the end of the universe in the year 100 trillion, it undergoes its final evolution. The cold, dark nothingness at the end of time drives people to regress into the Toclafane—primitive creatures wired into metallic shells. They are rescued by the Master, who transports them from the future to wreak disaster on present-day Earth.

Toclafane Facts

- The Master names the Toclafane after the fictional "Bogeyman" character from a Gallifreyan fairy tale.
- The Toclafane have regressed to primitive human emotions—they enjoy killing without discrimination because "it is fun."
- The childlike Toclafane exhibit the human characteristic of vanity and desire to be "pretty" in their metal shells.
- The Master hopes that it will break the Doctor's two hearts when he discovers that the grotesque Toclafane are the future of humanity.

Toclafane Sphere

The Master's Secret Weapon

The Master befriends the vulnerable and impressionable Toclafane. Loyal to him without question, they carry out his every destructive instruction. The Master uses them to conquer the Earth and enslave the human race—the first stage in his plan to found a Time Lord Empire across the entire universe.

Merciless killing machines, the Toclafane speed through the air after their victims. They have lasers for long-range attacks and blades for up-close slicing and dicing.

Blades cause extra damage when the sphere rotates

The Toclafane are able to kill their ancestors without wiping out their own existence thanks to the Paradox Machine, a device the Master created by reconfiguring the TARDIS. It forms a temporal paradox that allows the universe to continue despite the apparent contradiction.

Wired into each metallic sphere is a withered human head—the last remnant of the creature's human form

All six billion Toclafane share one collective memory. It holds all the thoughts and experiences of the last humans and is haunted by the never-ending darkness and the terrible cold that they faced at the end of time.

Origin on Malcassairo

In the year 100 trillion, when the universe was coming to an end, the last humans fled the planet of Malcassairo in the search for Utopia—a perfect place, believed to have been built by the Science Foundation as part of the Utopia Project to preserve humankind. But Utopia was just a myth and the travelers found nothing but oblivion. Despair led them to evolve into the Toclafane.

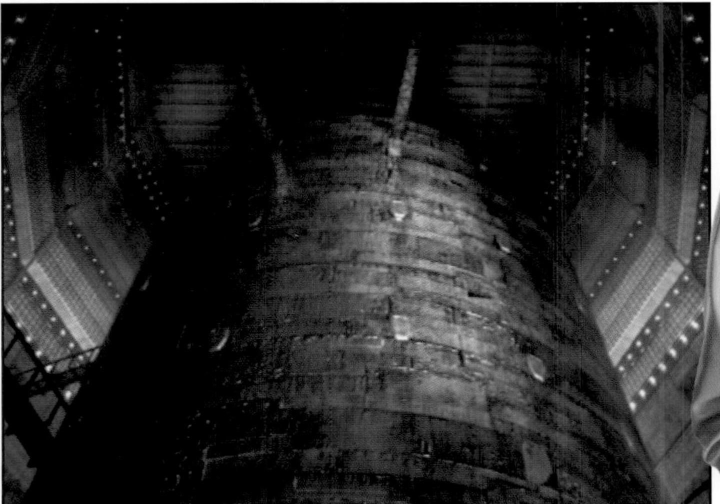

The space craft for the journey used an experimental engine, built using whatever was available at the silo, including gluten extract as a binding agent.

CHANTHO

Exoskeleton and mandibles evolved from insects

Highly formulaic speech pattern: every sentence begins in "chan" and ends in "tho"

Body survives by drinking its own internal milk

Chantho, the last of the insectoid Malmooth race, helped the humans to flee by working on the space shuttle as Professor Yana's devoted assistant.

Leaving Malcassairo meant escaping the Futurekind, a fierce humanoid race. Some feared that the Futurekind was what humankind would become if they stayed, but their actual destiny—the Toclafane—was no better.

World Domination

With the help of the Toclafane, the Master covers the Earth in work camps, churning out rockets for waging war. He is only defeated when the Paradox Machine is destroyed, reversing the invasion and returning the Toclafane to the future.

On the Master's orders, the Toclafane kill one-tenth of the Earth's population on first contact. Under his regime, they use terror to maintain order among the population.

The Heavenly Host

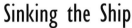

Razor-edged halo can be thrown as weapon

Wings unfurl to fly

Metal hand can deliver karate-style blows

Robot's default position is standing straight, with hands together and head bowed

LIFE RING

A GROUP OF TOURISTS from the Planet Sto in the Cassavalian Belt are on the luxury Max Capricorn Cruiseliner *Titanic*, en route to Earth to experience primitive cultures. On board they are served by golden robots known as the Heavenly Host, but the angelic-looking creatures are not what they seem.

Sinking the Ship

The *Titanic* is owned by Max Capricorn, who has a secret agenda to destroy the ship, kill the crew and passengers, and wipe out life on Earth. Capricorn has even bribed the dying Captain Hardaker to sabotage the ship to cause it to crash.

Magnetizing the hull draws meteoroids toward the ship that damage the Nuclear Storm Drive engines. As the *Titanic* plummets to Earth, the Nuclear Storm will explode on impact, destroying all human life.

Dying man has only six months to live

Newly graduated sailor on first trip

CAPTAIN HARDAKER

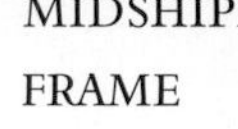

MIDSHIPMAN FRAME

Angels of Death

When a Host is asked to fix a passenger's necklace, it nearly breaks her neck! The Host follow orders from the highest authority and Capricorn has programmed them to kill everyone on board the *Titanic*.

Host Facts

- **Each Host has the strength of ten men.**
- **On board ship, the Heavenly Hosts' job is to provide tourist information and assistance.**
- **The Hosts' robotics can be temporarily deactivated by an electromagnetic pulse.**
- **The Doctor initiates Security Protocol One, which overrides any previous instruction and compels the Host to answer three questions.**

When the TARDIS crashes into the ship, the Doctor stows away on board. He realizes the ship is in danger, but the Host try to stop him from saving it.

The Doctor and the Waitress

Astrid Peth dreams of the stars—and the Doctor makes her dreams come true by taking her to experience the alien planet Earth. He recognizes a kindred spirit in the feisty young waitress and helps her see that nothing is impossible.

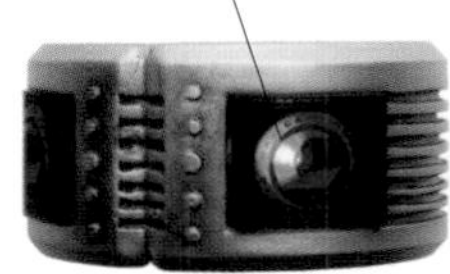

TELEPORT BRACELET

Head is only remaining organic part

Protective casing contains oxygen field

Mechanism produces steam

Titanic's engines can be remote-controlled

Life-support system constructed in secret on Sto

Vengeful Cyborg

Max Capricorn has vowed revenge on the Board that voted him out of his own company. He believes that he is the victim of anticyborg prejudice and hopes that using the *Titanic* to destroy Earth will ruin the company and land his former colleagues in jail for mass murder.

London is deserted—except for Wilfred Mott and the Royal Family. The Queen just escapes, as the Doctor pilots the *Titanic* safely over Buckingham Palace.

Max Capricorn Facts

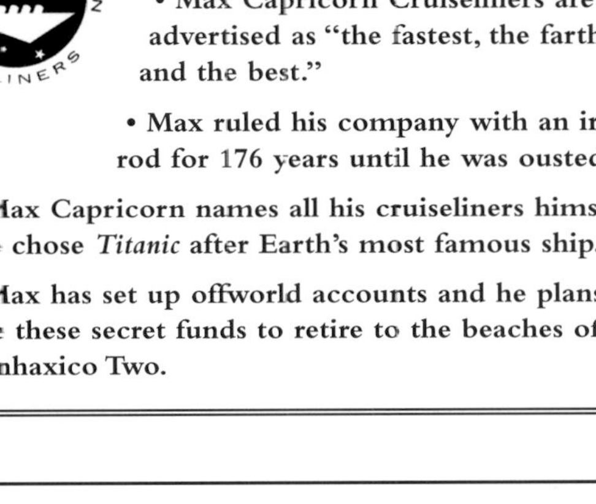

- **Max Capricorn Cruiseliners are advertised as "the fastest, the farthest, and the best."**
- **Max ruled his company with an iron rod for 176 years until he was ousted.**
- **Max Capricorn names all his cruiseliners himself. He chose *Titanic* after Earth's most famous ship.**
- **Max has set up offworld accounts and he plans to use these secret funds to retire to the beaches of Penhaxico Two.**

Astrid falls to her death while trying to save the Doctor. Her molecules are held in stasis and the Doctor sends them to the stars.

Adipose Industries

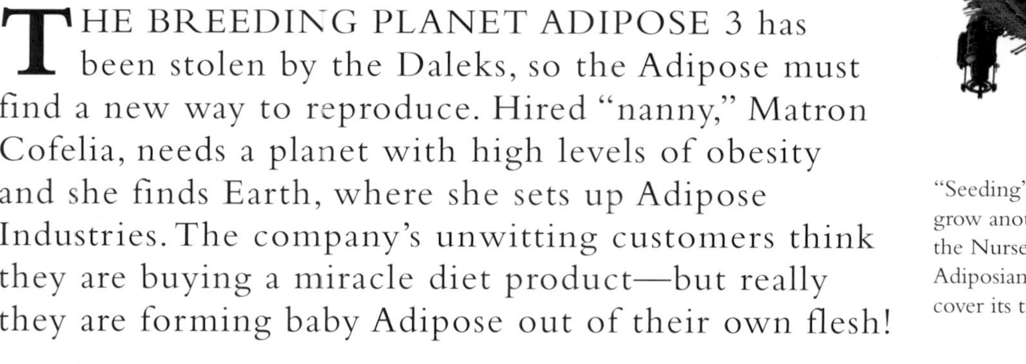

THE BREEDING PLANET ADIPOSE 3 has been stolen by the Daleks, so the Adipose must find a new way to reproduce. Hired "nanny," Matron Cofelia, needs a planet with high levels of obesity and she finds Earth, where she sets up Adipose Industries. The company's unwitting customers think they are buying a miracle diet product—but really they are forming baby Adipose out of their own flesh!

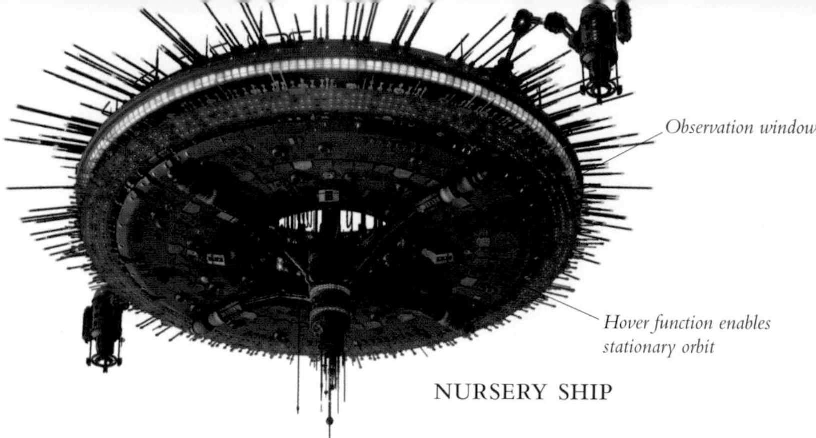

Observation windows

Hover function enables stationary orbit

NURSERY SHIP

"Seeding" a Level Five planet like Earth—using it to grow another species—is against galactic law. While the Nursery Ship collects the newborn Adipose, the Adiposian First Family murders Matron Cofelia to cover its tracks.

One million customers in the Greater London area sign up to the Adipose Industries special offer: £45 ($70) for a three weeks' supply of pills, plus a free gift of an 18-carat gold pendant.

The Adipose

The baby Adipose may appear friendly and sweet as they wave goodbye to Miss Foster, but some of them have already killed, albeit unwittingly. In a crisis, Adipose are programmed to consume their entire human host rather than just the fat.

Parthenogenesis changes people's fat into baby Adipose!

Adipose are created at 1:10 a.m. every morning

Miss Foster

Matron Cofelia of the Five-Straighten Classabindi Nursery Fleet adopts the alias Foster when she is employed by the Adiposian First Family to facilitate the birth of a new generation of Adipose. Her devotion to her charges is matched only by her callousness toward the humans she utilizes in her plans.

Has access to high-level technology

Will kill to achieve her goals

PENDANT

Pendant attracts fat, binds it together, and galvanizes it to form a body

Capsule bio-tunes itself to its owner so only affects that person

FAT-EATING PILL

Watch doubles as communicator between Miss Foster and her minions

WATCH

Miss Foster's pen has similar properties to the Doctor's sonic screwdriver

SONIC PEN

Adipose Facts

- **Each Adipose consists of exactly one kilogram (2.2 lb) of living fat.**
- **In a crisis, Adipose can form themselves from body parts other than fat, but converting bone, hair, and internal organs makes them sick.**
- **Newborn Adipose are small enough to fit through cat flaps.**

The Adipose Industries building is converted into a Levitation Post, ready to float ten thousand baby Adipose up to the Nursery Ship.

Vespiform

Although prized as a priceless gem, the Firestar is actually a Vespiform Telepathic Recorder. It is psychically connected to the Vespiform and holds his true identity.

THERE ARE MANY shape-changing insectivorous life-forms in the universe, but none is native to the galactic vector containing Earth. But in 1885, a member of one of these amorphous races—a Vespiform—arrives in India from its hive in the Silfrax galaxy, and takes on a human form to learn about the human race.

Susceptible to insecticides such as piperine, found in pepper

Vespiform is able to fly

Eight feet in length

Morphic residue is left behind when Vespiform transforms from human form

VESPIFORM

Eddison Hall and its estate are passed down the female line, along with the Eddison title.

An Insect Romance

A purple shooting star heralds the arrival of the Vespiform in Delhi. As "Christopher," he meets Lady Clemency Eddison. She conceives his child, but he is drowned when the Jumna River bursts its banks in the great monsoon, leaving Clemency heartbroken.

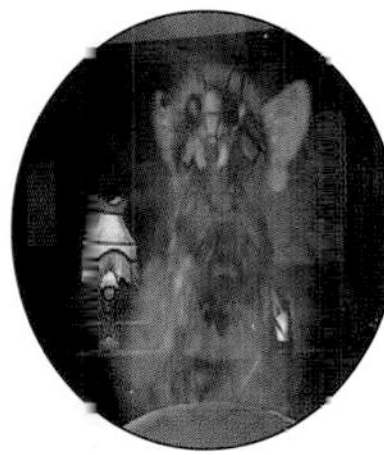

Anger breaks the genetic lock that prevented the half-human, half-Vespiform child from accessing his true identity.

Loss of sting renders wasp temporarily defenseless

Stinger can be regrown

STINGER

Full of deadly poison

REVEREND GOLIGHTLY

Spends 40 years unaware of his Vespiform heritage

Firestar was a gift from Christopher

LADY EDDISON

Reverend Golightly

In 1926, the Reverend discovers he is the half-Vespiform child given up for adoption when the Firestar beams his true identity into his mind. Like the insect he resembles, he attacks humans without compunction, but at the end, he lets Agatha Christie go.

The Doctor poses as Chief Inspector Smith of Scotland Yard to solve the mystery of the murdering insect. Justice of a sort is served when the Vespiform drowns in the lake.

Agatha Christie Facts

- **Agatha Christie was born in England on September 15, 1890, and became the "Queen of Crime," the world's best known mystery writer.**
- **By 1926, she had written only six books, but she went on to pen another sixty mystery novels as well as romances, plays, and over 150 short stories.**
- **Agatha Christie's most famous sleuths are the Belgian detective Hercule Poirot and the shrewd elderly spinster Miss Jane Marple from the village of St. Mary Mead.**
- **In 1926, Agatha disappeared for eleven days and never explained what happened. Doctors diagnosed amnesia, but some thought it was a publicity stunt or revenge on her cheating husband.**

Pyroviles

Fiery breath can incinerate humans

Cold water shatters hot stone

Internal magma holds body together

Stone carapace, the dorsal part of an exoskeleton

EARTH FEELS THE HEAT as the Pyroviles wake up! The fire-loving stone creatures shattered when their escape pod landed on Earth and they lay dormant for thousands of years under Mount Vesuvius, a volcano near the city of Pompeii, Italy. But in 62CE, an earthquake heralds their awakening. With much of their technology still intact, the Pyroviles plan to return to their planet, Pyrovillia. But it has been stolen by the Daleks so they must find a new home.

Reconstitution

With their bodies smashed into dust, the Pyroviles need a new form. They are inhaled as tiny particles by the citizens of Pompeii and then force themselves inside the brain, where they use latent psychic talent to bond with their host's body, gradually transforming it into stone.

The magma creatures travel from the heart of Vesuvius to Pompeii via the underground network of hot springs.

Burning Earth

Inside Vesuvius, the Pyroviles blaze with ideas. Their energy converter will harness the power of the lava in the volcano to create a fusion matrix and speed up the conversion of humans into Pyroviles. In their new empire, the Earth will burn and the oceans will boil.

Pyrovile dust is contained in the vapors from Vesuvius's hot springs, which are breathed in by the mystics of Pompeii to aid their visions.

Vesuvuis Facts

- **On August 23, 79CE, Mount Vesuvius erupted with the force of twenty-four nuclear bombs.**
- **The eruption lasted over twenty-four hours. Many were killed by hot gas and rocks.**
- **The Romans believed eruptions were caused by giants who had been buried under mountains by the gods.**
- **Like typical Romans, Caecilius the marble dealer and his family who meet the Doctor, regularly gave thanks to the household gods to avoid bad fortune.**

Pompeii was a popular vacation destination for Romans. It's unknown exactly how many of the town's 20,000 inhabitants died, but the scale of the disaster in 79CE was unprecedented.

Voice of the Pyrovile speaks through her

Entire body has become stone

Sibylline Facts

- **The name "Sibyl" was given to women who were thought to be possessed by the god Apollo.**
- **The Sibyl were believed to have the power of prophecy.**
- **Joining the Sibylline Sisterhood was a life-long commitment and was considered a prestigious and honorable occupation for Roman women.**
- **The Sibylline books were a collection of oracles that were consulted when Rome was in trouble.**

HIGH PRIESTESS

The High Priestess of the Sibylline shows her heart of stone when she tries to kill the Doctor. She is halfway between human and Pyrovile, but thinks that her painful transformation is a blessing from the gods.

The painted eyes are a symbol of the Sibylline.

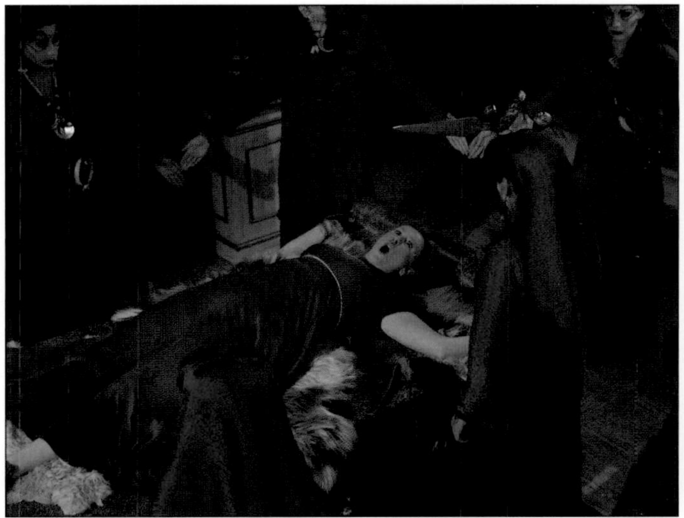

False Prophet

Thanks to her knowledge of history, Donna knows that Pompeii will be destroyed, but the Sibylline Sisterhood disagree. Scared and angry at this dissenting voice, the seers decree that she must pay for her words with death.

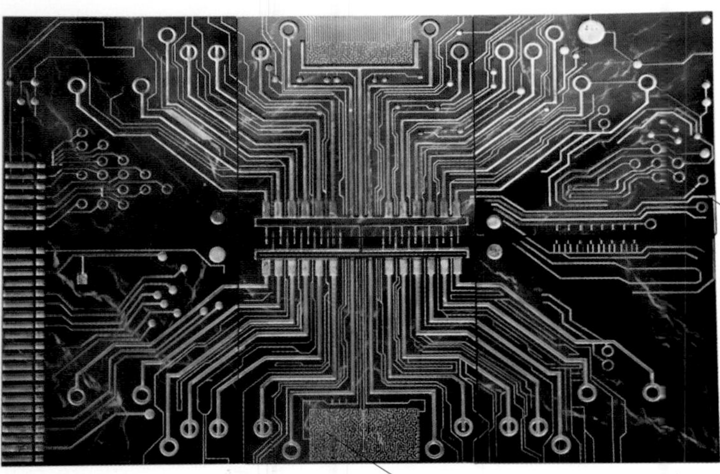

The six circuits are carved from marble

Design came to Lucius Dextrus in a dream—from the Pyroviles

ENERGY CONVERTER

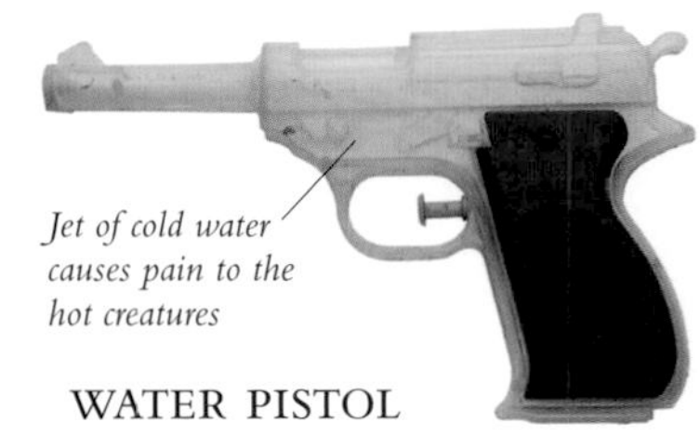

Jet of cold water causes pain to the hot creatures

WATER PISTOL

Pyrovillian Prophecy

Vesuvius's eruption is so powerful that it cracks open a rift in time. Ripples from the explosion radiate back to the start of the Pyrovillian timeline—the earthquake in 62CE. This disruption of time gives the Pyrovile-infected citizens like Lucius Petrus Dextrus the ability to see echoes of the future.

Pompeii's Chief Augur—a Roman priest and official

Concealed right arm has turned to stone

LUCIUS PETRUS DEXTRUS

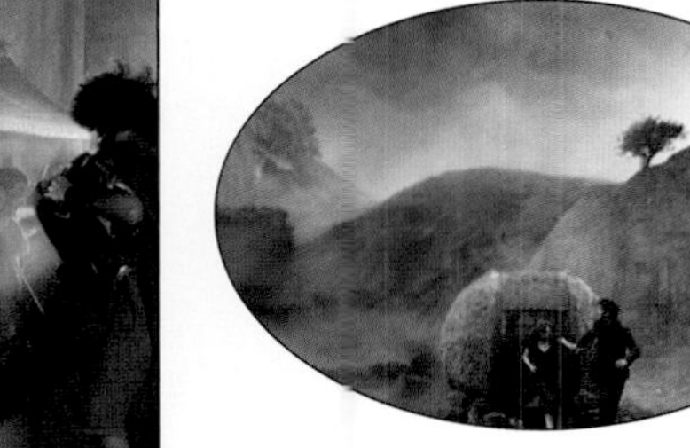

Not even the Pyroviles' escape pod would survive the eruption of Vesuvius. But since it is programmed to evade danger, it removes itself from the heart of the volcano and lands safely nearby with Donna and the Doctor.

The Doctor's Dilemma

Pompeii or the world? The Doctor has to choose. Vesuvius's lava will be used up in the Pyroviles' plan, but by stopping the aliens, the eruption goes ahead and the whole of Pompeii is destroyed.

Saving the Caecilius Family

History states that those who stayed in Pompeii died and the Doctor cannot change that. But history does not list every individual, so Donna encourages the Doctor to look beyond the letter of the law. He can save one family and he saves the Caeciliuses, which could have been what always happened.

Sontaran

SONTARANS CARE ABOUT NOTHING but war. They have been fighting their deadly enemy, the Rutans, for 50,000 years, and there is no end in sight. Their every action serves to further their cause, whether it is searching for a strategically advantageous position or increasing the number of Sontaran warriors to take part in the conflict. Combat is glorious for Sontarans and to die heroically in battle is their ultimate goal!

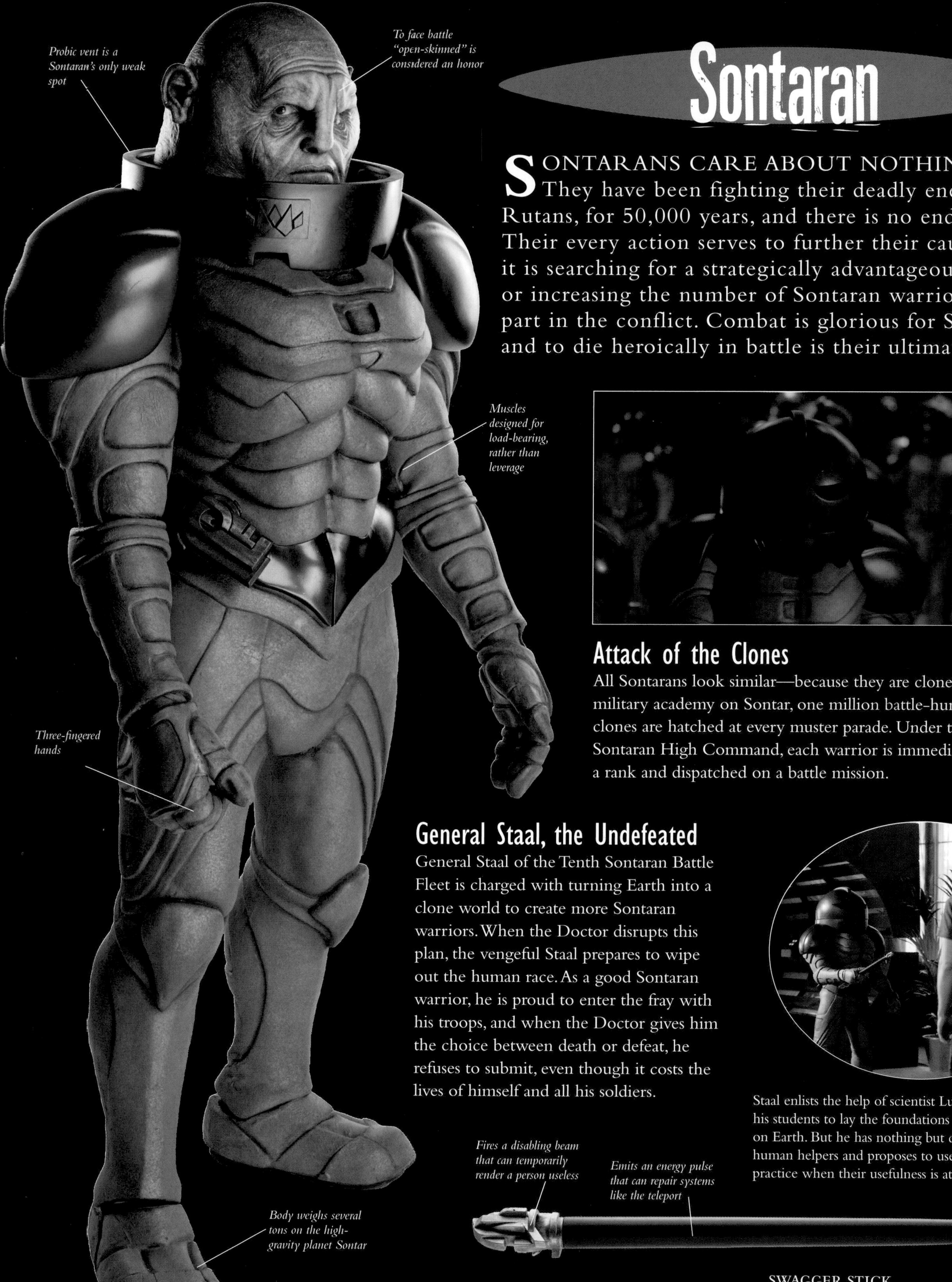

Attack of the Clones

All Sontarans look similar—because they are clones! At their military academy on Sontar, one million battle-hungry Sontaran clones are hatched at every muster parade. Under the charge of Sontaran High Command, each warrior is immediately given a rank and dispatched on a battle mission.

General Staal, the Undefeated

General Staal of the Tenth Sontaran Battle Fleet is charged with turning Earth into a clone world to create more Sontaran warriors. When the Doctor disrupts this plan, the vengeful Staal prepares to wipe out the human race. As a good Sontaran warrior, he is proud to enter the fray with his troops, and when the Doctor gives him the choice between death or defeat, he refuses to submit, even though it costs the lives of himself and all his soldiers.

Staal enlists the help of scientist Luke Rattigan and his students to lay the foundations of a clone world on Earth. But he has nothing but contempt for these human helpers and proposes to use them for target practice when their usefulness is at an end.

Fires a disabling beam that can temporarily render a person useless

Emits an energy pulse that can repair systems like the teleport

SWAGGER STICK

Sontaran Spacecraft

The Tenth Sontaran Battle Fleet consists of a Command Ship and a number of capsules that can be moved into position when Battle Status is enjoined. Sontaran ships are impervious to nuclear missiles.

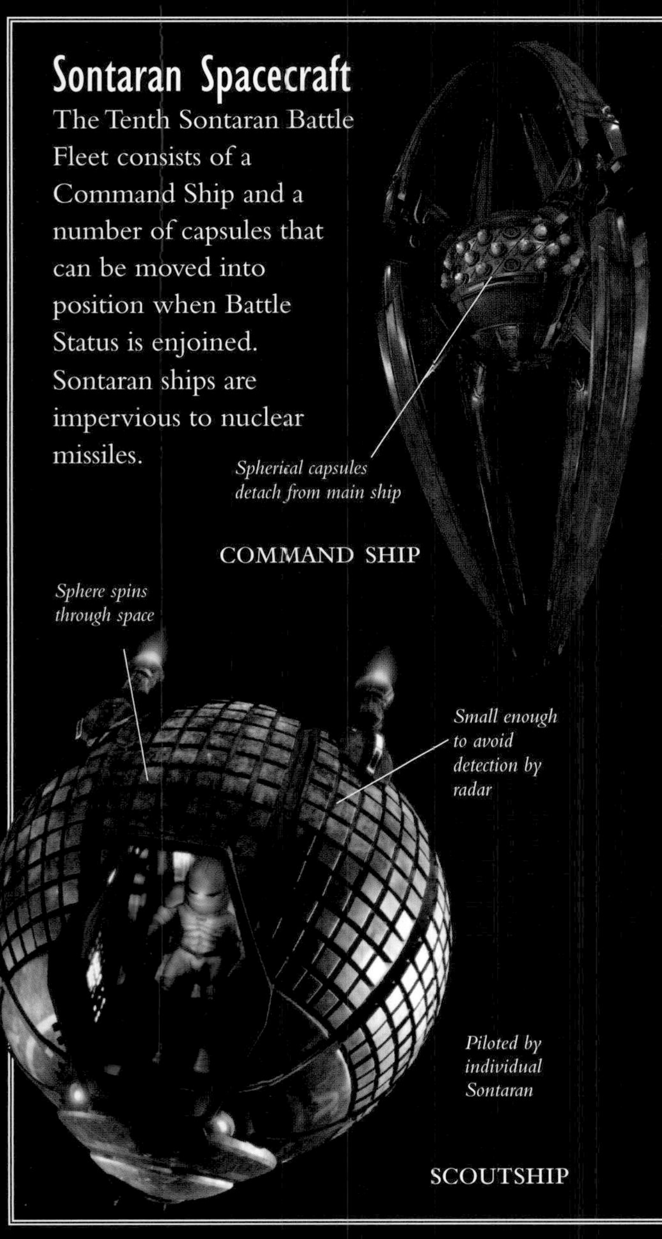

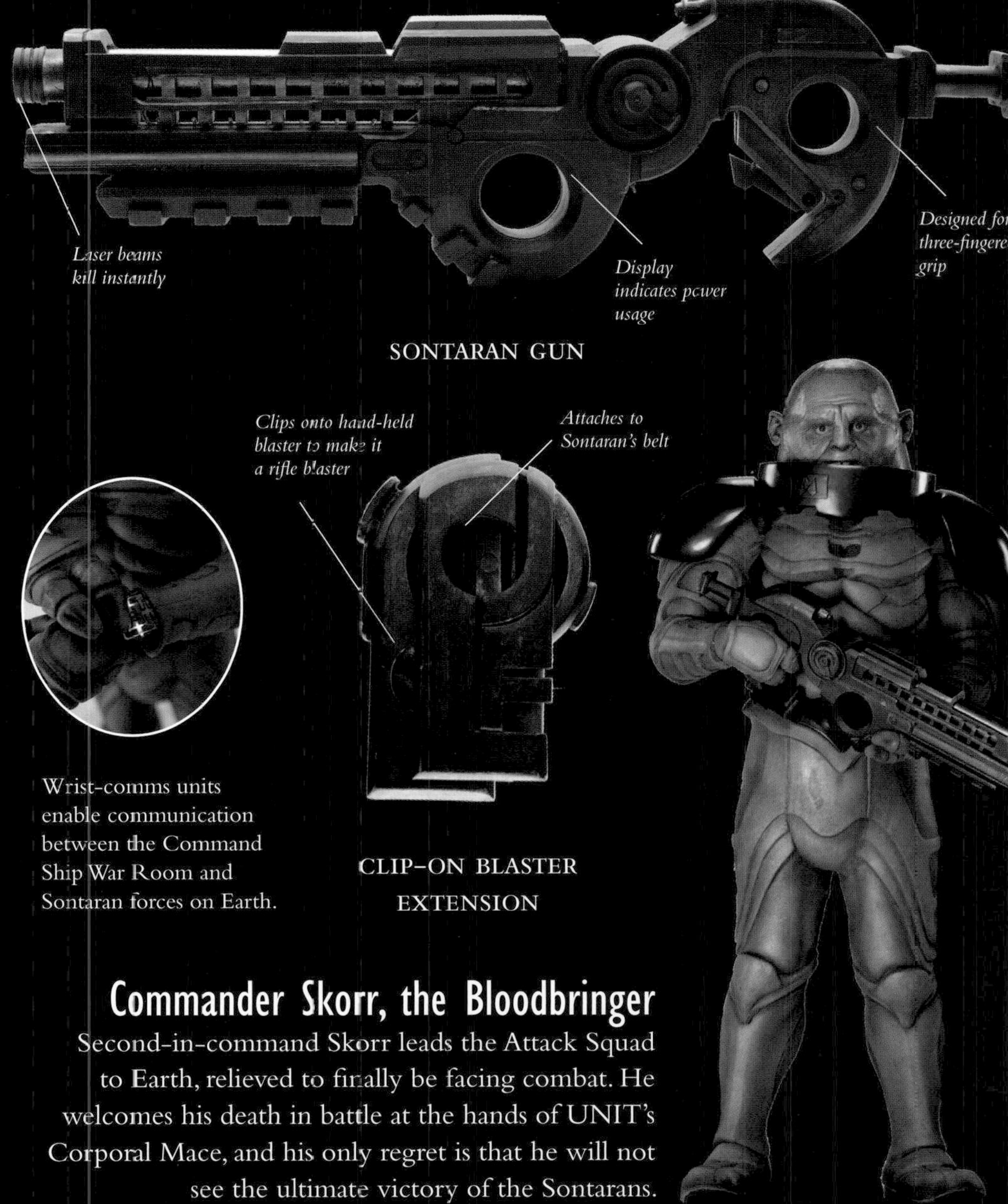

Wrist-comms units enable communication between the Command Ship War Room and Sontaran forces on Earth.

Commander Skorr, the Bloodbringer

Second-in-command Skorr leads the Attack Squad to Earth, relieved to finally be facing combat. He welcomes his death in battle at the hands of UNIT's Corporal Mace, and his only regret is that he will not see the ultimate victory of the Sontarans.

ATMOS

All ATMOS cars are equipped with this Sontaran-controlled satellite navigation system.

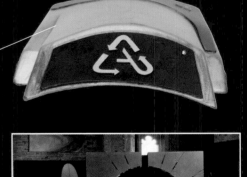

ATMOS Industries

The Atmospheric Omission System (ATMOS) is a driver's dream: in addition to being a satnav system, it reduces carbon emissions to zero using an ionizing nano-membrane carbon dioxide converter. But its true purpose is to release a killer gas that will change Earth's atmosphere into food for Sontaran clones.

Luke Rattigan

Teen genius Luke Rattigan is tired of being laughed at on Earth. So he is quick to create ATMOS for the Sontarans, mistakenly believing that his reward will be a planet populated solely by smart people.

The teleport between the Command Ship and Luke's Academy is the Sontarans' undoing—through it betrayed Luke is able to wreak revenge.

The Hath

By the 61st century, Earth's resources are dwindling but its population is increasing, so humankind must look for other planets to colonize. The fishlike Hath assist humans in their search and eventually the allies discover a suitable planet named Messaline. However, the death of the mission commander triggers a generations-long war between humans and the Hath.

Bony ridge protects the facial area

Nutrients need to be replenished frequently

Gills "breathe" liquid nutrients on land

Coveralls designed for manual work

Pockets now used to carry ammunition

Protective kneepads

Boots enable sure and silent movement

HATH GABLE

Messaline

The three moons of Messaline reveal a barren wilderness of bleak moors and treacherous bogs. The high levels of ozone and radiation make the planet's surface uninhabitable, so the visitors must build their colony underground.

Warrior Hath

The Hath are intelligent, emotional humanoid creatures and are capable of great loyalty to those who earn it. However, conflict breaks out easily between the Hath and other species due to their fearsome tempers, a trait that also makes them formidable opponents in battle.

The Hath and humans become bitter enemies in the search for "the Source," which they both believe to be the breath of their creator.

Hath Facts

- **Although Hath speech is difficult to decipher due to the bubbling of their nutrient flasks, humans and Hath are able to communicate.**
- **The Hath have a similar skeletal structure to humans, including ball-and-socket joints in their shoulders.**
- **Hath are experts in genetics and have a high level of technological knowledge.**
- **Natural pioneers, the Hath made their own way into space before teaming up with humans who could help further their quest by sharing technology and resources.**

The Hath have piscine genes in their ancestry, but technology allows them to live on land. Flasks of the nutrient liquid that they breathe operate similarly to an human's underwater oxygen tank.

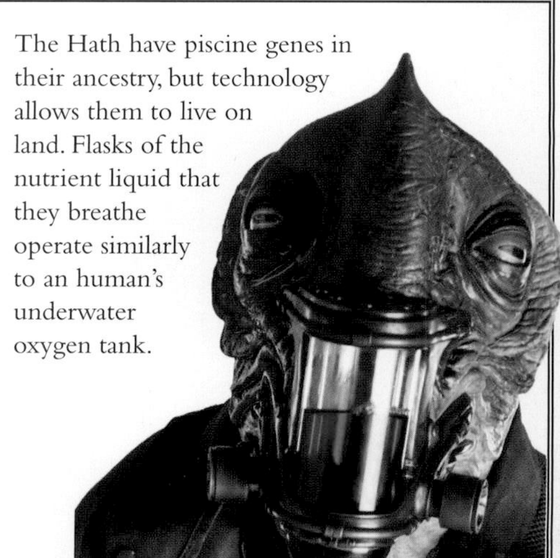

GENERAL COBB

General Cobb commands the human army

War

After the death of mission commander General Cobb, the humans and Hath quarrel over who should assume control of the operation and the colonists divide into rival factions. Progenation machines are reprogrammed to create soldiers, embedding military history and tactics in the generations that spring from them.

Colonists needed workers so the Hath created the progenation machine, which takes genetic material from the original pioneers and uses it to form fully grown beings of the same race.

Two hearts, like a Time Lord

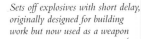

Sets off explosives with short delay, originally designed for building work but now used as a weapon

DETONATOR

The Doctor's Daughter

When the TARDIS lands on Messaline, a soldier forces the Doctor's hand into a progenation machine. A tissue sample is extrapolated and accelerated, and within minutes the Doctor becomes a father! The blonde teenager is genetically a Time Lord, but has been engineered to be a soldier.

Soldiers are not assigned names, so Donna calls the Doctor's daughter "Jenny" because she is a "genetic anomaly."

Ability to regenerate

Jenny

Despite their physiological likeness, the Doctor claims there is no real relationship between them. However, he grows to care for his "daughter" and Jenny learns compassion and wanderlust from her "father." When she is shot, her Time Lord DNA enables her to regenerate.

An expert in unarmed combat

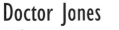

Doctor Jones

A doctor treats anyone, and when you are a space-traveler, that includes aliens. Martha resets Peck's dislocated shoulder and gains the trust of the injured Hath and his colleagues. In return, Peck insists on accompanying her across the perilous surface of Messaline, and ends up rescuing Martha from a deadly swamp.

Weapon of Hath design

Ammunition magazine

HATH PECK

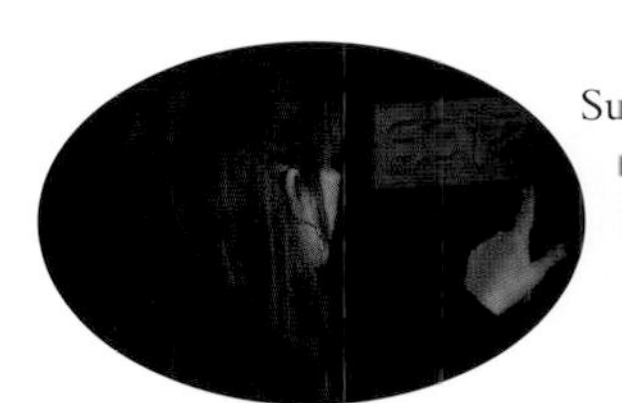

Super-temp Donna realizes the mystery numbers are the building completion dates. This means that, despite having been on Messaline for "generations," the colonists have actually only been there for seven days!

The Source

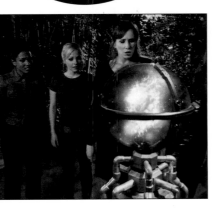

Tales of the Source have been passed down through generations of colonists. It turns out to be a terraforming machine—a device to make bare planets habitable. The gases it releases into the atmosphere accelerate evolution on Messaline, rejuvenating the ecosystem and creating abundant plant life.

The Library

Silence in the Library

When the human-hunting Vashta Nerada hatch in the Library, it seals itself, leaving a single message: "the lights are going out." The Library's creator, Felman Lux, cannot decode the seals and enter, but he exhorts his descendants to keep trying and to safeguard CAL.

BY THE 51ST CENTURY, there are many ways to experience narratives—holovids, direct-to-brain downloads, fiction mist—but people still love books! The Felman Lux Corporation creates a book repository so vast that it is an entire planet and needs no name other than "the Library." Whole forests are pulped to create new editions of a billion books, and each one is backed up onto the biggest hard drive ever created—an immensely powerful computer called "CAL"—that forms the core of the planet.

CHARLOTTE ABIGAIL LUX

Book-loving Charlotte Abigail Lux is terminally ill, but her father, Felman Lux, won't let her die. Instead, her mind becomes the main command node of the Library, which Lux builds for her eternal entertainment.

The computer is known by Charlotte's initials, "CAL"

SECURITY CAMERA

Charlotte watches the Library through living cameras

"4,022 Saved"

One hundred years before the Doctor arrives, the Vashta Nerada enter their deadly hatching cycle. There are 4,022 humans in the Library at the time, and nowhere safe for them to be teleported to, so CAL saves them all to her hard drive.

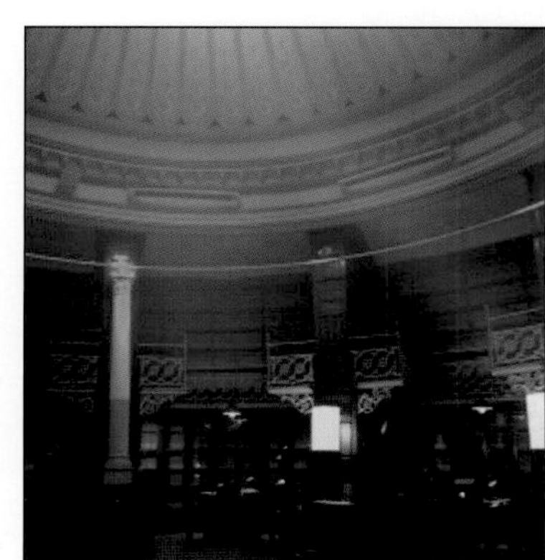

The kindly Doctor Moon looks after CAL in her dreams—just as the satellite above the library, a doctor moon, maintains the planet's computer core and checks for viruses.

Vashta Nerada Facts

- **Their name means "the shadows that melt the flesh" because they strip their victims to the bone in seconds. They are also known as "piranhas of the air."**
- **The Vashta Nerada are found on a billion worlds, including Earth, where they live mainly on roadkill.**
- **The creatures hunt by latching on to a living food source and keeping it fresh until they devour it.**
- **They normally live in the darkness, but can also be seen as the dust in sunbeams.**

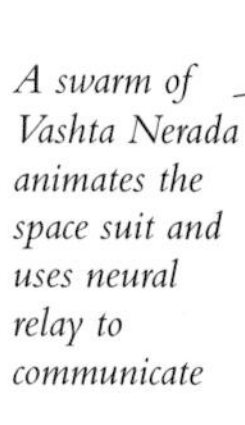

A swarm of Vashta Nerada animates the space suit and uses neural relay to communicate

More than a trillion Vashta Nerada live inside the Library. They hatched out of the newly printed books, which had been made from trees containing their microspores.

The man-eating swarms resemble an extra shadow

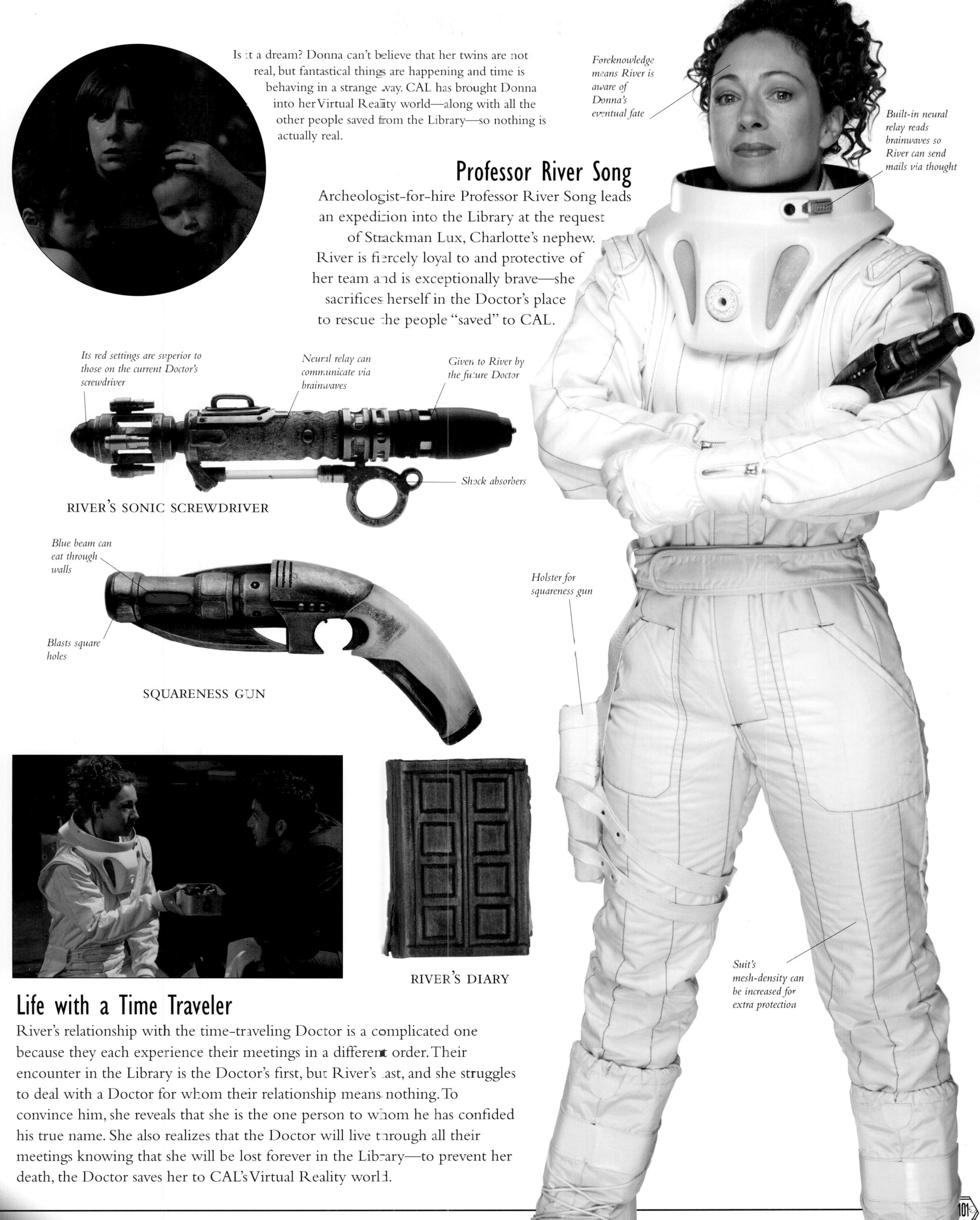

Is it a dream? Donna can't believe that her twins are not real, but fantastical things are happening and time is behaving in a strange way. CAL has brought Donna into her Virtual Reality world—along with all the other people saved from the Library—so nothing is actually real.

Professor River Song

Archeologist-for-hire Professor River Song leads an expedition into the Library at the request of Strackman Lux, Charlotte's nephew. River is fiercely loyal to and protective of her team and is exceptionally brave—she sacrifices herself in the Doctor's place to rescue the people "saved" to CAL.

RIVER'S SONIC SCREWDRIVER

SQUARENESS GUN

RIVER'S DIARY

Life with a Time Traveler

River's relationship with the time-traveling Doctor is a complicated one because they each experience their meetings in a different order. Their encounter in the Library is the Doctor's first, but River's last, and she struggles to deal with a Doctor for whom their relationship means nothing. To convince him, she reveals that she is the one person to whom he has confided his true name. She also realizes that the Doctor will live through all their meetings knowing that she will be lost forever in the Library—to prevent her death, the Doctor saves her to CAL's Virtual Reality world.

Dalek Sec

AS LEADER OF THE CULT OF SKARO, Dalek Sec is tasked by the Dalek Emperor with finding new ways for Daleks to breed and prosper. Following a failed plan to grow Dalek embryos, ambitious Sec comes up with a radical idea: purity has led to near extinction for the Daleks, so he decides their biological destiny lies with humans, in what he calls the Final Experiment.

In 1930 New York City is in the grip of the Great Depression with mass unemployment and thousands destitute. The Doctor and Martha show up here, soon after the Daleks arrive by emergency temporal shift.

Pig Slaves

An intelligence scan determines the fate of the humans captured by the Daleks. While those of superior intelligence are kept for the Final Experiment, the less bright prisoners are transformed into primitive pig slaves and used to abduct more people. The instability of the genetic graft means no pig-man survives more than a few weeks.

Energy Converter

Dalek Sec's plan to forge a new Dalek-human race requires a powerful energy source. A huge solar flare is due to pass by Earth, and will provide the necessary Gamma radiation. The Daleks must attract the flare and conduct its energy, so they engineer and build the tallest point in New York City—the Empire State Building.

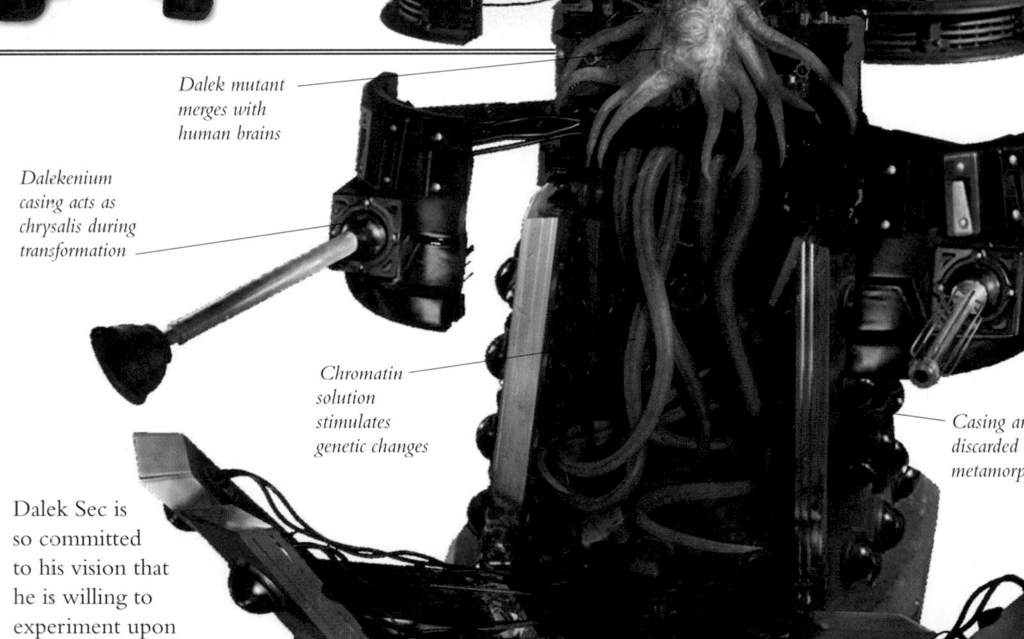

Dalek Sec is so committed to his vision that he is willing to experiment upon himself and becomes the first ever Dalek-human hybrid.

Becoming Human

The other three members of the Cult of Skaro, Daleks Thay, Jast, and Caan, believe that Daleks should remain pure, but Sec disagrees. He is convinced that the genetic merger will herald the beginning of a new era of Dalek rule, but the merger brings surprising results.

Human brain creates emotions

Tentacles from Dalek mutant

Exposed flesh makes hybrid vulnerable

Hybrid gains dexterity

Mr. Diagoras's suit is a remnant of a former identity

First-ever walking Dalek!

DALEK SEC

Dalek-Human Hybrid

Ambition, hatred, aggression, and a genius for war—that is what Dalek Sec thinks being human is all about. When he combines with the ruthless and ambitious Mr. Diagoras, he believes he is getting more of the same. But Sec discovers something unexpected—positive emotions. He decides that Daleks must go back not only to the flesh, but also to the heart.

Dalekanium is attached to mast

Empire State Building Facts

- **The Empire State Building, in New York City, was opened to the public in 1931.**
- **The cost of the Art Deco-style building was $24,718,000. It was expected to cost twice as much, but expenses fell due to the Depression.**
- **Construction took one year and 45 days, and finished ahead of schedule!**
- **The building has 102 floors and the top of the lightning rod is 1,421 feet (443.20 meters) above ground.**
- **It was the tallest building in the world for 40 years, until the World Trade Center was built.**

Death in Hooverville

Soloman, the leader of Hooverville, cares for the outcasts in New York's shanty town, but when he tries to extend the hand of friendship to the Daleks, he is exterminated. But his courage inspires something unique, when observer Dalek Sec feels compassion.

The purpose of Daleks is to be supreme! Sec's fellow Daleks disagree that their race should renounce their purpose by embracing emotions and becoming more human. They declare their one-time leader to be an enemy of the Daleks and he is exterminated while compassionately trying to save the Doctor's life.

Dalek Humans

Human DNA is spliced with Dalek Sec's genetic code, creating a new race. But some Time Lord gets in the mix, and so the human Daleks begin to question orders. This leads to their extermination, but not before they kill Dalek Thay and Dalek Jast.

Dalek Caan

With the Daleks Sec, Thay, and Jast all dead, Dalek Caan is the only surviving member of the Cult of Skaro—the last Dalek in the universe. Caan rejects the Doctor's offer of help and operates his emergency temporal shift and vanishes.

Davros

DAVROS IS RESPONSIBLE FOR THE DALEKS. The scientist foresaw a day when the chemical warfare that raged on his home planet would cause his people, the Kaleds, to mutate. Obsessed with the survival of his race, he experimented with their mutations and invented an armored machine to carry them. Ambitious Davros went further, making chromosomal changes to the Dalek embryos to remove their consciences and emotions. But his plan backfired when his creations declared him unnecessary to their plans and attempted to kill him.

Davros and the Doctor

The Doctor has a grudging respect for a number of his adversaries, but Davros is not one of them. The Time Lord has come to regard him as one of the most dangerous, and certainly the most insane, of his many enemies. The Doctor is appalled, but sadly unsurprised, to discover that Davros's reaction to the horror and devastation of the Time War is a desire to destroy all living things.

Davros taunts the Doctor, claiming that he is responsible for innocent deaths, despite his abhorrence of violence. Davros asserts that the Doctor takes ordinary people and turns them into weapons to die in his name.

Like many children with their parents, the Daleks' relationship with Davros is a combination of reverence and contempt: they look to him to solve their problems, but still believe that they are better off without him.

Davros Facts

- **Calling himself "the Great Healer," Davros once ran a funeral parlor, where he raised money to build a Dalek army by selling cryogenically frozen bodies as human food.**
- **Davros's home planet, Skaro, was destroyed during the Time War.**
- **Davros offers to reward loyalty in human followers by giving them immortality—by turning them into Daleks.**
- **The Doctor once asked Davros if he would wipe out all life if he had the opportunity—an idea Davros found fascinating and that came back to haunt the Doctor.**

Single lens replaces sightless eyes

Microphone and amplifier enable speech

Voice becomes more Dalek-like when angry

Heart and lung machine keeps Davros alive

Mechanical hand shoots energy bolts

Wheelchair generates its own power

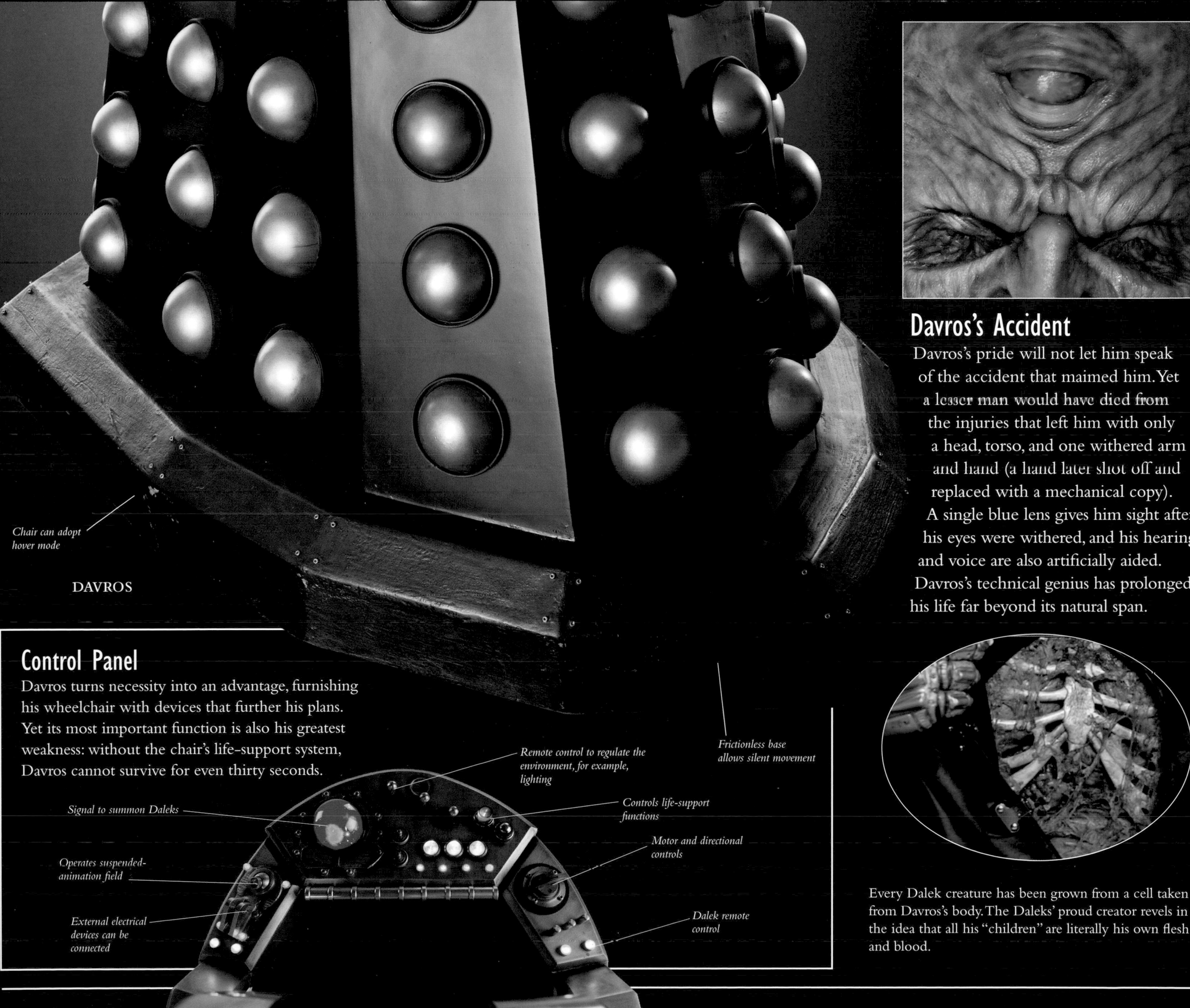

DAVROS

Control Panel

Davros turns necessity into an advantage, furnishing his wheelchair with devices that further his plans. Yet its most important function is also his greatest weakness: without the chair's life-support system, Davros cannot survive for even thirty seconds.

Davros's Accident

Davros's pride will not let him speak of the accident that maimed him. Yet a lesser man would have died from the injuries that left him with only a head, torso, and one withered arm and hand (a hand later shot off and replaced with a mechanical copy). A single blue lens gives him sight after his eyes were withered, and his hearing and voice are also artificially aided. Davros's technical genius has prolonged his life far beyond its natural span.

Every Dalek creature has been grown from a cell taken from Davros's body. The Daleks' proud creator revels in the idea that all his "children" are literally his own flesh and blood.

Davros's Empire

MEGALOMANIAC DAVROS has only one ambition—to see a universe ruled by Daleks. His warped mind believes that cooperation between species is impossible and ultimately only one race can survive and he is determined it will be the Daleks. His plans are based on the Daleks exterminating their way to victory, annihilating every other being in the universe. This apocalyptic shortcut will make Davros Emperor of an empty infinity.

The Reality Bomb

In order to build his empire and destroy all life-forms other than the Daleks, Davros creates the Reality Bomb. This fearsome technology cancels out the electrical fields that hold together atoms, thereby obliterating the fabric of reality itself. Davros brings the Doctor to his Command Ship, the Dalek Crucible, for a ring-side seat at what he believes will be his ultimate victory.

Lights flash in time with speech

The Supreme Dalek was charged with activating the Reality Bomb

Unique red coloring indicates supremacy

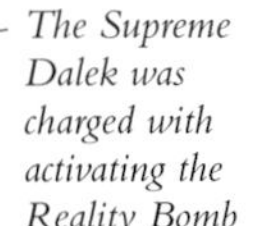

The Supreme Dalek

Although Daleks were engineered to have no emotions, the Supreme Dalek is guilty of pride when he believes that the Daleks have finally triumphed over the Doctor. His strength and determination sees him retain control as other Daleks falter, but he meets his end at Captain Jack's Defabricator Gun.

Dalek Caan

The only surviving member of the Cult of Skaro, Dalek Caan went insane when he jumped into the Time War to save Davros. The mind-altering experience brought him the gift of prophecy.

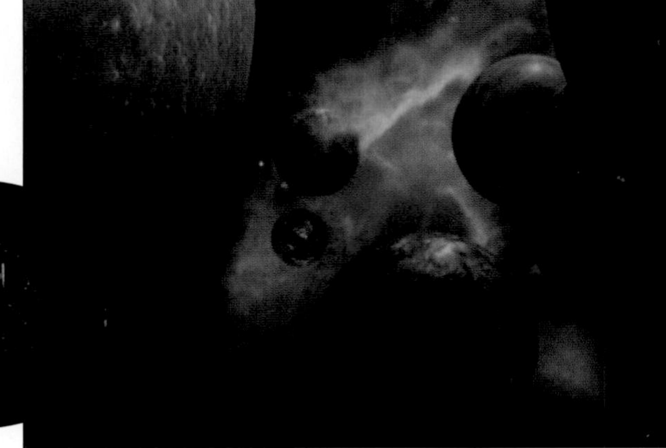

The Dalek Command Ship, the Crucible, has a core of deadly Z-neutrino energy

The Medusa Cascade

Twenty-seven celestial bodies, including Earth, Adipose 3, Pyrovillia, Callufrax Minor, Jahoo, Shallacatop, Woman Wept, Clom, and the Lost Moon of Poosh, vanish from their normal orbits and appear together in the Medusa Cascade. This is not chance, but careful design by crazed Davros. In their new formation, with the Dalek Crucible at their center, they create a transmitter designed to focus the wavelength of the Reality Bomb.

Masters of Earth

Once again, Daleks terrorize the citizens of Earth. This time, however, they are setting their sights higher than the destruction of the human race and Earth is supposed to play its role as part of the machinery of the Reality Bomb.

The Subwave Network

The Subwave Network is a piece of undetectable sentient software used to seek out and communicate with anyone who can help to contact the Doctor. With its power sufficiently boosted by the computer Mr. Smith, it is able to transmit to the Doctor, even though he is separated in time.

Ex-Prime Minister Harriet Jones feels responsible for Earth's citizens, and sacrifices her life to help contact the Doctor.

The Secret Army

The Subwave Network enables the Doctor to communicate with Captain Jack Harkness, Sarah Jane Smith, and Martha Jones—previous companions of the Doctor, collectively called "the Children of Time" by Davros. The Doctor is horrified when Davros claims he turns his friends into weapons to fight his battles for him.

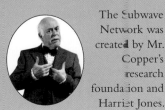

The Subwave Network was created by Mr. Copper's research foundation and Harriet Jones.

The Shadow Proclamation

Nearly all species recognize the authority of the Shadow Proclamation, an imposing galactic regulatory body and police force that both sets and enforces laws. Its directives proscribe alien interference with planets and their populations, and govern the rules of parlay between species.

Headquarters of the Shadow Proclamation

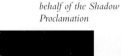

- **Protocol allow representatives to seize transportation and technology if required.**
- **The Shadow Proclamation has its own religious creed that includes a sole god.**

The Judoon are hired by the Shadow Proclamation as enforcers and bodyguards. The muscle-bound creatures are perfect for situations that require a show of force.

Distinctive albino appearance

Architect speaks on behalf of the Shadow Proclamation

ARCHITECT

The End of the Daleks

The Doctor abhors genocide, but his half-human, half-Time Lord incarnation has no qualms about destroying the whole Dalek race. He blasts the Dalekenium power feeds, annihilating the Daleks and their ship, and bringing an end to Davros and his designs on the universe.

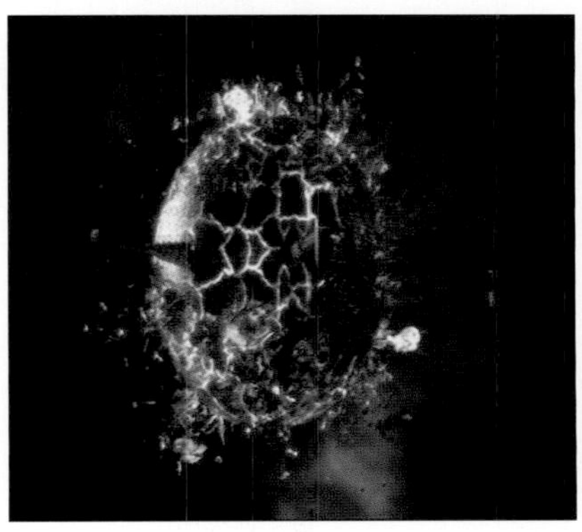

Creation of the CyberKing

WHEN THE CYBERMEN were sucked into the Void during the Battle of Canary Wharf, the Doctor thought he had seen the end of them. But a few survived and broke back into the world, using a time-traveling Dimension Vault stolen from the Daleks. They arrived in London, England in December 1851 and set about their business of abduction, murder, and creating the CyberKing—a giant battleship to lead their invasion of Earth and the conversion of the human population into Cybermen.

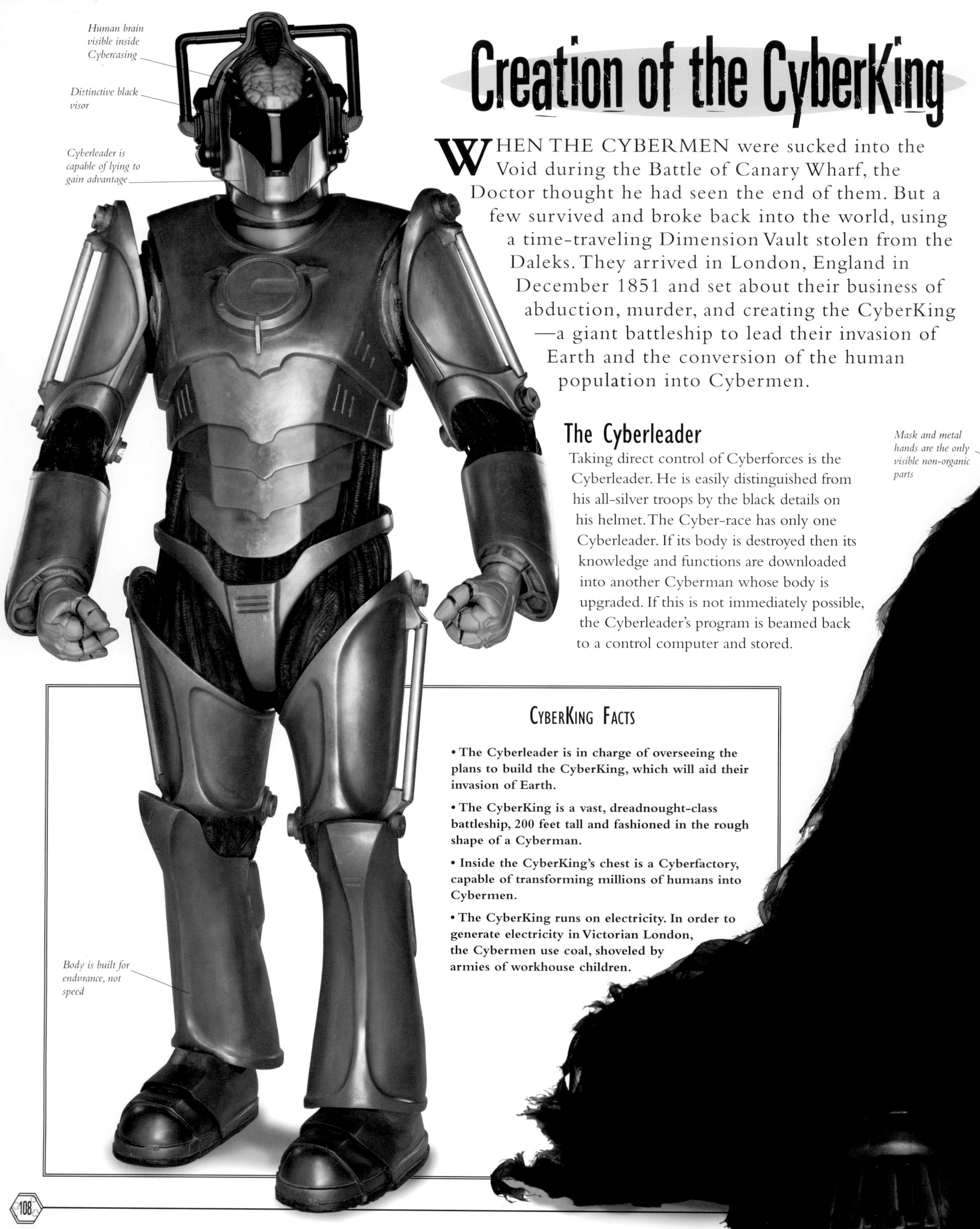

Human brain visible inside Cybercasing

Distinctive black visor

Cyberleader is capable of lying to gain advantage

Body is built for endurance, not speed

Mask and metal hands are the only visible non-organic parts

The Cyberleader

Taking direct control of Cyberforces is the Cyberleader. He is easily distinguished from his all-silver troops by the black details on his helmet. The Cyber-race has only one Cyberleader. If its body is destroyed then its knowledge and functions are downloaded into another Cyberman whose body is upgraded. If this is not immediately possible, the Cyberleader's program is beamed back to a control computer and stored.

CyberKing Facts

- **The Cyberleader is in charge of overseeing the plans to build the CyberKing, which will aid their invasion of Earth.**
- **The CyberKing is a vast, dreadnought-class battleship, 200 feet tall and fashioned in the rough shape of a Cyberman.**
- **Inside the CyberKing's chest is a Cyberfactory, capable of transforming millions of humans into Cybermen.**
- **The CyberKing runs on electricity. In order to generate electricity in Victorian London, the Cybermen use coal, shoveled by armies of workhouse children.**

Miss Hartigan

Mercy Hartigan, Matron of the St. Joseph's workhouse, deeply resents the men who oppress womankind. She accepts the Cybermen's offer of liberation, not realising they plan to liberate her from her feelings by incorporating her into the CyberKing. But strong-minded Mercy is a match for the metal monsters. Her Cybermind retains emotions and bends the Cybermen to her will, combining their logic and strength with her fury and passion.

The Other Doctor

After Jackson Lake's wife is killed by the Cybermen, he wants to forget. He finds an infostamp—a steel object for storing compressed data—but it backfires and streams facts about the Doctor into his head, causing him to believe that he is the Time Lord. But Lake's courage and ingenuity are genuine and gain him a companion—brave and resourceful servant Rosita throws in her lot with him when he saves her life.

Not only does Jackson Lake believe he is the Doctor, he also calls his screwdriver a sonic screwdriver and builds a TARDIS – a hot air balloon he names a "Tethered Aerial Release Developed In Style."

JACKSON LAKE

ROSITA

Cybershades

The Cybermen's latest innovation, the Cybershade, is created by placing the brain of a primitive creature, such as a cat or dog, inside a cybernetic form instead of the usual human. These Shades have less intelligence than their Cybermasters, but possess the speed and agility that Cybermen lack. They are able to outrun humans and scale vertical surfaces. Shades act like hounds to the Cybermen's huntsmen, tracking and rounding up prey.

The conversion of animals into Cybershades requires less power than producing full Cybermen. They act as the Cybermen's eyes and ears in London, providing visual and audio data, while allowing the remaining Cybermen to concentrate their resources on preparing the CyberKing factory and battleship.

CYBERSHADE

Index

LONDON, NEW YORK, MUNICH,
MELBOURNE, and DELHI

PROJECT EDITOR Elizabeth Dowsett
MANAGING EDITOR Catherine Saunders
PUBLISHING MANAGER Simon Beecroft
CATEGORY PUBLISHER Alex Allan
SENIOR DESIGNER Guy Harvey
DESIGN MANAGER Rob Perry
PRODUCTION EDITOR Siu Chan
PRODUCTION Amy Bennett

First published in the United States in 2007
Revised edition published in the United States in 2009 by
DK Publishing
375 Hudson Street, New York, New York 10014

10 11 12 13 10 9 8 7 6 5 4 3 2
DD533—02/09

The publisher would like to thank Gary Russell, David Turbitt, and Kate Walsh at the BBC, Margaret Parrish for Americanization, Marian Anderson for the index, and Jo Casey and Vicki Taylor for proofreading.

A catalog record for this book is available from the Library of Congress.

ISBN: 978-0-7566-5156-5

Color reproduction by Media Development and Printing, UK
Printed and bound in China by Hung Hing

For their work on the first edition, the publisher would like to thank Russell T. Davies, Gary Russell, Edward Thomas, Jonathan Allison, Matt North, Peter McKinstry, Arwel Wyn Jones, Adrian Anscombe, Adrian Rogers, Harriet Newby-Hill, and Kate Beharrell. Dorling Kindersley would also like to thank Amy Junor, Project Editor; Jon Hall, Designer; Guy Harvey, Senior Designer; Rob Perry, Brand Manager; Simon Beecroft, Publishing Manager; Alex Allan, Category Publisher; Hanna Ländin, DTP Designer; Rochelle Talary, Production.

Artworks: Dalek Flagship by John Maloney (pages 46–47); The Satan Pit by Richard Bonson (page 67), Sonic Screwdriver (pages 18–19) by Peter McKinstry.

Discover more at
www.dk.com